Dina's Choice

Dina's Choice

By

Chaya T. Hirsch

Also by Chaya T. Hirsch:

Shira's Secret

An Unlikely Match

Meant To Be

That Special Someone

Aviva's Pain

Malky's Heart

Losing Leah

Finding Leah

Dear reader,

For your convenience, a Hebrew/Yiddish Glossary of Jewish phrases and terms is available at the end of this book.

Chapter One

Dina Aaron glanced at her watch before scanning her phone for a missed call or text. Could it be she wasn't getting service at the airport?

Her gaze skimmed over the text she sent her mother no more than ten minutes ago: **Hey, Mom. I landed almost an hour ago. Where are you?**

Puffing out her cheeks, she knocked the back of her head against the wall and closed her eyes. *She forgot.* After being apart from her for nearly ten years, Dina's mother failed to show up. She shouldn't be surprised, but it stung. A lot.

Opening her eyes, she scanned the crowd again. Maybe her mother had changed so much that Dina didn't recognize her? Impossible, because they'd video chatted over the years and exchanged pictures. While Dina never considered herself close to the woman who brought her into this world, she certainly didn't feel like they were estranged.

Many people were hugging and kissing their family members, some of whom Dina recognized from her flight. She had to remind herself that her mother had done things like this countless times throughout most of her childhood. Forgetting to pick her up from school or forgetting to take her to a long overdue dentist appointment. She wasn't a bad mother, per se, she was just scatter-brained. It seemed Dina had no choice but to take a cab.

She froze in place when she caught sight of a familiar face. Was that…no way, that couldn't be *him*.

He was a tall man, twenty-one, the same age as Dina, with dark hair to his shoulders, and eyes the color of the deep ocean. He had a noticeable scar near his left eye. Dina would recognize that scar anywhere, because she was there when the small accident occurred. He had tripped when they played outside and hit his face on the bench in front of his parents' house.

What on Earth was he doing here? He must have just come off a flight. Except, the way his head moved right and left, it was as though he was searching for someone.

Then his gaze landed on the young woman standing there, her fingers wrapped around the handle of her black suitcase. Dina's breath caught in her throat. Those eyes…Gosh, she hadn't seen those ocean eyes in nine years. She forced herself to look at the rest of him, taking note of things that should be there but weren't. His *kippa*, for example. The strings of his *tzitzis*, for another. Dina heard from old friends and family that he left the faith a few years ago, but she refused to believe it. Now the proof stood less than twenty feet away from her.

And it hurt. A lot.

He stared at her for a moment, a surprised look on his face. Then he blinked and smiled, making his way over…to her? Dina looked around, but didn't see anyone behind her. He really *was* heading her way.

He smiled again when he reached her. "Hi, Dina."

"H—hi."

"Sorry, you were expecting your mom. She couldn't make it and asked if I could pick you up."

Her tongue was not functioning properly. She couldn't…she didn't…the last time she saw him, the last words she said to him, the last promise she held in her heart…

His eyebrows knit. "Um…oh, of course! You probably

3

don't remember me. I'm Sam Weiss. We used to be neighbors."

Did he seriously think she didn't remember him? After all those years they were friends?

Dina shook her head. "Right. Yeah. I know."

He looked relieved. "Good. I like to think I haven't changed that much in ten years." A soft chuckle.

Oh, he'd changed all right. Right before her eyes, she saw the twelve-year-old boy who used to play with her every day after school. The twelve-year-old boy who still wore his *kippa* and *tzitzis* and spoke excitedly of his upcoming *bar mitzvah*. Before her eyes, she saw the twelve-year-old boy whom she thought would grow up to be her husband.

Dina shook her head again. Silly, foolish childhood dreams.

"Can I take your suitcase?" he asked.

"Thanks." As she passed him the handle, his hand brushed hers. It took everything Dina had not to flinch. Orthodox Jewish men and women are not allowed to touch.

Coughing, he tightened his hold on the handle, then led her toward the parking lot.

"So...how's Florida been?" he asked.

It felt strange to be back in Brooklyn, New York. Dina had gotten so accustomed to Miami that it was like walking into another dimension. Things were similar, sure, but they were also very different.

"Good," Dina said.

He was quiet, as though he wanted her to elaborate. She *couldn't*. Why wasn't she able to act like a normal person around him?

"I've never been to Miami," he said as he approached a dark-colored car and unlocked it. "Just to Orlando a couple of times with my family. Disney World."

"Oh, yeah." She'd only been there once, when her father surprised his new wife and children. Like the other times, Dina felt like such an outsider. They always did everything they could to include her and help her feel part of the family, but she felt out of place. Rachel was only ten years older than she was and her four kids were quite young.

"You okay?"

Dina blinked and found herself standing in the middle of a parking lot. "What?"

"My car." He gestured to it, and she realized that he was already loading her suitcase into the trunk.

"Oh, thanks."

He nodded before heading to the driver's side. Dina stood

still for a moment. She'd have to ride in the passenger seat. She could sit in the back, but she didn't want him to think she was an overly religious girl who was scared to be alone in a car with a guy. Even though she was nervous to be alone in a car with *him*.

"Wait, I got that for you." He raced to her side and opened the door for her.

"Thanks." Dina climbed in and shut the door, wringing her hands in her lap. She didn't want to act strangely, but she knew she was. She was never good with social skills, something she'd been working on since she'd started dating earlier this year. Being around guys caused her extreme anxiety. But with Sam? It was magnified by a hundred.

"Do you want me to put on music?" he asked once he was settled in.

"Okay."

He glanced at her for a second. "Do you only listen to Jewish music?"

"No."

"Okay. Just wanted to make sure. So any station is fine?"

Dina nodded.

Thank God for the music, or this would have been an

awkward ride. Not that Dina minded the silence. Usually. It was different now.

"Recognize the neighborhood?" he asked when they were ten minutes away from Dina's house.

She peered out the window. "Nothing's really changed."

"Is that comforting?"

Staring outside for a few more seconds, she said, "I don't know."

He chuckled gently. "Yeah, I don't know either. I've been thinking about moving out of Brooklyn. But there's something comforting about staying in the city you grew up in."

"Unless you're trying to run away from something," her mouth said before her brain could stop it.

He nodded slowly. "Yeah, unless you're running away."

Are you trying to run away?

Dina wished she could ask him that question. Instead, she went with, "Do you live with your parents?"

"Nope. Moved out two years ago."

"Oh." That meant they weren't neighbors anymore.

"I'm there almost every day, though. I guess I can't break away from Sim-Sim."

He was referring to his little sister, Simi, who was five years old. Dina had never met her since she was born after she left.

"What about Dovid?" she asked. From what her old friends told her, Sam's twin brother was still religious.

"Yeah, he still lives at home."

Why did Sam leave the faith? It was as though Dina's heart would burst if she didn't find out. She wished she could ask him. She'd probably never know.

He parked the car in the Weiss's driveway. Dina's eyes were pasted on the house she grew up in. It looked exactly the same, except, maybe the steps had been repainted. The door was the same, too. She recognized the small dent she, Sam, and Dovid made when they played ball in front of the house. Her dad was furious. Her mom just laughed.

They got out of the car, and Sam retrieved Dina's suitcase from the trunk. This time, she made sure not to brush his hand when she took the handle from him. "Thanks for picking me up," she said.

"No problem." He smiled that sweet smile that made him look so young and carefree. "Oh, almost forgot." He dug his hand into his jeans pocket and produced a key. "Your mom gave me this to give you. Key to the house."

"Oh, she's not home?"

He shook his head.

That was disappointing. A part of Dina hoped her mom would throw her a surprise welcome home party.

"Something about getting her wig done?" he said.

"Oh, yeah. She told me this morning that she has a date tonight."

Dina had no idea why she mentioned the word "date" in front of Shmuel Weiss. Well, she supposed he was Samuel now.

He was about to respond, when the door of the house next door opened and a middle-aged woman came out. "Is that you, Dina?"

"Mrs. Weiss! Hi."

She ran over and enveloped Dina in her arms. "The last time I saw you, you were just *bas mitzvah*!" Mrs. Weiss pulled back and studied her. "Now look at you! You're such a beauty. Isn't she a beauty, Shmuel?"

He balanced on the balls of his feet. "Mom, don't embarrass her."

She squeezed Dina to her chest again. "You were always a beauty. I knew you'd grow up to be a gorgeous girl. Oh, I'm so happy you're back. Perry's been asking about you since she found out you were coming back. I have to say, I don't think she's ever made any good friends as you. And now you're back and can be best friends again."

Dina noticed the way Sam shuffled from one foot to the other. She didn't mind Mrs. Weiss's extreme enthusiasm. She'd always loved it.

"Okay, I made cookies," Mrs. Weiss said as she freed the young woman. "Go get settled back in your old home and I'll send Sam and Simi over with them. Just don't spoil your dinner. I heard your mom was slaving away in the kitchen all morning preparing a special treat for you."

"She was?"

She slapped her forehead. "Oh, why did I tell you that? Oh well." She took Dina's hands and squeezed them. "It's so good to have you back."

"Thanks. It feels good to be back."

The older woman waved as Dina walked up to her house. Before climbing the stairs, she turned her head. Mrs. Weiss was back in her house, but her son...her son's eyes were pinned on Dina. She quickly turned around and unlocked the door. Before closing it, she stole another peek at Sam. His gaze hadn't left hers.

Chapter Two

The kitchen smelled like it had been used today. Dina scanned around, at the walls, every inch of furniture, the kitchen appliances, and even the tiles. The place looked exactly like it did the day she left.

She was about to head to the fridge to see what goodies her mom prepared, when she caught a note on the door.

Dina, do not, under any circumstance, open this door!

She laughed. She hoped this would be the start of a new beginning for her and her mother. They hadn't really gotten along when Dina was a kid. That was why she chose to live with her dad when her parents got divorced. Dina planned to put all her effort into making things work here. She didn't want to move back in with her father and his new family.

But if things didn't work out, there was always dating…

She shook her head. Not until she got a new job and grew accustomed to living here.

After rummaging around in the pantry, Dina settled on a piece of chocolate. She would have gone for something healthier like fruit, but apparently the fridge was off-limits.

The small hallway that led to the stairs hadn't changed much, either. Except for a painting on the wall. Lifting her suitcase, Dina climbed upstairs to her room. She expected it to look exactly like it did the day she left nine years ago.

Sure enough, the familiar sight greeted her. There was the closet and matching dresser. Her bed was near the window, and her artwork hung all over the walls. Her mother never threw out a single one of her projects. There was also that ancient television set. Many Orthodox Jews don't have TVs in their homes, but others are more lenient, being careful what they watch. The only thing in Dina's room that changed was the long shelf that lined the wall. It was where all her stuffed animals sat before she moved them to their new home. She gave most of them away but she still had a few that would feel right at home here.

The smell was so familiar. It reminded her of her childhood. This place held so much innocence, so much hope and promise. Dina wondered what new hopes and dreams she'd have during her stay here. She wondered how many, if any at all, would come true.

Dropping down on her bed, she stared up at the ceiling. She smiled at what hung up there. Although she and Perry lived right next door to each other, they loved having sleepovers at each other's houses. They stuck glow-in-the-dark space stickers up there and pretended they were astronauts.

Dina's body sprang up when she heard a knock on the front door. Mrs. Weiss mentioned she'd send Sam and Simi over with cookies. She quickly glanced at the mirror of her dresser to make sure her hair was decent before making her way downstairs. When she opened the door, someone flung her arms around her.

"Dina! Oh my gosh, finally!"

For a second, she was thrown off-guard because she was expecting Sam. But the disappointment left her as she wrapped her arms around her best friend Perry. "I've missed you so much," Dina said.

"I can't believe you're actually here." They pulled apart and Perry scanned Dina from head to toe. She playfully shoved Dina's shoulder. "Ugh, why are you still so skinny?"

Dina scanned her as well, from her dirty blonde hair, down her blue eyes, the same shade as her brother's, down her slim frame, and to the bottom of shoes. She and Dina had video chatted many times and exchanged pictures, but it was different seeing her face to face. A small container with cookies was tucked under Perry's arm.

Dina returned the playful shove. "Look who's talking. You're as skinny as a stick."

Perry rolled her eyes. "For a second, I worried this would be awkward, but it feels like we've been with each other all these years. Here." She handed Dina the container with cookies. "From my mom."

"Please thank her for me."

She nodded before turning around and motioning behind her. Dina hadn't realized Simi standing there. The little girl clutched a worn-out, stuffed gray bear in one arm and had her thumb in her mouth. She pressed her cheek against her sister's skirt.

This cutie was definitely a Weiss—the ocean eyes said it all.

"Simi, please take your thumb out of your mouth." Perry gently tugged on her sister's hand. "You know you're too old for that."

Dina's Choice

With her face still pressed to Perry's skirt, she looked up at Dina.

"Hey, Simi," Dina said. "You don't know me, but Perry and I used to be best friends. I moved to Florida before you were born."

Simi buried her face in Perry's skirt.

Perry laughed. "She's a little shy. But don't worry, once she gets to know you she'll be nothing but a pest. Isn't that right, Simi?" She ruffled the little girl's hair.

"Nah, this girl doesn't look like a pest," Dina said. "She looks like someone who would really love some candy."

Simi's head perked up.

"I brought some back with me. Come on in and I'll let you choose whatever you want."

"She's already had a few cookies," Perry whispered to her friend.

"That's the good thing about being the fun neighbor," Dina said. "I get to spoil her."

Perry chuckled.

Once Simi was preoccupied at the cupboard with her choice of candy, Perry pulled Dina to the table. "Gosh, I still can't believe we're together again. There's so much I want to ask you, but I have no idea what to ask first."

Dina opened the cookie container. "I need to try these. Your mom always baked such awesome things."

"Ugh, don't remind me. I was always such a chubby kid."

Dina kept her eyes on the cookie, breaking it in half. "I thought you weren't home. Your mom said Sam and Simi were going to bring over the cookies."

Perry fell back on her chair. "Wow, Sam. I haven't heard that name in a long time."

Dina raised her eyebrows.

"Shmuel insisted everyone call him Shmuel as soon as he turned *bar mitzvah*."

Dina couldn't have known that, since she left a few months before his thirteenth birthday.

Now Perry's eyes were on her cookie. "No one ever calls him Sam. Well, not counting the people from his other life."

Dina bent her head a little closer to Perry's. "Perry…what happened to him? Am I allowed to ask that?"

Perry lifted her eyes to her friend for a second before focusing back on her cookie. "I don't know." She sighed. "He gets so upset when we try to talk to him about it. It feels like we're driving him away. So we don't ask. Well, other than my dad. He's pretty harsh on him. They don't exactly have the best relationship."

Dina loved how close she and Perry felt to each other. They were apart for nearly a decade, but their friendship remained just as strong.

Perry waved her hand, smiling. "Forget about Sam. Tell me more about you. Have you started dating yet?"

Now Dina rolled her eyes. "Don't tell me you're obsessed with dating like so many other girls."

Perry gave her a face. "I'm not obsessed. I'm just overly curious. So…how many dates?"

"You're lucky you're my best friend, or you would be way too nosy. The truth is, I've only been on like two dates. And they both were horrible."

"But that's why you came to New York, right? To date?"

Dina shook her head. "No…um…" She cleared her throat. "You know my dad remarried."

"Yeah. To a woman…well…"

"Yeah, she's like ten years younger than him. Anyway, with all her kids and everything, I felt out of place. I had to leave."

Perry nodded. "I can imagine."

Simi ran up to her sister, holding two different kinds of

candy. "You can only have one," Perry told her.

"But, Perry!"

"It's not nice to take so much. Pick one and put the other one back."

"I don't mind," Dina said. "Simi, you're welcome to whatever you want."

With a huge smile, she bolted over and threw her arms around Dina, though she was so small she hugged the older girl's legs. "Thank you!" And she ran back to the cupboard.

Perry frowned. "That kid is way too spoiled."

"Hey, I don't have any brothers or sisters. I need to spoil someone."

"You kind of do have brothers and sisters," Perry pointed out.

She was right, but Dina didn't know if she could have a relationship with her stepsiblings. She tried many times, but things always felt strained. Other times, it felt like she fought with them for her dad's attention.

Dina and Perry talked for what felt like hours. About what? Dina had no clue. But at some point, Perry checked her watch and said she and Simi needed to go home for supper.

Perry hugged Dina one more time. "I'm really so glad

you're back."

"Me, too."

Dina stood at the door, waving as they left. She couldn't help but look at their house, searching for…she shut her eyes. No, she needed to stop thinking about him. He wasn't the guy he used to be. He wasn't the guy she was looking for.

Her stomach rumbled. She had no idea when was the last time she ate. As she was about to reach for the fridge's door handle, there was a voice behind her. "What do you think you're doing? Didn't you read the sign?"

Dina whirled around. "Mom!"

Her mother held out her arms. "Hi, sweetie."

Dina walked into them a little hesitantly. Her mom's arms came around her, a little hesitantly, too. Dina expected things to be a little awkward. They hadn't seen each other face to face for a long time.

Her mother lowered her arms and placed them on Dina's shoulders, studying her face. "I can't believe how much you've grown. You're so beautiful."

"Thanks. You look amazing."

Mrs. Aaron pulled her bag off her shoulder and dropped it onto the table. "Sorry I couldn't pick you up from the airport.

The date I have tonight was planned last minute and my wig stylist could only squeeze me in this afternoon."

"It's fine," Dina told her, forcing all thoughts of Sam out of her mind. She also didn't know what to make of her mother dating. It never used to matter to her because she lived so far away and their lives hadn't affected one another's. But if her mom met the right one and decided to get married, and if he brought along a suitcase filled with kids…Dina didn't want to think about it.

"Sorry, you must be hungry." Mrs. Aaron marched over to the refrigerator.

"Yeah, I didn't eat much on the plane."

Her mother turned around, her back pressing into the fridge door, and grinned. "I prepared a special treat for you."

"Thanks, but you didn't have to."

"Are you kidding? You and I have been apart for so long and I want to show you how happy I am to have you here with me." She closed her hand over the door handle. "I know I wasn't much of a cook when you were growing up and that your father cooked all the meals, but I've gotten much better. I made your favorite dish. At least, it was your favorite dish when you were a kid." She bent inside and pulled out a large baking pan. Walking over to the dairy counter, she lowered it. "I just need to warm it up in the oven…" She muttered to herself as she turned on the oven.

The smell of pasta and cheese attacked Dina's nose. She knew exactly what dish her mother was referring to, and her mouth watered.

After shoving the pan into the oven, Mrs. Aaron smiled. "So? Have you guessed yet?"

Dina tapped her chin as though she was trying to solve the world's most difficult math equation. "Hmm, I smell pasta and cheese. Could it be my mother's trying to win me over by making me lasagna?"

Mrs. Aaron chuckled. "Is it working?"

"Yeah, but you don't have to try so hard to win me over, Mom."

The older woman busied herself with placing plates and forks on the table. "I feel like I need to make it up to you. I wasn't the greatest mother."

Dina waved her hand. "It's fine. I turned out normal. Well, at least I think I did," she added with a light laugh.

Her mother moved closer and kissed her forehead. "I got married so young, Dina. I was only eighteen. Your father swept me off my feet. Sometimes I wish…" She shook her head. "Never mind."

"Sometimes you wish what?" Dina asked gently.

Her mother scanned her face, as though trying to decide if she should have this discussion with her daughter. She shrugged. "I sometimes wonder if we had waited a few years, maybe our marriage would have lasted." She stroked her hair. "I'm sorry we put you through all of that."

Dina didn't know what to say. She and her mother had never been close, yet here she was sharing very personal thoughts with Dina. Dina didn't want to say the wrong thing. At the same time, she wanted to have a close relationship with her mother.

Mrs. Aaron must have sensed her daughter's unease because she said, "Well, never mind that. You want to help me with the salad?"

"Sure."

They worked on a simple salad of lettuce, tomatoes, cucumbers, peppers, and a dressing. Dina usually didn't mind the quiet, but right now she felt stifled. Her mom seemed preoccupied with her thoughts—maybe about the date?

"Are you eating here or is the guy taking you out?" Dina

asked.

"I asked him not to take me out because I want to eat with you. He's probably going to take me to an old movie."

Dina tried to scrutinize her mother's face to learn if she was serious about this man, but she couldn't tell. She didn't feel comfortable enough to ask.

"Sweetie." Mrs. Aaron's eyes were on the tomato she was cutting. "Do you want me to talk to matchmakers?"

"Nooo, not yet. Maybe never."

She lifted her eyes to Dina's.

"Okay, maybe not never. I just can't deal with that right now. I have to decide if I want to find a job or apply to graduate school. I still need to get settled back in—"

Mrs. Aaron patted her daughter's arm. "That's okay. I just wanted to ask. Take all the time you need."

Dina knew her mother didn't really mean that. Mrs. Aaron might have regretted getting married so young, but she was probably a little worried that Dina was still single. Twenty-one is not old, but there are so many singles out there and mothers tend to worry. Dina couldn't imagine getting married, though, at least not right now. Many of her classmates had a child or two already. Dina didn't feel pressured, but she wondered how they were so calm, so sure of themselves. To share the rest of your life with one person? How do you know when you meet the right one? As a child, Dina thought she had all the answers: marry Sam Weiss, continue being best friends with Perry, and live happily ever after. She was still best friends with Perry, but the rest of her dream had been flushed down the toilet.

Once the salad was done, Mrs. Aaron and Dina sat at the table to eat. The lasagna was delicious. Dina had a few memories of her mom trying to cook meals when she was a kid, but they always failed. She remembered how her father would laugh and take over. She wasn't sure when things between them went south. She supposed she lived in blissful, childhood ignorance. All she knew was that one day they were one big happy family, and the next her dad was moving to Miami.

"This is awesome, Mom," Dina told her. "There's hope for you yet."

Mrs. Aaron laughed. "Why, thank you. Oh by the way, the Weiss's have invited us over for this Shabbos. Both meals. Bracha's so happy you're back. She couldn't stop talking about it for days."

"Yeah, she's great. She sent over those cookies." Dina

pointed to the counter, trying to ignore the pounding of her heart. Would Sam be there? He wasn't an observant Jew, but he might still join his family for the meals. A part of Dina was dying to see him again, but the other part wanted to never look at him again.

Mrs. Aaron cut a small slice of the lasagna. "How's your father doing?"

"You mean, how he and his new family are doing," her daughter mumbled.

"I'm sorry, sweetie." She reached for Dina's hand.

Dina shook her head. "I'm not bitter. Rachel's a nice person and her kids are good kids. I just feel..." Her mouth clamped shut. She didn't feel comfortable talking to her mother about this. She wished she did, though. Hopefully one day.

"I can't say I understand what you're going through, but I just want you to know that I'm here for you. Okay?" Mrs. Aaron gave Dina a smile.

Dina returned it. "Thanks."

Mrs. Aaron wiped her mouth, her eyes on the clock on the wall. "Is that the time? I need to get moving."

Dina watched her mother scramble about. Mrs. Aaron had been married before. She'd been divorced. Yet, she was still brave enough to try again. Dina didn't know why the thought caused her such unease.

Mrs. Aaron kissed the top of Dina's head. "I'm so happy you're here, Dina'la."

"Me, too. Have fun on your date."

"Thanks." She waved before shutting the door behind her.

The house was so quiet. Dina wasn't used to it because of her stepsiblings. She got up and washed the dishes. She had no clue how her life would turn out here in New York, but she hoped she'd be happy.

Chapter Three

"Ten minutes, Dina!" her mother called from downstairs.

Why couldn't Dina's hair cooperate? The wavy auburn strands refused to stay in place. She usually didn't care because she was used to eating with just the family, but now that they were guests at the Weiss's, she needed to look her best.

Okay, she *wanted* to look her best. And that was not because of Sam.

Okay, fine, it was because of Sam. Which was totally ridiculous. He wasn't that same boy. How long would it take her brain to understand that?

And why did her brown eyes look so tired?

"Dina!" Mrs. Aaron called again.

Dina gave up, throwing her comb onto the dresser. Before leaving her room, she swept one of her stuffed animals off the shelf—a one-eyed blue monster—and tapped its nose. "I look pretty despite my crazy hair, right?"

It gave her a blank look. She sighed. Even a stuffed animal knew she was a hopeless case.

She sprinted down the stairs before her mom called again. Mrs. Aaron already had the Shabbos candles set up.

"Did you take the cake out of the fridge?" Dina asked.

"It's on the counter. Don't look so nervous—everyone will love it."

Dina didn't care whether or not Sam would like the cake she baked. Not at *all*.

Mrs. Aaron waved her hands over the candles before covering her face and reciting the blessing. When she was done, she said, "Good Shabbos."

"Good Shabbos."

The women recited *Kabbalas Shabbos*, the short prayer to welcome in the Sabbath, then headed to the Weiss's. It'd be some time before the men returned from the synagogue, but she and her mom didn't want to arrive too late. Dina dug her nails into her palms as they climbed the short steps to the front door. Sam wouldn't be at the synagogue because he wasn't religious. That meant there was a good chance he'd be at the house. Dina didn't want to speak to him. Except, that was a lie.

Mrs. Aaron knocked on the door and smiled at her daughter. "Mrs. Weiss is such a sweetheart. She invites me over practically every Shabbos."

The door opened and Simi appeared. She wrapped her little arms around Mrs. Aaron's legs. "Hello, Simi!" she said.

Dina's eyes strained toward the inside of the house. She didn't see Sam.

"Dina gave me Fruit Roll-Ups and candy corn when I went over!" Simi jumped up and down, grabbing onto Dina's skirt. "Did you bring any with you?"

"Simi, is that the Aarons? Please let them in."

Simi yanked on Dina's skirt some more. "Did you?"

"I'm sorry. I'll bring some tomorrow, okay?"

She beamed before grabbing Dina's hand and pulling her inside. Once again, her eyes searched for Sam. She didn't see him anywhere.

Mrs. Weiss came out, wearing a stained apron over her Shabbos robe. "Good Shabbos! Perry will come home soon. She's babysitting for a woman down the block." She glanced down at herself. "Woops, sorry. I was just finishing up the salad." She reached behind to untie the apron, but it was stuck.

"Let me help," Dina offered.

"Thanks, Dina."

"Mommy, Dina said she's gonna bring over some candy tomorrow!" Simi said.

Mrs. Weiss stroked her daughter's head. "Did you say thank you for the other candy she gave you?"

Simi's eyebrows squeezed together as she thought. "I think so!" She beamed once again and skipped out of the room.

"She's so adorable," Dina said as she untied the apron.

"Thank you. She's quite a handful. Not as bad as Shmuel was at her age, though. That boy…" Mrs. Weiss shook her head with a frown.

Dina couldn't help but smile at how true her words were.

Her mother held up the baking pan. "Dina baked this for your family."

Mrs. Weiss yanked the young woman into her arms. "You're an angel. I'll cut some for dessert." She took the pan from Mrs. Aaron. "Please make yourselves at home."

Dina couldn't understand where Sam was. Could it be he went to pray with the others? Maybe he wasn't as far removed as she thought. It caused her heart to beat with hope.

When Mrs. Weiss returned, they talked about various

topics, including Dina's life in Miami. Forty minutes later, the door opened and the men walked in. For a second, Dina couldn't believe the sight in front of her. She thought Sam stood there dressed in white and black, the traditional garb religious men wear on Shabbos. But she quickly realized it wasn't Sam standing before her but his twin brother Dovid. They looked so identical, but she always knew which was which. She had always prided herself in telling the difference when they were kids. Most people didn't bother trying because it was practically impossible.

"Good Shabbos," the men said as they walked in.

The women returned the greeting.

"Hello, Dina," Mr. Weiss said in the booming voice Dina remembered so clearly as a child. "Got sick of the sun in Miami, huh?"

Dina laughed. "I wish."

"Hi, Dina," Dovid said in a shy voice.

Suddenly, Dina grew just as shy. "Hi."

The room was bathed in silence.

Mrs. Weiss moved forward. "So who's hungry?"

Everyone started shuffling into the dining room. Dovid stepped in line with Dina. "I heard you were back," he said with a shy smile. "It's been so long since I've seen you."

"I know. It's like I came back in a time machine. Everything feels the same, but at the same time…"

"Different. I know what you mean."

They smiled at each other.

"So other than Perry, who else is supposed to arrive?" Dina asked him.

"Just her. Though I wonder how long that'll take. She loves babysitting for the Berman kids. We practically have to yank her away." He laughed.

"What about your brother?" Dina asked, then immediately regretted it when the laugh vanished from his face.

"Oh. Shmuel doesn't really come over for Shabbos." He focused his attention on his sleeve, straightening it out, though it wasn't really wrinkled.

Dina didn't know why she hoped Sam was returning to observant life. He had chosen the life he wanted to live. They were on two very different paths. She needed to forget about him and move on with her life.

"I think Dovid should sit near Dina," Mrs. Weiss announced when they entered the room. Dina's cheeks heated up. Was she trying to…?

Dina's Choice

Dina glanced at Dovid and saw his cheeks were red, too. "She always does this when single girls come over," he whispered to her. "Sorry in advance."

Dina…and Dovid? She had always seen him as a brother. She didn't think she could ever feel about him the way she felt about Sam. She didn't even know if it was ethical to date the twin brother of the guy she liked. Nah, there was no way that was okay, not when they looked so similar.

Dovid pulled out her chair for her. "Thanks," she said.

He smiled before taking the seat next to her. There was no way he felt anything for her. He knew very well how she felt about his brother when they were kids. The only one who didn't know was Perry. Dina had been too embarrassed to tell her.

Once everyone was settled at the table, they started singing *Shalom Aleicheim*, welcoming the Shabbos. Dina's eyes trekked to Dovid as his voice filled the room. Both he and his brother had beautiful voices when they were kids. She was glad to see Dovid still had the gift, and wondered if Sam did as well.

She noticed Mrs. Weiss's gaze flitting from her to Dovid. Once again, her cheeks heated up. She didn't want the older woman to get the wrong idea.

Simi sang at the top of her lungs. Though her pitch was a bit too high, Dina could tell she was just as talented as her brothers.

Just when they finished the last verse, the door burst open and Perry rushed inside. "Am I late?"

"You missed the entire meal," Mr. Weiss said with a grin.

Perry rolled her eyes. "Stop teasing me, Dad."

They all headed to the kitchen to wash for *challah*—the braided bread eaten on Shabbos. When Dina returned to the table, she was tempted to switch seats and sit near Perry. But she realized choosing another seat would probably offend Dovid.

After the blessing was made on the *challah*, they each received a slice. Dina closed her eyes for a second and savored the deliciousness. "Mrs. Weiss, your *challah* is just as good as I remember it," she told her. "The best *challah* I have ever tasted in my life."

Mrs. Weiss waved her hand. "Thank you, but my baking skills are pretty average."

Dovid shook his head with a smile. "My mother's never been good at taking compliments."

"Like another young man sitting in the room?" Mrs. Weiss

said.

Dovid shrugged. "I am my mother's son."

Mrs. Weiss, Perry, and Dovid left to the kitchen to fetch the first course, shooing Dina away when she offered to help. Apparently, she was a very important guest at this table. They returned with the *gefilte* fish.

"So tell me, Miss Aaron," Mr. Weiss said as he spread the horseradish over his fish. "What's life like down in the Sunshine State?"

Everyone pinned their eyes on her. She shifted in her seat, never one to be comfortable in the spotlight. "It's really nice. I used to go to the beach almost every day when we first moved. And it was great that I didn't have to worry about cold weather, though I really missed the snow."

"Well, don't worry about that," Perry grumbled. "You'll soon see enough snow here. It's only November and the weather's gotten so cold."

"Yeah, I saw on the news the snowstorm you had last year. It looked crazy."

"More than crazy." Dovid took a bite of his fish. "You can't even imagine what it was like. It took me an hour and a half to get to work, when it usually only takes twenty minutes."

"And remember that city bus that was stuck at the corner of our block?" Perry said. "The bus stop is like seven blocks away."

"I know," Dina said with a laugh. "I used to live here, remember?"

Perry's face brightened. "Oh my gosh, do you remember the time we once snuck onto the city bus when we were like eight?"

The memory flashed in Dina's mind. "We pretended we were the kids of the woman before us. The driver thought we were with her."

"Yeah, he should have asked her to pay for us, though. We were way above the age limit."

"What's this I hear?" Mrs. Weiss asked. "You snuck onto a city bus *alone*?"

Perry's face went stone white for a second. Then she giggled. "Just one of our many youthful adventures. It was Dovid's idea."

"Me?" He pointed his fork at his chest. "I wasn't involved in that. I would remember it."

Perry's eyebrows furrowed. "You weren't? But I distinctly remember...?" Her voice trailed off as she thought.

Dina's Choice

Dina played around with the last bit of her *gefilte* fish. "It was Sam's idea. I mean, Shmuel. It was Shmuel's idea."

"Well, that sounds more like it." Mrs. Weiss shook her head. "That boy caused me more gray hairs than the two of you combined."

"He does have his mother's spirit," Mr. Weiss said.

"Maybe a little too much," she mumbled. Then she pasted on a smile and started collecting the dishes. "So where did the joy ride bring you?" she asked Dina and Perry.

Perry looked at her friend. "I have no idea."

Dina thought for a few seconds. "I don't remember either."

"I'm pretty sure Shmuel would remember," Dovid said. "He has such a good memory, I sometimes wonder if he's actually a robot."

"Well, I can attest that he most certainly is *not* a robot." Mrs. Weiss stood up with a stack of plates. "It was because of him that I had that small complication during my pregnancy. I should have known that was only the beginning of the anxiety he would cause me."

They all chuckled, but their laughs tapered off. It was obvious the Weiss's were very hurt by the life their son had chosen for himself. Dina only wished she knew what caused this. Maybe she could help him. But at the same time, it was none of her business.

Simi made a random comment about one of the neighbors, and everyone laughed again. Trust her to ease away the tension of the room.

When they were all slurping chicken soup, Dina's mother asked her, "What do you plan to do for a job?"

"I'm not sure. I have to see if it's worth it for me to go for my master's."

"What did you major in?" Dovid wanted to know.

"Web design."

He nodded slowly. "You can probably find a job where you can work from home."

Dina returned the nod. She wasn't sure she wanted to work from home. True it was very convenient, but she would be all alone. Her mom worked as a secretary at the local Bais Yaakov, and while their apartment wasn't very large, she would still feel lonely. She worried she'd go insane if she didn't have at least some sort of social stimuli, even though she disliked being social.

The rest of the meal went by quickly. Dina couldn't help but try every single dish on the table. Mrs. Weiss's cooking was just unbelievable. Dina's family had been invited to the Weiss's house for Shabbos every so often, and Mrs. Weiss would send leftovers home with the Aarons. Dina's father even asked for some recipes when he saw how much his daughter loved them.

Once the meal was over, they remained at the table, chatting. Mr. and Mrs. Weiss were discussing something with Dina's mom, and Perry left with Simi to bring some food over to the elderly neighbor across the street. Dovid and Dina sat there in silence.

He smiled at her, looking like he wanted to say something but not sure what. Dina took him out of his misery by asking, "Where do you work?"

"In the human resources department at the hospital."

"Oh, cool."

He smiled again.

Dina played with her ring. "What exactly does Sam do? I mean, Shmuel. I seriously need to stop calling him that."

"That's okay. I call him that sometimes, too. I guess it's hard to let go of a nickname I used to use all the time as a kid."

"That's the only name I know him by," she said. Then she shook her head. "Gosh, I can't believe how much has changed. I mean, you're like all grown up. The last time I saw you two, you were studying for your *bar mitzvahs*."

"And the last time I saw you, you had leaves in your hair."

She laughed. "Sam really did love climbing trees, didn't he?"

"Excuse me? I believe a certain somebody equally loved climbing trees, too."

"And Perry did, too. Until she fell off a branch and broke her arm."

They smiled at the memory.

"And I just followed Sam," Dovid said. "Like I always did. I guess it took me a while to forge my own identity. Even so, I still find it hard to be my own person. Sorry if I'm not making any sense. Maybe it's a twin thing."

"No, I think I understand. Part of who you are is being a twin. If you weren't a twin, you wouldn't be *you*."

"And I guess it's a little easier to be my own person now, since Sam lives such a different life."

"It's really nice that your family accepts him. Some families wouldn't."

He played with his glass cup. "Yeah. I mean, my dad's pretty strict with him, but we try not to drive him away. It won't do any good but cause him to fall even deeper. I guess we all secretly hope he'll return one day, but I seriously doubt he will. Call it twin intuition."

"I'm sorry."

He lifted his eyes to her and smiled. "Don't be. You didn't do anything wrong."

In the short time Dina had been back in New York, it seemed all her conversations revolved around Sam. That had to stop, because she needed to move on.

"So what else is new?" she asked.

He shrugged. "Nothing much."

And they were quiet again. Luckily, Perry and Simi returned and took care of the awkward silence. But a minute later, Mrs. Weiss hurried into the living room with Dina's cake.

"Dina, I'm so sorry! I forgot to bring out your cake for dessert."

"It's okay."

"We'll have some now." She returned to the kitchen and came back a few minutes later with her husband, carrying plates with slices of cake. They handed one to each guest. It was a chocolate cake with chocolate filling. Dina had found the recipe in a magazine last year.

They all dug in.

"This is amazing," Dovid said.

"My gosh, so good," Perry agreed.

Dina blushed. "Thanks."

"You have talent," Mrs. Weiss told her. "This is delicious."

"High praise coming from my wife," Mr. Weiss said.

"More, more, more!" Simi jumped up and down.

"Thanks." Dina smiled as she finished off her cake.

Chapter Four

Dina's mom stopped by her room at 9 AM and woke her, telling her she was going to the synagogue. She'd meet her at the Weiss's house after praying.

Dina groaned and rolled over to her side. She didn't know why she was able to sleep for hours on Shabbos. If it was up to her, she'd sleep all day. But she forced herself to get up at ten. After dressing into a dark purple, ruffled shirt and black skirt, she took her prayer book and prayed. When she finished, she looked around the apartment. It was so quiet. She didn't know why it bothered her—all she ever wanted when she lived with her father and his new family was peace and quiet.

It was almost eleven. The men should finish praying in half an hour. Dina was pretty sure Mrs. Weiss needed help with preparations. She knew Perry decided to go to the synagogue—

she told her last night that she went nearly every week.

Mrs. Weiss opened the door after Dina's second knock. "Dina! Good Shabbos." She yanked the young woman in for a hug.

"Good Shabbos, Mrs. Weiss."

"I'm sorry, but the men haven't returned yet."

"I figured. I came over to help."

Mrs. Weiss yanked her in for another hug. "You are such an angel. I actually can use some help. Perry wanted to stay home, but I insisted she go *daven* for the both of us and take Simi with her." She led Dina into the house. It smelled delicious in there. The kitchen was slightly messy, with vegetable peels all over the floor.

"I worried there's not enough food." Mrs. Weiss handed Dina a knife. "So I decided to make a quick salad. Do you mind cutting up these cucumbers?"

"Sure."

She threw Dina an apron. "Please don't ruin your beautiful outfit."

Dina didn't have to worry about awkward silences with Mrs. Weiss. The older woman could talk about anything and keep the conversation interesting. It was a real gift. Perry had inherited that from her. In a span of ten minutes, Dina had been updated on the major events going on in their neighborhood.

"Thanks," Dina said as she threw the sliced cucumbers into the bowl. "Now I'm all caught up in the news and can gossip with everyone else," she joked.

Mrs. Weiss laughed. "I know I don't have to worry about you. You wouldn't talk badly about anyone. You were such a good kid." She frowned. "Well, when Shmuel wasn't getting you into trouble. The three of you were almost inseparable. Well, and Perry, too, when she was brave enough." She poured in the dressing. "So what do you think of Dovid?"

Dina froze. "Oh. Um…"

"He's such a good boy. And he really wants to get married."

"But he's only twenty-one."

"Almost twenty-two."

"That's still young."

"True. But I want to see him and Perry happy."

Dina played with some cucumber peels. "What about Shmuel?"

Mrs. Weiss sighed, tossing the salad. "I don't even know

what to think of Shmuel anymore." She sighed again. "I guess I just want him to be happy, even if he's chosen a different life from the one we provided for him."

Dina wished Mrs. Weiss told her what caused him to stray. She wished she could ask.

Mrs. Weiss undid her apron. "Dina, I need to run over to Mrs. Glick for a few minutes to give her some lunch. Do you mind? It'll just be five minutes."

Dina remembered the elderly woman far too well. The truth was, she had scared Dina as a kid. She just had one of those personalities that didn't mesh well with children. She lived alone now.

"I'll clean up here," Dina told her.

Mrs. Weiss hugged her again. "Thanks. You really are an angel."

Dina gathered the vegetable peels and threw them in the garbage. She was about to rinse off her hands at the sink when there was a knock on the door. Mrs. Weiss was back already? Dina thought she took keys with her.

Opening the door, she came face to face with Sam Weiss.

"Sam."

He was dressed in a dark blue shirt and dark gray pants. His hair sat neatly on his shoulders, as though he made an effort to look presentable.

He seemed equally stunned to see her. "Oh. I was expecting my mother."

"She had to run off to Mrs. Glick's for a few minutes."

"I see."

Quiet.

"Your parents invited my mom and me for Shabbos," she told him.

"I know."

Quiet again.

"I'm helping your mom out," she said.

He nodded. "That's very kind of you."

Quiet yet again.

Dina widened the door. "Sorry, come in. You don't have a key?"

"Yeah, but I figured my mom would be home so I didn't bring it."

"That makes sense."

He stood awkwardly in the kitchen while she wiped the counter. She felt his eyes on her back. She finished cleaning up, but pretended to be busy.

"It's really nice of you to help out my mom," he said after a few minutes. "She makes it seem like she's Super Mom and can do it all, but it's pretty hard work cooking for Shabbos every week."

Dina's gaze met his.

"I used to help her a lot when I was younger," he said.

She put the dish towel aside. "I didn't know that."

"It was after you moved."

For some reason, Dina heard the unspoken words in her head. *Because I was so lonely after you left and needed to distract myself with something.*

Except, that was her imagination. Those were the words she wished he would say.

"I thought you don't come over for Shabbos," she said.

"I don't."

Dina waited for the explanation why he was here, but it didn't come. Once again they were bathed in silence.

"Can I help with anything?" he asked.

Glancing around the kitchen and the dining room, she couldn't find anything to do. She wished she would, because she didn't want to stand there like that.

Sam walked to the doorway between the kitchen and dining

room and peeked into the dining room. Mrs. Weiss should win an award. The white tablecloth had exquisite, intricate designs. The *challahs* were covered with breathtaking embroidery—no doubt made by Mrs. Weiss. There was a large plate with a smaller plate in front of every chair, the silverware sparkled as if they were polished a few minutes ago, and the glass cups were just as pretty. Dina had been so nervous last night she didn't pay attention to any of it.

"It's been a while since I came over for a Shabbos," Sam said, his gaze on the table. "I almost forgot how beautiful it looks."

"Then why don't you?" Dina asked.

A dark look passed over his face.

"Sorry," she apologized.

"How are you liking New York so far?" he inquired.

Dina was momentarily thrown off by the sudden change of topic. "Um…I'm not sure."

He laughed lightly. "You're not sure if you like it here?"

"I'm not sure how I feel. Mixed emotions, I guess."

"Can you elaborate?"

"Not really."

She didn't intend to be rude, she just found it difficult to be open with him. It was as though a lock clamped over her heart whenever he was near.

"Fair enough," he said. Dina couldn't read the expression on his face. She didn't know if he was hurt, offended, or indifferent.

Once again, they stood in awkwardness. Dina started to regret her decision to come over and help. She wished she didn't feel that way. She wished she could treat him like she would any other guy. Last night, she had hoped to see him, but now she realized it hurt too much.

"Where did my mom say she was going?" he asked.

"Mrs. Glick."

"She's probably keeping her with her stories. She's a nice woman, but she does tend to talk too much."

"I never really liked her as a kid," Dina admitted.

"I know."

Her eyes met his for a second before he focused on one of the magnets on the fridge.

When Dina heard keys outside, she nearly jumped for joy. The front door opened and Mrs. Weiss entered. She did a double take when she noticed Sam. "Shmuel! What a surprise! What are you doing here?"

Dina's Choice

He glanced at Dina for a second before saying to his mother, "I was in the neighborhood and decided to drop by."

It seemed Mrs. Weiss didn't believe his words. That meant Sam came over specifically. Why was that? A sudden thought hit Dina. It couldn't be because of her, could it?

"Is there enough food?" he asked his mother.

She waved her hand. "Don't you know me by now? There's always more than enough food. I know the real reason you're here. You want to take home some leftovers."

He grinned. "You know me."

Mrs. Weiss stood by Dina's side, taking her arm. "Thank you so much for cleaning up, Dina. You're such an angel."

She laughed, embarrassed. "You've said that three times already."

"But you really are an angel." Mrs. Weiss kissed Dina's cheek. "I'm glad you're back. You and your mother are invited for Shabbos every week."

"That's so nice of you, Mrs. Weiss. I actually was thinking of inviting your family for Shabbos next week."

"See? You're such an angel."

"You're going to scare her away, Mom," Sam said with a smile.

She tightened her hold on the young woman's arm. "I'm not letting this girl go anywhere."

Voices were heard outside. A few seconds later, the door opened and everyone else piled in, including Dina's mom. "Good Shabbos," they all greeted.

"Shmuel?" Dovid asked.

"Shmuel's here!" Perry flung her arms around her brother.

He chuckled, lifting her a few inches off the ground. "There's my annoying little sister."

"Shmuel! Shmuel!" Simi jumped up and down as she grabbed onto his plants.

"And there's my adorable little sister." He swept her off the ground and threw her over his shoulder.

"Wee!"

"You're going to ruin her dress." Mrs. Weiss frowned.

"Then I'll just buy her another one."

Simi giggled as he tickled her upside down.

"Maybe next time you could dress a little more appropriately for Shabbos," Mr. Weiss said.

Sam looked at him but didn't utter a word.

"I think he looks really handsome." Perry softly punched his arm. "It beats those raggy jeans you always wear."

"Agreed," Dina's mom said.

Sam glanced at Dina for a second before continuing to tickle Simi.

"Well, let's eat," Mrs. Weiss said. "But first I need to get Simi out of that dress."

"Do I have to take it off, Mommy? I feel so pretty in it. Like a princess."

The dress was light purple with poofy sleeves, ruffles, and a small petticoat.

"You *are* a little princess." Perry rolled her eyes. "You don't need a dress to prove it."

Everyone laughed.

Simi frowned. "I don't get it."

That caused everyone to laugh again.

The little girl folded her arms across her chest. "It's not fair. I never get what you grownups say."

Sam patted her nose. "Trust me, it's better to be a kid. No one expects anything from you." His gaze flicked to his father, who scowled.

Mrs. Weiss took Simi's hand. "We'll be back in a few minutes. Please make yourselves comfortable at the table." She led Simi to one of the back rooms. "Did you have fun in *shul?*"

she asked as they walked away.

Mr. Weiss sat down in his usual chair at the head of the table and Mrs. Aaron took his left. Mrs. Weiss would take his right. The rest of them just stood there awkwardly.

"I want to sit near my best friend." Perry grabbed Dina's hand, pulling her to the chair next to hers. That left Sam and Dovid to sit across from the girls.

Mr. Weiss, Dovid, Perry, and Dina's mom discussed what happened in the synagogue this morning. The man reading from the Torah made quite a few mistakes. When Dina peeked at Sam, she discovered his gaze was locked on hers. He quickly looked away. A few seconds later, she caught him looking at her again.

"Shmuel, maybe next time you can stop by a little earlier and join in the *davening*," Mr. Weiss said.

"Thanks, Dad. Maybe next time I will."

There was no mistaking the sarcasm rolling off his tongue. It appeared as though his father wanted to retort, but he kept his mouth shut.

"You should come next week," Perry whispered to Dina. "There are a lot of single guys there." She poked her with her elbow.

Dina's Choice

"Ha."

"Come on. They'll take one look into the women's section, see your awesome hair, and they'll fall in love right on the spot."

Dina rolled her eyes. "You haven't changed."

She once again found Sam's eyes on her. Had he heard what his sister said? His gaze moved to her hair before looking away.

Dina was hit with a memory, one that took place when she had just turned twelve. She, Sam, and Dovid were in their backyard digging around in the ground, pretending to be scientists searching to discover new species.

"Your hair's kinda pretty, Dina," Sam had said.

Dina's hand had immediately gone to her braided hair. "What?"

Sam had turned to his brother. "Don't you think it's pretty?"

Dovid had looked at Dina's hair and shrugged. "I don't know."

"Well, I think it's pretty." Sam had flashed her a big smile.

It hadn't meant anything back then because Dina didn't really understand what Sam meant. She looked at him again.

Did he still think it was pretty?

It doesn't matter.

Mrs. Weiss and Simi returned. Mr. Weiss stood to make a blessing over liquor. Everyone else stood up as well. Then they each received some of the liquor. Sam requested for more, which prompted a frown from his father.

"Just a little more, Dad," he said, and it seemed as if it took a lot of effort to keep his voice calm. "I'm not an alcoholic," he muttered.

"I'm glad to hear that." His father's tone was sarcastic. He didn't pour him more. Sam pressed his lips together.

"Time to wash," Mrs. Weiss quickly said.

Simi ran over to Sam, who lifted her in the air a few times before dropping her to the ground. "Wee! Did you get me the doll you promised?"

"Not until Mommy tells me you've been a good girl in school."

"But I am a good girl! My teacher gave me three stars this week."

His eyes widened. "Three stars? Wow. I definitely need to consider buying you that doll."

"Yay! But you have to hurry. Because my friend Menucha

said her mommy was going to buy her the doll. I want to get it first!"

"Don't worry. The doll I get you will be much better than Menucha's."

"I love you so much, Shmuel!" She hugged his knees. "You're the bestest brother in the world."

"Hey. I think Dovid's a pretty cool brother, too."

Simi glanced at Dovid and nodded. "Yeah. I have the two bestest brothers in the world."

Dovid gave his twin an appreciative nod.

Once they all washed and had eaten the bread, Mrs. Weiss, Perry, and Dovid brought in the first course. A choice of *gefilte* fish or egg salad. Both Sam and Dovid went for the egg salad. While Dovid could tolerate some *gefilte* fish brands, Sam couldn't stand them at all.

"It's a good thing I decided to make the egg salad after all." Mrs. Weiss winked at the younger twin.

"Thanks, Mom," Sam said.

They discussed many topics, including current events, news in the community, and various other things. Dina glanced at Sam several times and noticed his eyes occasionally wandering to hers. But like before, he quickly looked away.

When it was time for the *cholent,* a slow-cooked stew eaten on the Sabbath, Sam stood up. "I'll bring it in, Mom," he offered before disappearing into the kitchen.

"That was his job when he still lived here," Mrs. Weiss informed her guests before leaving to the kitchen.

Dina followed her.

"Dina! You don't have to help—you're our guest."

"Thanks, but let me take care of it. You've prepared such a beautiful meal. You deserve a break."

The older woman beamed, then turned to her son. "See? Such an angel. Thanks." She squeezed Dina's hand before returning to the table.

Sam took off the lid and inhaled the smell. "I've really missed this."

Dina brought over the large glass bowl Mrs. Weiss had prepared. "Me, too. My dad makes awesome *cholent,* but it's nothing like your mom's. Just don't tell him I said that. He takes pride in his *cholent.*"

He smiled. "Thanks for letting my mom take a break. You've got a kind heart." He poured the *cholent* into the bowl.

"Thanks."

"You don't have to thank me." He lifted the bowl. "It's the

way you are."

Dina took the cucumber and pasta salads and followed him into the dining room. Mrs. Weiss handed each person a plate filled with *cholent*. As soon as everyone took a bite, they sighed.

"Well, you've done it again, Bracha," Mr. Weiss complimented his wife. "This is just as delicious as last week."

Everyone else agreed.

"Thanks, but I must say my *cholent* tasted much better when Sam helped me out."

"Mom," he said.

"I'm serious. I don't know what you did, but it brought the dish to a whole new level."

Sam shrugged.

"I didn't know you like to cook," Dina said.

"There are a lot of things about me you don't know." He looked directly at her.

The table grew silent.

Mr. Weiss cleared his throat. "So how about that strange weather we've been having? I don't recall November weather being so unpredictable last year."

"It's because the world is coming to an end," Perry joked. "Didn't you hear?"

Sam didn't remove his gaze from Dina. She couldn't read the expression on his face.

"Excuse me." She got to her feet and made her way to the kitchen, placing her palms on the table and gulping in some air. Her heart was beating so fast it would catapult out of her chest. What had he meant when he said that? And why had he looked at her so intensely?

"I'm just going to grab a drink," Sam said.

Oh no. He was coming to the kitchen. Dina hurried to the sink and ran her hands under the faucet.

Sam strode in and opened the fridge. Instead of returning to the table, he headed toward Dina instead. She stood there with water dripping from her hands.

"Why did you stop writing me letters?" he asked.

"What?"

"After you left. We exchanged letters for nearly a year. Then you stopped responding."

It had been his idea to write letters instead of emails or texting because he claimed it felt more special. Seeing your name scribbled on the envelope, the anticipation you felt as you ripped it open, wondering what lay inside...

"I didn't stop the letters," Dina said. "You did."

Dina's Choice

His eyebrows knit together. He reached for a dish towel hanging on one of the kitchen chairs and tossed it to her. "No. It was you who stopped the letters."

Dina shook her head. "I remember it clearly. I wrote to you about the play my class was having, complaining that my teacher was forcing me to have a line. You never answered."

His eyebrows relaxed. "I…" He ran his hand through his hair. "I remember that. Are you sure I didn't write back?"

She nodded, remembering how she had rushed to the mailbox every day after school, hoping to find his familiar handwriting written on one of the envelopes.

"Oh. Sorry."

"It doesn't matter," she lied. "We both knew it couldn't last long anyway."

It looked as though he wanted to disagree, to say he couldn't care less that he wasn't allowed to have any sort of communication with a girl. But he turned around and returned to the dining room.

All that time…it had been a misunderstanding. Dina had thought he didn't want to have anything to do with her. She should have written him another letter, but she had been worried she was doing something wrong by talking to a boy.

Orthodox Jewish youths are frequently told they are not allowed to converse with the opposite gender. And Dina had been such an obedient kid.

The meal was finished and everyone thanked the hosts for having them. As Dina and her mother walked to their house, Dina said, "Do you know what caused Sam—I mean Shmuel—to go off the *derech*?"

Her mother shook her head. "Bracha never confided in me. It's a shame. He seems like a nice boy. He gives his parents so much heartache." She sighed, shaking her head again.

"Yeah," Dina whispered as her mother vanished into the apartment. "A real shame."

Chapter Five

Dina's mother dashed into the living room with her teaching bag. "Why am I always late? The principal yelled at me twice this month."

Dina glanced up from her laptop and leaned back against the couch. "Can I ask you a quick question?"

"Sure, honey." Mrs. Aaron opened her bag and rummaged inside.

"I don't really need to go for my master's, but some bosses want their employees to have it. I guess there's more competition. But many bosses don't require a master's. Do you think it's smarter to get a job instead of applying to graduate school?"

Her mother continued rummaging in her bag.

"Mom?"

Her head snapped up. "I'm sure you'll figure it out. You're a smart girl. Now I really need to run." She raced out the door.

Dina stared at the closed door, disappointment nestling in her stomach. She just wanted her mom's advice.

Leaning further back on the couch, she rubbed her hand down her face. This whole future thing was causing her more stress than she thought it would. She bent forward, pulling up social media to check what her friends were up to back in Miami. She'd never been the popular type, and was never surrounded by a group of girls, but she was very close to two girls, Miri and Yehudis. They had spent the whole week in Los Angeles. Dina flipped through the pictures they posted, smiling and commenting. She felt a deep pang in her stomach. As much as she needed to leave Florida, she missed it terribly. She was very glad she and Perry reconnected—Dina didn't know what she'd do without her.

She spent the rest of the afternoon doing more research (which brought her nowhere), browsing the Net, and watching a few TV shows. She wasn't very into TV because there was a lot of inappropriate junk out there, but she managed to find a few good shows. Now she understood why many members of the community are against TV and why her parents had strictly monitored what she watched growing up.

At around 5:30, her phone beeped. Scanning the screen, she learned it was a text from Perry. **Can you come over? Fashion emergency!**

You're asking *me* for advice?

Uh, are you not my best friend? Come over!

Dina laughed, remembering how bossy Perry could be sometimes. Before she had a chance to knock on the Weiss's door, it flew open and Perry grabbed her arm. "I thought I had it all planned, but of course everything had to fall through at the last minute!"

"What on Earth are you talking about?"

She yanked Dina up the stairs and into her room.

"Where is everyone?" Dina asked.

"Dad's at work. Mom's shopping. Dovid took Simi out to some kid concert." She stormed to her closet and yanked the door open. "Okay, what do I wear?"

Dina sat down on the bed. "To where?"

"To my date. Duh, where else?"

"You didn't tell me you have a date."

Her eyebrows shot up. "I didn't? Sorry! I must have been so caught up in it that it totally slipped my mind."

Dina waved her hand. "That's okay. You're not used to spilling all you guts to me."

"You're right. That needs to change right now. I'll tell you all about him once I find a decent thing to wear. Can you believe it? I picked out the *perfect* outfit last night and just realized the shirt has a *huge* stain on it. Like HUGE. So now I've got nothing to wear."

Dina tried to hide her laugh.

Perry threw her hands on her hips. "Are you laughing at me?"

Her best friend nodded. "I miss how you used to stress over anything."

Perry frowned as she turned to her closet. "I don't stress over *everything*. Just the important things."

Dina scooted back on the bed until she hit the wall. "Show me what you've got."

To say Perry's closet was stuffed to the max would be an understatement. The thing looked like it was ready to explode. Perry shoved aside shirt after shirt after shirt.

She looked back to give Dina a face. "Stop laughing. I wish I could see how you stress out before a date."

No need. Dina was pretty sure she wouldn't be going on

any dates in the near future.

"What do you think of this?" Perry held a light green shirt with floral designs over a white skirt lined with green at the hem.

"That's beautiful," Dina said.

"I haven't worn this since last year. And green's a weird color isn't it?"

"No, why would it be weird? You know it's my favorite color."

"Great. You're biased." Perry shoved it back in the closet.

"No way. Put that on and let's see how you look."

"I already know it won't look good." She pushed aside another shirt.

"I'm not letting you get away with not putting it on. Let me see."

She groaned. "Fine, but it's a waste of time." She headed into the bathroom.

"Why are you stressing out so much?" Dina called. "Is there something special about this guy?"

"Maybe. Oh my gosh, did I gain weight? This skirt doesn't close. Never mind, I got it. I might have to suck in my stomach the whole night, though. See, I told you this skirt's not good."

Perry opened the door and walked out.

Dina blinked a few times. "Perry, you look amazing."

Her friend hurried to the mirror. "I do?" She turned to her right and left, a large smile breaking out on her face. "Wow, I *do* look amazing."

"Show off," Dina joked.

"Nope. Confident." Perry touched her stomach. "Ugh, where did this come from? I wish my mom wasn't such a good cook and baker. Disappear, stomach."

"So are you going to tell me about this guy?"

Perry walked over to her bed and was about to sit down, when she winced. "Ugh, I can't move in this skirt. Fine, I'll stand."

"Maybe you should change it. You don't want to be uncomfortable throughout the whole date."

"Please. If women's clothes were meant to be comfortable, we'd all be wearing robes." Perry leaned against the windowsill. "So, his name is Naftali Josowitz. He and I have been going out for two weeks now."

"Nice. So things are starting to get serious?"

Perry studied her nails. "I think so. Maybe that's why I'm stressing out so much. I mean, what am I thinking, dating someone seriously? I don't think I'm ready for this. I'm just twenty. I have like no job and no degree…I don't know."

Perry worked at a dentist's office. Dina asked, "Do you want to go to college?"

Her friend shook her head. "This may sound backward, but I want to be a stay-at-home-mom."

"Nothing's wrong with that." She was lucky she knew what future she desired. Dina still had no idea.

"You okay?" Perry asked.

"What?"

"You just got this very serious look on your face."

Groaning, Dina lay on the bed. "I'm just worried about my future. I don't know if I should go for my master's or get a job. My mom's been a great help," she said sarcastically.

"Well, the two of you are just starting to form a relationship. Maybe she doesn't yet feel comfortable enough to give you her two cents."

"I wasn't asking her to write my Nobel Peace Prize speech."

"Do you want my advice?" Perry asked.

"Please."

"Look for a job. Then after you can see if you need your

master's. You can always go to college while having a job. Some employers even pay their employees to go to school. And there are always online classes and night classes. Lots of options."

Dina smiled as relief washed over her. "Thanks. See, this is why you're my best friend."

Perry gestured to her outfit. "And this is why you're *my* best friend."

They laughed.

"You know," Perry said, "my uncle has helped some people get jobs. Maybe he can help find you one. I can give him a call."

"Really? Thanks, that'd be awesome."

Perry walked back to the mirror and examined herself, a proud and excited smile on her face. She started working on her hair.

"You think he's *the one*?" Dina wanted to know.

Perry sighed. "I don't know. I was up all night thinking about him. I wish I had someone to talk to about this. I don't have any older sisters, just twin brothers who know absolutely nothing about the important things in life. Seriously, who needs them?"

Both girls burst out laughing.

Dina's Choice

"What about your mom?" Dina asked.

She yelled over the hair dryer, "My mom has so many other things to worry about. I don't want to burden her with this, too."

Dina wondered if she was referring to Sam.

When Perry shut off the hair dryer, Dina said, "I wish I could be more helpful. You know I'm bad at these things."

Perry rolled her eyes. "If I had your looks, I wouldn't need all this advice."

The color drained from Dina's cheeks. "What are you talking about?"

Another eye roll. "Dina, you're beautiful. Don't you know that?"

Her hands flew to her flaming cheeks. "What? No—"

"You're not even wearing makeup and you look so pretty." Perry leaned forward to apply foundation.

"How do you know I'm not wearing any makeup?"

Perry gave her friend a face in the mirror. "You don't fool me." She rubbed the foundation. "And the ridiculous thing about it is that you don't even realize it, which makes you more…likeable." She shook her head. "Guys would grab you on the spot."

Dina folded her arms over her chest. "No guy is going to grab anyone. A guy should earn the respect and love of a woman, no matter how she looks."

Perry cheered. "Preach it, Dina." Now she was applying eye shadow. "Still, I feel like I need to work extra hard because I'm average looking."

"Perry—"

"I saw the way both Shmuel and Dovid looked at you."

Dina's face was so hot it could cook an egg. "Shmuel and Dovid," she said as nonchalantly as possible. "You mean, the boys who thought it was cool to throw me over the gate into the house next door to see if I can find any stray dogs?"

Perry giggled. "Wow, I remember that. Didn't you scrape your knee or something?"

"It wasn't a scrape. It was a gash. Seriously, my mom should have sued yours."

"Is the boo-boo still there?"

Dina folded her arms again. "I might have a little scar."

"But you like the scar."

She knew Dina too well. It reminded Dina of her childhood, and how fun the years were. It was a reminder that while she was an adult now, she still shouldn't let go of the child inside her.

"Sam's long gone." Perry applied mascara. "But Dovid's an option."

"Perry, no way—"

"Wouldn't it be awesome if we were sisters?"

Perry was the second one trying to set Dina up with Dovid. "We already are sisters."

She dropped her mascara and stared at Dina in the mirror, her jaw hanging open. She got off her chair and ran over to embrace her. "Oh my gosh! What you said was so awesome. I feel like we're sisters, too."

Dina put her arms around Perry, not knowing until this moment how much her words meant to her, too.

"And Dovid's like my brother," Dina said as she pulled back. "Ew."

Perry wrinkled her nose. "Yeah. Ew." She sat back at the mirror. "I just need to finish my mascara…and success! I'm done."

"Let's see how pretty the lady looks," Dina said.

Perry stood before her friend, and Dina couldn't help the huge smile conquering her face. "You look awesome. Really beautiful."

"Thanks. Some of us need help while others are just natural beauties."

Dina playfully narrowed her eyes. "Some of us are born with the personality while others are as boring as a doormat."

"What? You're not boring! Who said you're boring?"

"A guy I dated back in Miami. The guys I dated there were such jerks."

"You need a good matchmaker. Ooh, I'll give you the number of the one we use. Maybe she'll set you up with one of Naftali's brothers or close friends—we'd be together forever!"

Dina lay back on the bed. "I can't believe you might get engaged. You're going to abandon me."

"*Engaged?* Okay, deep breaths, Perry." She breathed in and out heavily before giving Dina another one of her famous looks. "Who said anything about getting engaged?"

Dina held out her hand and began ticking off on her fingers. "Girl meets boy. Girl and boy like each other. Girl and boy go out on a few dates. Girl and boy start dating seriously. Girl and boy get engaged—"

"You've run out of fingers."

"—then girl and boy get married and live happily ever after."

Dina's Choice

Perry puffed out some air. "I only hope it will all come true."

***

It was nearly midnight and Dina's mother hadn't come home. She glanced at her phone, reading over the five texts she sent her since nine o'clock. Should she be worried?

Clicking on her mother's name, Dina waited as the phone rang. Once again, she got her voicemail. "Mom, where are you? I haven't seen or heard from you since you left to work this morning. I'm starting to worry. Please call me."

Dina hadn't lived with her mother long enough to know if this was normal for her, but she couldn't help the unease pricking her skin. To not be home at midnight? And why wasn't she answering her phone?

Dina didn't know who to call. She didn't know any of her mother's friends, other than Mrs. Weiss. But it was too late to call her now.

An hour later, her worry magnified by a hundred. She grabbed her phone and called her mom once more. There was no answer yet again.

Dina trekked to the window and peeked out into the dark night. "Mom, where are you?"

Chapter Six

Dina bolted up in bed when she remembered her mother hadn't come home last night. She hurried down the stairs and made a short stop in the living room. Her mother was asleep on the couch.

"Mom!"

Mrs. Aaron moaned as her eyes fluttered open. A puzzled look crossed her face. "Dina?" She sat up, rubbing her head. "I have such an awful headache. I shouldn't have slept on the couch."

"Where were you all night?" Dina asked.

Her mother blinked a few times. "What?"

"You were gone all night. I called you a million times and sent you a gazillion texts."

Mrs. Aaron reached for her phone that was sitting on the

coffee table and pressed the power button. It didn't turn on. "Sorry, sweetie. My battery ran out."

"I was worried."

She gave Dina a surprised look. "Why were you worried?"

"Because it was nearly one o'clock in the morning and you weren't home?"

The older woman rubbed her head. "Dina, please stop yelling. My headache."

"I'm not yelling. I was just worried. I hardly slept at night because I thought you were murdered and thrown into the river."

"Don't be so overdramatic. I met an old friend on the way home from work and we decided to go out. We lost track of time. I was so tired when I got home that I crashed on the couch."

Dina fell onto the adjacent recliner and ran a hand down her face. "I was so scared."

"I'm sorry, honey. I should have called. I shouldn't have let my battery die. But you're not a little kid anymore. You don't have to worry if Mommy isn't there when you need her. You have to learn to be independent and take care of yourself."

Dina just stared at her. "This isn't about my being

independent. It's about…" She shook her head as she stood up. "Never mind. You're exactly the same as you were when I was a kid." Irresponsible, selfish, and totally clueless.

Before her mother had a chance to respond, Dina made her way to her room and flopped down on the bed. Maybe coming back to New York wasn't the greatest idea. Seeing Sam, discovering that her mom was exactly how she'd been before. Dina would have been happier back in Miami.

A few minutes later, Dina was dressed and left her room. She needed to go out and do…she didn't know what. But she couldn't stay in that house.

"She totally blew up on me," she heard her mother say. "I don't understand what I did wrong…"

She was on the phone.

"Yeah, at least all of yours are out of the house. Who said children bring us joy? They seem to only give us heartache. I'm glad I only have one."

Tears entered Dina's eyes.

"No, despite everything, I wouldn't give her up for anything," Mrs. Aaron said, then laughed. "Even though it's very tempting."

Dina grabbed her jacket and left the house. She marched up

the block, blotting away the tears seeping out of her eyes. She didn't know what came over her. She supposed she was hoping to have a close relationship with her mom. Other than Perry, she wasn't close to anyone. Did her mother even want her there? She had told her friend that all her daughter brought her was heartache. Why? Because Dina dared worry about her when she hadn't come home last night?

She loves me—I know she does. But maybe not everyone is cut out to be a mother. Maybe Mrs. Aaron just *couldn't*, no matter how much she tried. *If I ever get married, I'll be the best mother in the world.*

"Ouch!"

Someone grabbed her arm before she tumbled to the ground. Dina's temple pounded from the strong blow, and it took a second to see through the tears. A tall man stood before her. Sam Weiss. Dina yanked her arm away.

"Dina, are you okay?"

She quickly turned away, embarrassed for him to see her that way.

"Did I hurt you?" he asked.

"What are you doing here?" Her back was still turned.

"My parents live here."

"No, they live down the block. We're a good few houses away from there."

He was quiet for a few seconds before he said, "Yeah, it's hard to find parking near the house." He placed his hands on her shoulders. "Are you crying?" he asked gently.

Dina squirmed away from his touch.

"Sorry, I didn't mean to touch you. But can you turn around?"

She shut her eyes. She didn't want him to see her tears. But he'd already seen enough. Opening her eyes, she turned around.

His entire face softened. He raised his hand like he wanted to touch her, but he dropped it to his side. "Are you okay, Dina?"

The way he said her name, so gently and full of feeling...she couldn't take it. "I'm fine," she said, a little too abruptly.

Pain passed over his face, but he pushed it away. "Did I hurt you? I'm sorry, I wasn't paying attention to where I was going."

"No, I'm not hurt. Just because I'm a woman, that doesn't mean I'm made of porcelain."

Now he appeared even more hurt. He turned away. "I

never insinuated you were. Even I felt a sting on my arm." He walked away.

Dina released a breath. "Wait."

He faced her.

"Sorry. I didn't mean to snap at you. I'm just upset."

He took a step closer, looking into her eyes. "What are you upset about?"

Those ocean eyes. They could make Dina expose her whole heart to him. She pulled her eyes away. "It doesn't matter."

"Are you sure?"

She still didn't meet his gaze.

"Dina." His soft, warm fingers brushed the bottom of her chin. Before she could think, he lifted her chin, forcing her gaze to meet his. "What's going on?"

She freed her chin from his grasp. "I told you, it doesn't matter. A person is allowed to be upset once in a while."

"Of course. But sometimes that person needs to talk to someone about it."

"To you?" she asked.

He held out his hands. "Why not? We used to tell each other everything."

"Not everything."

"Okay, obviously there were things you couldn't talk to me about. But you were always open about what was going on at home."

Dina narrowed her eyes. "How do you know I'm upset because of something that happened at home?"

"I don't. I was just giving you an example."

Great.

He took another step closer. "What's going on at home?"

She stepped back. "We're not twelve years old anymore."

"I know."

"You're not…you're not the same."

"Neither are you."

She turned away. "I need to go."

"Wait." He gently grabbed her arm.

She pried it free. "Stop touching me."

"Sorry. Habit."

Because he touched many other girls on a daily basis? Dina's hands fisted at her sides.

"I just want to make sure you're okay, Dina."

She glared at him. "Don't worry about me. Worry about yourself and the life you've chosen." She marched away before he could say anything, and didn't look back.

Dina's Choice

As she continued up the block, she wracked her brain, trying to remember if anyone on the streets had seen them together. The last thing she needed was people seeing a man touch her. Even though it felt nice.

No. No. No. No.

Dina didn't know where she was walking to, and found herself in a Judaica book store. Browsing the titles, she wasn't really playing attention to anything. She kept replaying the conversation she had with Sam over and over in her head. When she tried to blot it out, the conversation with her mother took over.

"Be quiet," she muttered.

"Excuse me?" a middle-aged woman browsing the next aisle asked.

"What? Oh, um, can you recommend anything good?"

Her eyes swept over the young woman. "You're looking for a husband?"

Did she seriously just ask her that? As if that was the most important thing on Dina's mind.

The older woman walked over and pulled a book off the shelf. "I bought this for my daughter two months ago, and now she's engaged! It's a wonderful book."

Dina refused to look at it.

"You should give it a try. It helps young people understand the opposite gender and what they can say or do to make a good impression. It covers every stage of a relationship, from initial meetings, dating, opening up, establishing emotional connections and when it's time to get engaged. It's written by a great rabbi."

Dina wondered if the woman actually worked there and was trying to make a sale.

She shoved the book into Dina's hands. "Trust me. Buy it." She walked away.

Curiosity took over the better of Dina. She glanced at the book. It was called *You, Me, and the Life that Could Be.*

That was either a ridiculous title or an interesting one. Dina flipped through the pages. Was this a sign? Maybe she'd learn something important from this book.

Before she could change her mind, she purchased it. If it turned out to be garbage, at least she'd have a good laugh.

***

Dina didn't want to go home and face her mother. She decided to stop by the Weiss's and learn how Perry's date went.

She lifted her hand to knock on the door, when it opened.

Dina's Choice

Sam was about to crash right into her. Again.

He faltered back. "Sorry. I definitely don't want to do that to you again."

There was something in his eyes. Pain. Nothing to do with Dina, though.

"Are you here for Perry?" he asked.

"Yeah. You're leaving?"

He folded his arms across his chest and balanced on the balls of his feet. "Uh huh."

"But didn't you just get here?"

He looked back into the house. "Let's just say some days are more welcoming than others. Enjoy the rest of your day." He stormed off.

Dina watched him walk up the block and round the corner.

"Did Shmuel leave?" Simi dashed out the door. "Why did he leave? We were supposed to play Horsey."

Dina reached for her before she hopped down the stairs. "Hey, are you supposed to leave the house by yourself?"

"No. But Shmuel said he was gonna play Horsey with me."

"I think he had to leave." She swung the little girl onto her hip and walked into the kitchen.

"Mommy, why did Shmuel leave?" Simi freed herself and

raced to the counter, where chocolate chip cookies were cooling off. She munched on one.

Mrs. Weiss smiled brightly at Dina. "Hi, Dina. Here, please have a cookie."

"Thanks, they look delicious." She devoured one in less than a minute. Simi grabbed another cookie before skipping out of the room.

"That girl." Mrs. Weiss shook her head. "She takes up too much of my energy. I'm not that young anymore."

"I'd be more than happy to sit for you," Dina offered. "Even when you're home. You don't have to pay me."

"Oh, Dina, you're so kind. I might take you up on your offer, though I insist on paying you."

Dina waved her hand. "I honestly don't mind doing it for free. You and your family have been so welcoming. I feel like I owe you."

Mrs. Weiss played with Dina's hair. "Well, we can work that out later. Thanks for the offer."

"Okay. Is Perry home?"

The older woman looked toward the doorway before lowering her voice. "She's been upstairs in her room all day, very upset. She won't talk to me or her father. I'm worried she had a bad date last night. Do you think you can talk to her? Lift her spirits?"

"I'll try."

"Thank you."

Perry was sitting on her bed with her back pressed to the wall. Her legs were pushed up to her chest, her arms looped around them. She was staring at the spot in front of her. A half-empty bag of jellybeans sat near her.

Dina took a hesitant step closer. "Perry?"

Her head snapped in her friend's direction. Dina expected Perry to tell her to get lost, but a look of relief captured her face. She motioned for Dina to come in. "Can you close the door?"

Her voice that was usually so full of life sounded dead. Dina nodded as she shut the door and sat down near her. "You okay?"

Perry snorted. "Do I look okay?"

"I'll rephrase. You look like someone died."

"Not someone. Something."

"I don't follow."

Perry buried her face in her knees. "I'm talking about my future. My future just died."

Her friend gently rubbed her shoulder. "Does this have anything to do with your date last night?"

Perry didn't say anything, only sobbed into her knees. Then she nodded.

"Did something bad happen?"

"The worst!" Her muffled voice cried.

"Did he say something offensive? Do something wrong?"

She continued to moan.

"Did he end things?" Dina asked.

She nodded. "The matchmaker will call any minute. I feel like such a loser. And I won't be able to stand the look on my parents' faces. They really wanted things to work out with Naf—with *him*."

"Why?"

"His dad and my dad went to school together. My mom and her mom know each other. Our families would mesh so well together."

Dina continued rubbing Perry's back. "All of that doesn't matter, Perry. This isn't about your parents or his parents. It's about the two of you."

"It doesn't matter. He doesn't want me."

"But you told me last night that things were starting to get serious."

She scoffed. "Joke's on me, huh?"

"Well, that's the last time I'm giving you fashion advice."

Perry's head sprang up. "No way. That was like the best outfit I've ever worn. Even Naf—*he* said so. Gosh, I can't stand the name now. It's ruined for me forever."

Dina took her hand. "You'll find the right one. I know you will. And anyway, you have time. You're only twenty."

Perry dug her face in her knees. "But I want him! And how is being twenty a good thing? It just means I'll have more years of disappointment and heartbreak."

Simi skipped into the room "Perry, did you take my jellybeans?" She made a short stop when she noticed the state her older sister was in. "Perry's crying?"

"Get out of my room," Perry snapped.

Simi's eyes widened. "But you're crying. You're sad. Why are you sad?"

Perry dug her face in her knees again.

Dina took the bag of jellybeans and took Simi's hand, guiding her out of the room. "Perry's a little sad now and wants to be left alone. Here are your jellybeans. Go play, okay?"

"But I don't want Perry to be sad."

Dina squeezed the little girl's hand. "I'll try to make her happy again, okay?"

She nodded before skipping away, munching on her jellybeans.

When Dina was back in Perry's room, she reached into her bag and pulled out the marriage book. "Perry, have you read this book?"

Perry lifted her head. "No. What is it?" She wiped her eyes and took it from Dina.

"I don't know, really. Some woman at the store practically forced me to buy it. You can borrow it."

She opened the flap. "I'm so useless I need to learn from a book."

"We're all useless," Dina said. "Useless and clueless when it comes to guys. But that's normal. And maybe that's why that rabbi wrote the book."

"Okay, thanks." Perry placed it on her night table.

"Are you ready to talk about it?" Dina asked.

"I guess. But I'm not really sure what happened. I thought we were having a great time. Then in the middle of nowhere, he just said, 'I don't think this is a good idea. Sorry, I'll drive you home.' And being the fool that I am, I was like, 'What's not a

Dina's Choice

good idea? The restaurant? Okay, let's go somewhere else.' And then he got all stiff and said, 'No, I mean us. We're not a good idea.' And I just stared at him. It's like his words refused to make sense in my head. I don't know how long I was staring at him like a fool until it finally sunk in. And then I started crying like a big baby right there in the middle of a fancy restaurant. He was so mortified he told me he was going to call me a cab."

"Jerk," Dina said.

"He paid for it, though."

Dina snorted. "Ever the gentleman."

"I just don't get it." Perry's face was back in her knees. "I don't know what I did wrong."

Her best friend rubbed her back again. "Forget about him, Perry. He's a loser. You deserve much better."

"Thanks. I'm so embarrassed by the whole thing. I wonder what he told the matchmaker and what she'll tell my parents." She raised her head. "You know, it's weird that he ended it right to my face. Most people tell the matchmakers to end it for them."

"Well, I guess he's got some boldness in him. And Perry, now you can tell your parents about this before the matchmaker does. Your parents will hear your side of the story before his. You know, in case he says something ridiculous."

She shook her head. "No, he'd never do that. You're getting the wrong impression of him—he's a good guy. I guess he's just not for me. Now I'll just have to trust that Hashem will send the right one."

Dina leaned back against the wall. "Do you think it's possible for you to never marry your soulmate because your soulmate is the one getting in the way?"

Her eyebrows scrunched. "Huh?"

"Everyone has a soulmate," Dina explained. "Hashem brings us together when the time is right. But what if one of them is the one who's holding back? Like...let's say he's off the *derech* or something."

Perry's eyebrows shot so high they practically disappeared into her hairline. "Are you talking about Shmuel?"

"No!" Dina said too quickly. "No way. I told you he's like a brother." Complete lie.

Perry looked relieved. "Good. I honestly don't know. But I don't like thinking about it. Mom's so worried Shmuel will marry a non-Jewish girl."

Dina swallowed the lump in her throat. "Has he...brought home any girls?"

Dina's Choice

She shook her head. "No, but Dovid visited his apartment once. It was obvious a girl was living there."

Dina's heart pounded in her head.

Perry touched her friend's shoulder. "You okay?"

Dina nodded.

"You look pale."

"I was…um, it's my mom."

"What?"

Relieved at the change of subject, Dina told her what happened between her and her mother. "Do you think I overreacted? I mean, it's not like my mom's my kid or anything. She doesn't owe me any explanations."

"True," Perry agreed. "But she should have at least called you to let you know. I would be worried, too." She wrapped her arm over Dina's shoulder. "She's not used to having you around. I'm sure things will be better soon."

Dina hoped she was right.

"By the way." Perry opened the drawer of her night table and pulled out a piece of paper. "I spoke to my uncle about helping you find a job. He wants you to call him."

"Thanks." Dina hugged her. "I'll call him as soon as I get home."

Chaya T. Hirsch

***

Perry's uncle, Yaakov Weiss, promised he'd get in touch as soon as he could. Dina hoped things would work out.

Mrs. Aaron entered the kitchen while her daughter was cooking spaghetti on the stove. She did a double take. "Are you cooking?"

The young woman laughed lightly. "Well, if you can call pasta and sauce cooking. I, um, wanted to apologize about this morning. I shouldn't have blown up on you like that."

Her mother walked over and put her arms around Dina. "You shouldn't be the one apologizing. I forgot what it's like to have someone at home worrying about me. I've been on my own for so long." She kissed the top of Dina's head. "I didn't mean to worry you. I'm sorry."

Dina focused on mixing the spaghetti. "It's okay. Um…"

"Yes?"

"Do you think I should start dating?"

"If that's what you want, sure. I already have a few matchmakers' numbers in my phone."

"For you or for me?" Dina asked.

"For you."

Dina lifted an eyebrow. "Are you *that* eager to get rid of

94

me?" she joked, though she couldn't shut out the phone conversation she'd overheard that morning.

"Goodness no." Her mother chuckled. "I wish I could keep you here forever."

Dina's face brightened. "Really?"

Mrs. Aaron put her hands on her daughter's shoulders. "But I worry about you. I worry your father and I have ruined marriage for you. Not all marriages end up in divorce. I hope you know that."

"I *do* know that. I'm not a little kid."

She squeezed Dina's shoulders. "I know. But these things stick with a person, carries on even into adulthood. I just want to make sure we haven't left you with any permanent damage."

"Oh, you have," Dina joked again.

Her mom laughed. "Stop, Dina. I'm being serious here."

"I'm fine. I trust that Hashem will take care of me and everything will work out."

Mrs. Aaron smiled. "Good. In that case, I'll call the first matchmaker in my contacts."

"Do you have the matchmaker Mrs. Weiss uses?"

"I don't think so. Why? Is she top-notch?"

Dina shrugged. "No clue. But Perry thinks if we use the

same matchmaker, we could get set up with boys who are related or friends. Her dream is for us to live near each other and raise our kids together."

Her mother grinned as she shook her head. "Perry is so loyal to her friends. But I don't think life works that way. You can very well marry guys who can't stand to be in the same room."

Dina's eyes widened.

"That doesn't mean you will! Gosh, I'm such a terrible mother." She kissed Dina's cheek. "Everything will work out. I'll call Mrs. Weiss tonight for the number."

"Thanks. So how are things going with the man you're seeing?"

"Meh." Mrs. Aaron sat down at the table with an apple. "I broke things off with him."

"Why?"

She shrugged. "I'm not really interested in getting married right now. I want to focus on myself, on you."

"You don't have to do that."

She bit into the apple. "It's not something I find pressing at the moment. Maybe once you're married off, I'll feel more inclined to get married again. But for now, I'm content with just having you in my life."

Dina smiled. "Thanks."

Chapter Seven

There were two very important things happening to Dina today. One, she had an interview with an advertising agency. Perry's uncle had been able to set her up with someone in only two days. And two, she had a date with a young fellow by the name of Mordechai Lowy.

When her mother had told her she was going to call matchmakers, Dina thought it would take a few days, maybe weeks, until everything fell into place. But it turned out that Mrs. Aaron and Perry's matchmaker had been in the same class in high school. She'd only had to hear some basic things about Dina before finding—in her words—the perfect guy for the young woman. Dina was so nervous she could barely touch her breakfast.

Her mother passed Dina's chair at the kitchen table to place her coffee mug in the sink and stopped to rub her daughter's shoulder. "It'll be okay. Just do you best and I'm sure it'll work out."

"Are you talking about the interview or the date?"

"I was referring to the interview, but I suppose the advice can work for both."

Dina played around with her scrambled eggs, her stomach rebelling against her.

"You have to eat something, honey," her mom said as she scrubbed her mug. "You'll need your strength."

Ordering her stomach to behave, Dina gathered some scrambled eggs and put it in her mouth. She had no idea if it tasted good. The only thing she focused on was not throwing up.

Mrs. Aaron kissed the top of Dina's head. "Good luck, Dina. Call me after to let me know how it went." She threw her teaching bag over her shoulder, opened the door, and waved before she left.

Dina forced herself to eat a few more spoonfuls before tossing the rest into the garbage. Her interview called for nine o'clock, and it was only 8:15. Although she and her mom had driver's licenses, they couldn't afford a car. She'd have to take a bus to the office. It had been a while since she'd been on a New York City bus, and she had no idea how long it'd take to get there. But the last thing she needed was to come late and make a bad impression. Shrugging into her jacket, she walked out of the house.

The city bus stop was about seven blocks away. When Dina arrived there, she found many people waiting. That was probably a good thing—it meant the bus hadn't arrived for some time and should be here any moment.

Hugging her arms, she told herself to relax. Not only was she stressed over the actual interview, but she felt another load of stress because she didn't want to taint Perry's uncle's name. He didn't know Dina, but he went out of his way to do this favor for her. If she bombed the interview, it would be a bad reflection on him. It wasn't healthy to think those thoughts, but she couldn't help it.

Finally, the bus arrived. Dina should have expected it to be packed like a can of sardines. Some of the other people chose to wait for the next bus, but Dina couldn't afford to do that. She couldn't be late to the interview.

She found a spot at the back of the bus and clung to a pole. With her free hand, she took out her book of Psalms. Not only would the prayers help with the interview, but it relaxed Dina as well. It was as though she felt Hashem's presence when she whispered the words. Whatever happened, she knew it would be for the best.

About forty minutes later, the bus reached Dina's stop. She was relieved she chose to leave early, since she hadn't thought the ride would be that long. Clearly, she hadn't gotten used to Brooklyn yet.

As luck would have it, the boss wasn't in yet. One of the other employees settled Dina down in the conference room with some water. She waited for him for ten minutes, which didn't help her nerves. But as the interview went on, she began to relax. The man seemed like a nice guy, and he even had gone to the same *yeshiva* as her father, though he didn't know him. Still, it was always nice to find common ground.

The agency had dealt mostly with print ads all these years, but now they wanted to add another branch—creating websites for many of their clients. They were looking to hire at least two web designers.

Since Dina didn't have any experience yet, he told her that if she were to get the job she'd work under the other web designer who had more experience. He thanked her for her time and told her he'd be in touch within the next few days.

Outside the office, Dina inhaled the largest gulp of air she had ever inhaled in her life. One down, one more to go.

With an abundance of nerves and adrenaline coursing through her, Dina decided to take a stroll around the neighborhood. She'd been to this part of Brooklyn many times as a kid. Her great aunt used to live here and she and her parents would visit her all the time. But it was a little foreign because it felt like forever since she'd stepped foot here. But all Orthodox Jewish communities look similar. Stores all around, *shuls* and schools, and of course the people.

Her date was at six o'clock. Her outfit was already laid out on her bed, her shoes had been chosen, and her jewelry was on her vanity. Even though she was practically ready, she wanted to get home and mentally prepare herself. This would be the third guy she went out with and she didn't want the date to be as disastrous as the other two. As she climbed on the city bus and found a seat, she called her mom to let her know how the interview went.

***

"Are you sure you have the right outfit on?" Perry asked Dina over the phone.

Dina's Choice

"For the hundredth time, yes!"

"Take a selfie and send it to me."

"I already sent you a picture last night."

"But that was *before* you put it on. Let me see how it looks on you."

Dina tried not to grit her teeth as she did what her friend asked. Before she sent the picture, she checked her reflection in the mirror. A white shirt with a pretty design and a black skirt. Once Perry received the text, she sent Dina a row of "thumbs-up" emojis.

"Told you," Dina said.

"You're at an advantage. Anything you wear will look good on you."

"Oh, be quiet."

Dina heard a male voice on the other end of the line. Then Perry said, "I'm just helping Dina get ready for her date…Yeah, Dina Aaron. Do you know any other Dinas?"

Was she talking to Dovid? Or was it Sam? She could never discern their voices over the phone.

"Dina, Dovid asks who the guy is," Perry said.

"Does your whole family know I have a date?" Dina asked.

"No. I just happen to be in the living room and Dovid

overheard."

"Why does he want to know the guy's name?"

"Dovid, she wants to know why you want to know his name...okay. Dina, he said he just wants to make sure you're going out with a good guy. Aw, isn't that *so* sweet? Dovid's like the older brother you never had—ouch!"

"Sorry," he said.

"Since when did you get so strong?"

"Um, Perry? As much as I enjoy talking to you, I need to get ready."

"For your *date*!"

"I rolled my eyes."

"I know you did," Perry said. Then she sighed. "I always dreamed of getting engaged at the same time as my best friend. It would be awesome to go through the process together."

"Um, who said anything about getting engaged?"

"You know what I mean. Anyway, I wish you the best of luck. And you'd better call me as soon as you get home. Oh, Dovid wants to know the guy's name."

"Right. Mordechai Lowy."

"She said Mordechai Lowy. Do you know a Mordechai Lowy...? Dina, he doesn't know him. But he wishes you lots of luck as well."

"Thanks to the both of you. Now I really have to go!"

Dina applied makeup and did her hair, reviewing the information Mrs. Feder had sent her last night. Mordechai Lowy was twenty-four and worked at his father's bakery, doing the bookkeeping and helping out with whatever he could. He had wanted to work at one of the top firms in Manhattan, but his parents really needed his help, since they were getting closer to retirement. Dina found that to be a really good quality, to put your dreams on hold to help out your family.

The doorbell rang. Shoot, he arrived and Dina wasn't ready. With a shaky hand, she quickly touched up her makeup and put on her jewelry. Her heart beat so fast and hard she thought she might throw up. *Remain calm. He's just a guy. You're just going out on a date.*

"Dina, can you please come down?" her mother called from downstairs.

Dina clasped her bracelet around her wrist, grabbed her bag, and made her way downstairs. His back came into view when she reached the foot of their stairs, and her palms grew clammy. She had no idea why she was more nervous this time than she had been on her previous dates. Maybe because back then, she still had innocence and hope. She'd been through two bad dates and now she knew it could very well happen again. She just wished she could have a good time.

"There she is!" Mrs. Aaron hurried over and took her daughter's hand, pulling her into the kitchen. "Here is Mordechai."

"Hi." He gave her a dimpled smile. He was a little taller than her, slim, with light brown hair and green eyes. He wore a plaid shirt and dark pants.

"Hi," she returned the greeting.

"You kids have a good time," her mother said with a wide smile.

Mordechai opened the front door for Dina, and she thanked him. "Sorry, but my car is a few blocks away. Do you want me to bring it over? Parking is so bad here."

"That's okay. Let's walk together."

He smiled again and led her down the block. "I'm really sorry we have to walk. I circled the block three times before giving up."

"It's okay. I'm wearing flats."

He glanced down at her shoes and nodded. "Smart choice."

"Thank you."

They laughed.

He cleared his throat as his eyes did a quick sweep of the area. "Any nosy neighbors watching?"

"I'm sure there are plenty."

There was silence for a few seconds before he said, "So what's Miami like?"

Dina told him about her old life until they reached his car. He opened the door for her, and she once again thanked him. His car wasn't in the best shape, but it didn't bother her. She didn't even have a car. And she knew he was trying to help out his parents with their bakery.

"By the way," Dina said. "I was very impressed when I learned you're helping your parents with their store. I know you want to work at a top company."

He pulled out of the curb. "Thanks. My family is the most important thing in my life. My brother lives in Israel and my sister in Ohio. A lot of the responsibility falls on my shoulders. But I'm very happy to take it all on."

"That's really great."

"Thanks."

Silence.

"I'm sorry if I'm a little quiet," Dina said. "I'm so nervous."

"You're not quiet. You're great. And it's okay—I'm really nervous, too."

"Can I ask how many dates you've been on?"

He thought for a few seconds, tapping his fingers on the steering wheel. "Not a lot. Maybe eight."

Dina raised her eyebrows. "You call eight not a lot?"

"Why? How many have you been on?"

"Two, not including this one."

"There's nothing wrong with that. Having more experience helps a little—I no longer get lost or leave on a date with an empty tank." He chuckled softly. "But I still get very nervous."

She leaned her head back, glad they felt similarly.

"Is it okay if we go to a coffee shop instead of a hotel lounge?" he wanted to know.

"Sure."

They were quiet for a bit.

"So can you tell me what your hobbies are?" he asked.

"I like to draw."

"That's cool. You're a web designer, right?"

"Yeah. I actually had an interview this morning," she told him.

"How did it go?"

"I think it went well. I won't hear back for another few days. But I really hope I get it. The boss seems like a nice guy, and it's a small office. It's a little far from my house and I'll have to take the bus, but it's not a big deal. What about you? What are your hobbies?"

"I really like sports," he answered. "And music. I play guitar."

"That's cool. Do you like to bake? Or do you not do any baking at your parents' store?"

"I usually don't go near the baking. My mother is so particular. But if we're having an extremely hectic day or when the holidays are coming up, I would help her. But I definitely haven't inherited the baking gene."

"I bake here and there," Dina said. "But I probably won't be winning any awards."

He laughed. Then he pulled up to the coffee shop and parked in the small parking lot. The two of them entered and waited on line at the counter.

"Have you been here before?" he asked.

"I don't think so. I'm not sure if it existed when I lived here."

"Probably not. They have delicious coffee, though."

"I'll take your word for it." Dina didn't want to tell him she wasn't much of a coffee fan.

When their turn arrived, Mordechai ordered a coffee with a name Dina had never heard of and she settled with vanilla. He also bought two large jumbo cookies. They found a table at the back and sat down. Dina did a quick sweep of the area and discovered another couple on a date. They were hardly exchanging more than one word to one another. Dina wondered what she and Mordechai looked like to other people.

"Thanks for the cookie," she said. "It looks delicious."

"Trust me, it is."

"So you come here often?" she asked.

"I buy coffee here almost every morning. But not the cookie or other baked goods. I nosh on the food at the bakery practically the whole day. Which is terrible."

"You don't look it," she complimented.

"Thank you. By the way, I forgot to mention that you look very nice."

Her cheeks heated up as she murmured a thank you.

As Mordechai told Dina a funny story that happened to him yesterday, the door opened and a familiar man walked in. Sam Weiss. He wasn't alone. A woman was with him. They were holding hands.

Dina didn't realize she was staring at the doorway. Mordechai turned around. "What's wrong?"

She tore her gaze away from Sam. "Nothing. Sorry."

She wished she could disappear. She didn't want Sam to see her. She tried to move in sync with Mordechai so he blocked her view, but from the way his eyebrows rose, she knew he thought she was behaving strangely. He turned around again. "Are you sure you're okay, Dina?"

Her eyes snapped to Mordechai and she forced them to remain there. "Yeah, I'm fine."

Except she was anything but fine. As Mordechai talked about a person in his life who had inspired him, Dina's gaze slipped to Sam. He stood a few feet away, clutching his coffee in one hand. His other hand clasped the girl's. He turned his head and saw Dina. Surprise registered on his face. Then his gazed moved to Mordechai and he frowned.

Why was Sam there out of all the places in Brooklyn? And at a kosher coffee shop? Dina was pretty sure there were countless others with much better-tasting coffee than there.

He and his girlfriend found a table a few feet away. The woman sat in the seat facing Dina, but Sam said something to her and she lowered herself in the opposite seat. Now Dina had a good view of Sam, and he had a good view of Dina. She heard his girlfriend giggling from where she sat.

"And he inspired me to be a good person," Mordechai was in the middle of saying. "To always think about the person next to you, even if it seems like he has it all put together. You really never know what a person is going through. I would have liked to be a social worker or maybe a therapist, but I have a mind for accounting." His eyebrows came together. "Did you hear what I just said?"

Dina blinked at him. "I'm sorry, what?"

"I was just telling you about one of my rabbis in high school. How much he inspired me."

She felt like such a horrible person. Here she was on a date with a pretty good guy, and all she was doing was stressing out because Sam Weiss and his girlfriend sat a few tables away.

"I was listening," she lied. "It's amazing how he inspired you."

He smiled. "Thanks. What about you? Has anyone ever inspired you?"

Sam's girlfriend leaned forward and whispered something in his ear. He grinned at her, but his gaze was locked on Dina's.

She felt something deep in her stomach, but didn't know what it was. As much as she wanted to tear her eyes from his, she couldn't. It was as though they were glued there.

Mordechai turned around. Then he faced Dina and scrunched his eyebrows. He cleared his throat. "Have you tasted your cookie?"

Sam opened a bag of potato chips, took one out, and launched it at his girlfriend, trying to aim it in her mouth. She missed and the chip cracked into little pieces as it splat on the table. They both laughed like it was the funniest thing in the world.

Mordechai shifted in his seat.

Oh my gosh. What was wrong with her? Dina had never been so rude before. Keeping her focus on Mordechai, she said, "My coffee is really good."

He gave her a slight smile. "I'm glad you like it."

Silence.

He tapped his fingers on his coffee cup.

More silence.

"You have good taste," Dina continued.

He nodded, continuing to tap his cup.

As much as Dina tried to force her eyes to remain on

Mordechai, they sprang to Sam. He and his girlfriend's heads were bent together, and they were whispering fervently. As though they had so much to talk about but not enough time. As though they were utterly in love.

Mordechai shifted in his seat again. "I guess we should head back."

Already? When Dina glanced at her watch, she realized an hour hadn't even passed yet. But the truth was, she was glad to leave. She would rather not witness another moment of Sam with his perfect girlfriend.

Mordechai gathered their cookies and placed them in the small bag the woman at the counter provided. They left the shop and headed to the car. They were both quiet on the ride to Dina's house.

"I'm sorry if I was quiet," she apologized. "I was very nervous."

She hated that she lied, but what could she say? That she was distracted by Sam and his girlfriend? Mordechai would dump her on the spot.

He shrugged. "No problem. I understand. Hopefully it'll be easier the next time."

Dina mentally sighed in relief. Mordechai still wanted to

give her a chance. Maybe she hadn't made as bad of an impression as she thought.

He walked her up the stairs to her apartment. "Thanks," she said. "I had a good time." At least she did until Sam had showed up.

He nodded. "Good night."

Dina's mother peeked her head into the hallway as Dina closed the door behind her. "How did it go?"

Dina walked into the kitchen, dropping her bag on the table. "I don't know."

"Uh oh."

Mrs. Aaron sat down and motioned for her daughter to join her. "What happened?"

Dina didn't want to tell her about Sam. "I don't know. I just…froze."

"Did he make you uncomfortable?"

The younger woman shook her head. "He was very nice. I thought I ruined it, but he told me he's sure the next date will be easier. I'm not sure if that meant *my* next date or *our* next date." She rubbed her forehead. "I'm too tired to make sense of it. I'm going to bed."

Her mother kissed her cheek. "I'm sure things will make

more sense in the morning. Good night, sweetie."

"Good night."

It was most certainly not a good night. Every so often, whether she was in the shower, propped up on her bed reading, or trying to fall asleep, the only thing Dina saw before her eyes was Sam. Sam with his hand interlocked with his beautiful girlfriend. Sam with his head bent closer to her, whispering like they were two lovebirds.

She smashed her pillow over her head. Why did any of it matter? She didn't have feelings for Sam. Not anymore. She couldn't. She needed to move on with her life. Clearly he had—in the opposite direction from where she was headed. He wasn't allowing Dina to ruin his life, so why did she give him permission to ruin hers?

Chapter Eight

Perry woke Dina up at seven in the morning for the much-needed details about her date last night. Dina told her what she told her mother, and Perry reassured her friend that it probably wasn't as bad as she thought. She was sure Dina would go out with Mordechai again.

Dina didn't want to stay home in case the matchmaker called, so she and Perry spent most of the day shopping. Not something Dina enjoyed doing, but it definitely took her mind off last night. The *other* part of last night, that is. Sam still hadn't left her mind.

But she couldn't avoid home forever. As soon as she walked into the kitchen where her mother was working on dinner and took in her expression, Dina knew her mom had heard back from Mrs. Feder. She leaned back on the counter with her arms crossed. "Let me have it."

Mrs. Aaron lowered the knife onto the cutting board and took her daughter's hand. "Mordechai isn't interested in continuing. I'm sorry, Dina."

Though she wasn't surprised, Dina hadn't expected it to hurt. Her pain transformed into anger a second later. If Sam wouldn't have walked into that coffee shop, she probably would have had an amazing date. But no, the guy who was no longer religious decided last night to grab coffee with his girlfriend at the kosher coffee shop *she* happened to go to. Ridiculous.

"I feel like we never really had a chance," she told her mother. "I wish I could try again."

"Do you want me to speak to Mrs. Feder? Ask Mordechai to reconsider?"

"I don't know. Maybe. Just not tonight. Give him some time."

Mrs. Aaron nodded. "Whatever you want, sweetie."

Dina's phone rang. Glancing at the screen, she saw an unfamiliar number. "It's no one," she told her mom. Then her eyes widened. "Oh my gosh, it's Mr. Hershkowitz. He's probably calling to let me know whether I got the job." She quickly answered the call. "Hello?"

"Hello, is this Dina Aaron?"

"Yes." Her voice was hoarse.

"Hi, this is Mr. Hershkowitz. I interviewed you yesterday for the web designer position?"

"Yes." Her voice was even hoarser. And shaky.

"I am pleased to inform you that we would love to have you join us."

"Really? I got the job?"

He chuckled. "You got the job."

"Thank you."

"How early can you start?" he asked.

"As soon as possible."

"How does tomorrow sound?"

"Perfect."

"Excellent. I'll see you tomorrow at 8 AM."

"Thanks, bye!"

Mrs. Aaron wrapped her arms around Dina. "*Mazel tov!*"

Dina's cheeks hurt from smiling. "Thanks, I didn't think I'd get it."

Her mother hugged her tightly. "I knew you would. You just need to have confidence." She looked into her daughter's eyes. "I'm so proud of you, Dina."

Dina's heart burst with warmth. "That means a lot to me, Mom."

***

First days are supposed to be difficult, so Dina tried not to let the setbacks during her first hours of work bother her. It's the usual complications one might experience on her first day, like accidentally putting the wrong paper in the copying machine, forgetting to save her work on the computer and having to start all over again. But other than those minor things, Dina was having a wonderful first day.

At around two in the afternoon, she received a call from Mrs. Weiss, asking her if she could babysit tonight. The family would be attending their cousin's wedding and they needed someone to look after Simi.

"I'd love to," Dina told her.

Dina didn't leave work until after six and the ride was about half an hour. She quickly ate something at home before popping over to the Weiss's. Perry opened the door. "You look gorgeous," Dina complimented.

She was wearing a navy dress with sequins and her hair was pinned up in an elegant updo. Her face held just the right amount of makeup.

"Thanks," Perry said. "Come on in." She shut the door, then yelled into the house, "Simi! Dina's here."

The little girl rushed over, that same ratty-looking stuffed bear hanging off her arm. "Yay!"

"What's all the shouting?" Mrs. Weiss entered the living room. "Ah, Dina. Thank you so much for agreeing to babysit on such short notice. Shmuel was supposed to, but he got caught up with something." She took the young woman's hands and kissed her cheek. "Still such an angel."

"Thanks. We'll have loads of fun."

Simi pumped two fists in the air. "Yay!" Her poor stuffed bear plunked to the floor. "Beary!" She swept it off and hugged it close. "I'm sorry, Beary."

Mr. Weiss walked in. "Hello, Dina." He turned to his wife. "Bracha, we need to get moving."

She nodded. "Dovid, are you ready?"

Dovid appeared in the doorway. "Ready."

Dina couldn't help but stare. Dovid looked so…handsome. His suit was nicely pressed and fit him perfectly. His hair was combed neatly and his blue tie brought out his eyes.

His gaze landed on Dina. "Dina?"

"She's here to babysit Simi," his mother explained.

"Oh, I see." He walked over and whispered, "Want some pointers?"

Dina found her brown eyes lost in his ocean ones. "S-sure."

"She loves Candyland. You can make her do anything you want as long as you bribe her with that game. Make sure you know where her stuffed bear is at all times or else she will throw a tantrum. And the most important thing? You must read her a bedtime story."

Dina nodded. "Thanks."

"Dina, I forgot to ask," Perry said, "how was your first day?"

"Good."

"You started work today?" Dovid asked. "That's great."

"Thanks."

Mr. Weiss looked impatient. "We really need to get moving, gang. My sister will kill me if we miss the *chuppah*."

"It's not fair!" Simi clung onto the bottom of her mother's skirt. "I wanna come!"

"Sweetie, we told you you're too young."

"But my friend Menucha went to her cousin's wedding. Why can't I go to mine?"

Dina's Choice

Dovid crouched down, though he made sure his knees didn't sweep the floor. "Simi, sometimes grownups don't invite kids to places. It's just the way things are. But you want to know why tonight is special for you?" He gently jabbed his finger into her stomach.

She scowled. "Why?"

He raised his eyes to Dina. "Because you're going to spend the whole night with Dina. And you are going to have a blast."

"Your brother's right," Dina told Simi with a huge smile. "Your family will *wish* they were here with us."

Simi's eyes moved from her brother to Dina, looking doubtful. Then she smiled. "I don't want to go to that wedding anyway."

"Great, great." Mr. Weiss waved his arms toward the door. "Let's move. And Simi." He hoisted her into his arms. "Are you going to be a good girl?"

She beamed. "I'm always a good girl, Daddy."

He kissed the top of her head. "Yes, you are." He gently lowered her to the floor, the nodded to Dina. "All our numbers are on the fridge. Call if you need us."

Dina returned the nod.

Once they all said goodbye and left, Simi and Dina faced

each other. "Simi, tonight is your night. We'll do whatever you want to do, but within reason."

The little girl's eyebrows crinkled. "What does that mean?"

"It means as long as we don't get in trouble, do something wrong, or hurt anyone, we'll do whatever you want."

She jumped up and down. "I want to play Candyland!"

Dina silently laughed to herself. "Okay. You sit on the couch and I'll join you with the game and some snacks."

"Fruit Roll-Ups and candy corn!"

"Your wish is my command."

After grabbing the game and the nosh, the two girls spread the board on the coffee table and sat on the floor. Perry and Dina used to be obsessed with the game when they were Simi's age—Okay, they even played it when they were well above Simi's age. Sam and Dovid had never liked it much.

Simi talked about her life in preschool. Dina actually found it quite interesting. She hardly remembered much from that age, other than playing Candyland with Perry and a few other memories.

"And I got a star because I helped a girl in my class," Simi was in the middle of saying. "She hurt her finger and I carried all her things for her. The whole week!"

Dina's Choice

"You're such a *mitzvah* girl," Dina said.

"That's what my teacher said! Are you a teacher, too?"

"No, I do web design."

"What's that?"

"Drawing, but for the computer." Sort of.

Her eyes widened. "You like to draw? I love to draw! Can I get my drawing supplies and we can draw?"

"Sure, I'd love to. But don't you want to finish the game?" Dina was having major nostalgia and didn't want it to end.

Simi made a face at the game. "No, I wanna draw!" She zoomed away, into one of the back rooms. She emerged a few minutes later, lugging a huge art set.

Dina hurried to take it from her. "That's the biggest art set I've ever seen in my life."

"Sam and Dovid got it for me for my fifth birthday. But we can't play here. Mommy will get mad if we get the floor dirty. We have to go to the basement."

"Okay."

They were about to head down there, when there was a knock on the door. Dina glanced at Simi. "Is someone supposed to come?"

The little girl's face shined with hope. "Maybe Mommy and

Daddy came back to take me to the wedding?"

Dina peeked through the peephole and nearly dropped the art set. Sam stood out there. Why in the world was Dina seeing him wherever she went?

"It's Sam—Shmuel," she let Simi know, putting down the art set.

"Shmuel! Shmuel!" Simi jumped up and down.

Why was he here? Before her eyes, all she saw was him holding his girlfriend's hand and laughing with her.

As soon as she opened the door, Sam swept Simi off the floor and threw her over his shoulder, causing her to hang upside down. "Sim Sim!"

When his gaze landed on Dina, surprise registered on his face. "Oh. I didn't know you were here." He looked into the house. "My family left already?"

"Like twenty minutes ago."

"Oh, I guess I'm super late." He tickled Simi as he strode in, causing her to yelp.

Dina shut the door and followed them into the room. "I don't get it. You're here to babysit Simi?"

He scanned his phone. "I told my mom I might be late, but…oh. She texted me that she found someone else. I don't know why I'm just seeing the text now." His eyes moved to hers. "I guess you're off the hook then."

Dina rubbed her arm. "I don't feel comfortable leaving when your parents expect me to stay here until they return."

"Why, do you not trust me?"

It took a second for Dina to realize he was teasing her. She forced the images of him and his girlfriend at the coffee shop out of her head. "I guess you can go," she told him.

"No way. I came all the way here to hang out with Sim Sim. What are you guys in the middle doing? I see she's already persuaded you to play Candyland. As I recall, you were quite the Candyland queen at her age."

Dina didn't know why she liked the fact that he remembered that.

She shrugged. "That was a million years ago."

"No, we're gonna draw and paint!" Simi said.

"Can you please put her down?" Dina said. "Her face is getting red."

"No, I want to stay like this! You both look so funny upside down."

"Dina's right," Sam told her. "You're going to get dizzy." He flipped her over but didn't lower her to the floor. He hoisted her onto his hip. "Does Princess Simi want to draw?"

"Yeah! We were gonna go to the basement!"

"The basement it is!"

Dina slowly followed them down the stairs. Why was he there? Dina didn't want to talk to him or even look at him.

Mrs. Weiss had set up a corner in the basement for Simi to do her art projects. Old tablecloths and plastics covered the floor and a few smocks hung on a row of hooks. Sam handed one to Dina. "I think this is Perry's."

"Thanks," she muttered.

He fastened one around Simi, then on himself.

For the next hour, they painted and drew. Sam and Dina didn't interact much because they were both focused on Simi. But every so often, Dina felt his eyes on her. She looked at him, but he immediately moved his eyes. She caught his a few times, though.

Then it was time for Simi to get ready for bed. Sam read a magazine in the living room while Dina gave her a bath and dressed her into bunny pajamas. They both settled down on her bed. "Time for a story?" Dina asked.

"Yeah, but can Shmuel read it? He always makes funny sounds."

Dina's Choice

"Maybe Dina makes funnier sounds," he said.

Dina shook her head. "Please, the honor is yours."

He plucked a book off the shelf, lifted Simi, and slid into bed with his sister in his arms. He read to her with so much love, Dina couldn't help but watch. Simi giggled at his funny voices and frowned at the sad parts. Sam was so into it, it was as though the story came to life. Right there in that moment, Dina realized that Sam would be a wonderful father one day.

He finished the story and tapped Simi's nose. "Now it's time for the princess to go to sleep."

She snuggled under her blanket with her stuffed bear. "Good night, Shmuel and Dina."

"Good night," they wished before leaving her room.

"She's so cute," Dina said as she and Sam walked through the hallway and into the living room.

"Indeed she is." He flopped down on the recliner.

Dina stood there for a few seconds before sitting down on the couch. Even though Simi was down the hall, it felt as if they were alone together. Dina didn't want to be alone with Sam Weiss. But she certainly couldn't leave.

"So what were you doing at Hyatt Street and East 5th?" he suddenly asked.

"That's where I work," she replied. "You saw me?"

"Yeah, you were waiting for the bus."

"Oh."

He leaned forward. "It's going to get dark pretty early in the next few weeks. If you ever need a ride, I'd be happy to give you one."

"Thanks, but I'm okay."

"I'm serious, Dina. The area where the bus stop is isn't the best neighborhood."

"I can take care of myself."

He kept his eyes on her for a few seconds. "Give me your phone."

"What?"

"Please, just give it to me."

She passed it to him. He punched something in before handing it back to her.

"That's my number," he explained. "If for some reason the bus doesn't come and it's getting late, call me. I'll drive you home."

Maybe this made her feel a bit like a damsel in distress, but it felt good that he had offered. Like he was taking care of her. Of course she could take care of herself, but everyone needs help once in a while. Though Dina was pretty sure she'd never call him. To ride alone with him in a car again?

"Thanks," she said.

Quiet.

"How long do weddings usually take?" he asked. "It's been quite a few years since I've attended one."

"It varies. Does your family plan on staying for the whole thing?"

He shrugged. "It's my first cousin, so probably."

"Were you not invited?" Dina wanted to know.

"Of course I was."

"So why aren't you there?"

His eyes flicked to hers before they focused on his shoes.

She knew the answer. Because everyone would stare at him, the cousin who went off the *derech*. He would feel uncomfortable.

"Perry told me you're in a band?" she asked.

He nodded.

"Where do you play?"

"Wherever we can get a gig. Bars, clubs. Parties."

"Weddings?"

"We don't play that kind of music."

"What about Jewish weddings?" Dina asked.

He scoffed.

"What's wrong with Jewish weddings?"

"I'd like to think we're more talented than the bands who play at Jewish weddings." He raised his eyes to hers. "Oh, don't give me that face. You know most Jewish singers aren't the greatest."

"Some are," she argued.

"Most aren't."

"You can be one of the ones who are," she pointed out.

He shook his head but didn't utter a word. Then he said, "Come to one of my gigs. You'll see the quality of my music."

"Me, at a club? You know that's not my scene."

He reached into his pocket and produced a USB flash drive. "Then listen to this."

Dina held out her palm, and he dropped it inside "What is it?" she asked.

"Listen to it when you get home."

She put the flash drive in her bag.

They were both quiet again, until Dina broke the silence. "Is your girlfriend Jewish?"

His eyes flicked to hers again. "Not that it's your business, but yes she is Jewish."

"Not religious."

"Neither am I."

"You don't need to remind me," she snapped.

"I suppose the man you went out on a date with is *frum*," he said sarcastically.

"Of course he is. Why would I go out with someone who's not religious?"

Again, he didn't say anything.

"Why did you go to a kosher coffee shop?"

He shrugged. "Just felt like it."

"When there are numerous ones all over the neighborhood, ones that probably serve better coffee and at cheaper prices."

He sat back and folded his arms over his chest.

"Do you only eat kosher?" she asked.

He glared at her. "Am I prying into your life? Am I asking you about your date?"

Now she folded her arms. "There's nothing to ask. You ruined it for me."

He sat up. "*I* ruined your date?"

Dina didn't meet his eyes. "Yes, you did."

"I would love to hear how."

She didn't respond.

"Well?"

Her mouth was firmly shut.

He stood up from his recliner and dropped down next to her. "Is it because I was with Gloria?"

Dina's eyes flashed to his. So the woman had a name. "Like I care about your little girlfriend."

"She's really pretty, isn't she?" he said.

Dina glared at him.

"But you know something, Dina? You're much prettier."

She scooted away. "Whatever you're doing, it's not working."

He moved closer. "You were jealous. That's why you think I ruined your date with Religious Boy."

She scoffed. "I was jealous of your Glinda?"

"Gloria," he corrected.

"You think I don't know that?"

"You were jealous of Gloria. But you know something else? I was jealous of Religious Boy."

"His name is Mordechai."

"I don't care what his name is."

She was about to say something when the door opened and

the Weiss's piled in. They looked surprised to see Sam there.

"Shmuel." Mrs. Weiss walked over and hugged him. "I thought you said you weren't going to make it. I asked Dina to babysit."

"It was just a misunderstanding."

"Is Simi in bed?" Mrs. Weiss asked.

"Yeah," Dina replied. "She was a perfect little angel."

Mrs. Weiss's smile held nothing but love and pride.

"How was the wedding?" Sam asked.

"Beautiful," Perry answered, then sighed in a dreamy and sad manner.

"You were missed," her father mumbled. "Many people asked about you."

Sam looked at him but didn't say anything. The room fell into an awkward silence.

"I want to show you something," Dovid told his brother. "It's in my room."

Sam looked more than relieved to leave.

Mrs. Weiss cleared her throat, then smiled to Dina. "Thank you so much for looking after Simi. Is twenty dollars okay?"

"That's more than enough. Thanks."

She handed the young woman the money and hugged her.

She and her husband exited the living room, leaving Perry and Dina alone.

"So," Dina said, "did you see any potential boys?"

An unreadable expression passed over her friend's face. But it disappeared a second later and was replaced with humor. "Sure did," she said, "and I'm pretty sure I've caught some mothers' attention. I mean, look at me." She held out her hands and did a little twirl.

Dina laughed. "You definitely look amazing. I'm sure you'll be married off in no time."

That same unreadable expression passed over Perry's face. Dina was about to ask her what was wrong, when she released the biggest yawn Dina had ever seen. "Wow, sorry," she apologized. "I'm so tired. And I need to wake up early tomorrow."

"I'd better go," Dina said.

They hugged and wished each other good night, and then Dina left the house. As she made her way to her apartment next door, she had an eerie feeling that someone was watching her. Looking up toward Sam's old room, she noticed the shade was pulled up, a head peeking out. When she moved her eyes to the next room, Dovid's, she saw that the shade was pulled up as well, and another head was peeking out.

She quickly turned away and entered her house. Her mother was already asleep. Dina climbed up to her room and emptied the contents of her bag like she always did when she came home. The USB flash drive toppled out. She had almost forgotten about it. She settled down at her computer and plugged it in. When the pop-up window appeared, she saw a list of songs. One of them caught her attention. It was called, *Girl I Can't Have.*

Her heart sped up as she clicked on the song and listened to it. She recognized Sam's voice immediately. He was lead singer and backup guitarist in the band. He sang about a girl he'd loved his whole life but couldn't have. First she had moved away. They had kept in touch, but then she broke contact. Next he talked about how they'd chosen different paths in life...

Her heart sped up even more. The song...it was about Dina. About the two of them.

Shaking her head, she leaned back in her seat. No, it was probably not about her. He must have just loosely based it on their lives. Aren't songs always melodramatic? Whatever the case, Dina couldn't deal with it right now. She just wanted to go to sleep and not think about her feelings.

Chapter Nine

As soon as Dina entered the kitchen the next morning, her mother rushed over to gather her in her arms. "Mordechai Lowy agreed to go out with you again!"

"What?"

The older woman nodded vehemently.

"Okay," Dina said, pulling away. "I don't know why it's such a cause for celebration."

Her mom frowned. "How about, 'Thank you, Mom, for convincing the matchmaker to convince the boy to go out with me again because I made a mistake on my date?'"

Dina rubbed the side of her head. "You're right. I'm sorry. I really appreciate you doing this. But I woke up in a bad mood."

"Oh? What's going on?"

She pressed her lips together. "I don't know. I guess it's just one of those mornings." She poured herself a glass of orange juice, trying to block out the words Sam said to her yesterday. *"You know something, Dina? You're much prettier. You know something else? I was jealous of Religious Boy."*

And that song. It had played in her head over and over again all night. She had only listened to it once, but she practically knew the words by heart. It wasn't about her. It *couldn't* be.

"When's the date?" Dina asked her mother.

"It's up to you. He's available all week."

The song started playing in her head again. *No, get out.* "Tomorrow night sounds good," she told her.

Mrs. Aaron smiled brightly. "Great. I'll call Mrs. Feder."

"Okay, thanks. I need to head to work. Have a good day, Mom."

"You too, sweetie."

The day passed uneventfully. At five o'clock, Perry sent Dina a text, asking if she could come over after work. **Of course you can**, Dina texted back.

Perry was waiting for her friend on the living room couch when Dina walked in, chatting with Mrs. Aaron and eating some pastries. The marriage book Dina had given her last week sat on her lap. She leaped to her feet when she saw Dina. "Finally! I've been waiting for an hour."

"Sorry. The bus took forever to come."

"Thanks so much for the cake, Mrs. Aaron," Perry said before grabbing Dina's arm and dragging her up to her room.

Perry just stood near the window, wringing her fingers. The book was tucked under her arm.

Dina lowered herself on her bed. "You okay?"

Perry continued wringing her fingers.

"I see you brought the book."

Perry held it in her hands, studying the cover. "Dina, this book…it made me do something really silly."

Dina's heart sank. "What did you do?"

She started pacing Dina's room. "Oh, why did I do it? Ugh! I hate myself."

"Perry, just calm down and tell me what you did. It's probably not so bad."

Perry plopped down near Dina on the bed and covered her face. "Naftali was at the wedding."

"Naftali *Josowitz*?"

Perry nodded, her face still buried in her hands.

"Okay..."

"The book talked about how sometimes you have to take risks in life. Don't always play it safe. Get out of your comfort zone. But I doubt the rabbi actually meant walking over to a guy and asking him why he doesn't want to marry you."

Dina's eyes nearly popped out of their sockets. "What?"

Perry lowered her hands and turned to face her friend. "He was at the wedding. I guess he was from the other side. He and I nearly collided in the hallway. I don't know what happened, but something just snapped inside me. I spent a good portion of the smorgasbord looking for an opportunity to get him alone. Then I saw him heading to the bathroom." She shook her head as though she couldn't believe herself. "I literally ran after him and called his name. He turned around, so shocked to see me. So then I said to him, 'Why don't you want to marry me?' Just right out and said it. He stared at me, totally frozen. So of course I felt like a real loser. I said to him, 'Look, you and I got along really well. We have so much in common, have the same goals and are on the same page. The only thing standing between us is fear. Fear of the unknown. Fear of the future. Fear to feel.'" Perry looked into Dina's face. "Then I just marched away." She covered her face and moaned. "Ugh, why did I do that?"

Dina lowered her friend's hands and noted the tears seeping out of her eyes. "Perry, that wasn't loserish of you. That was so brave!"

Perry blinked. "Really?"

"Yeah. Kudos to you for not being afraid to walk up to a guy and give him a piece of your mind. Didn't it feel good?"

A smile formed on Perry's face. "Yeah." She laughed. "It actually felt really good. I was holding that in for so long."

"I'm jealous of you," Dina admitted, "to be brave enough to actually tell a guy what you think."

Perry eyed her friend suspiciously. "What guy...? Oh, you're talking about Mordechai Lowy."

"Yeah," she quickly said, "I'm talking about him. But you want to hear something? Mrs. Feder convinced him to go out with me again."

Perry squealed. "Told you she's a good matchmaker. That's awesome. When are you going out?"

"Tomorrow night. Perry, what do you think Naftali will do now?"

She scoffed. "Probably tell all his friends to steer clear of the Crazy Girl."

"Or maybe you gave him a lot to think about."

"Sure. I scared him away. Whatever, it doesn't matter. I'm just happy I let it out. Now I can move on with my life."

Dina leaned forward to hug her. "I'm proud of you."

"It's all because of that book you gave me." Perry reached for it handed it to Dina. "Have you read it?"

"Not yet."

"It's really a good book. Made me realize things about myself and opened my eyes to things I've never even considered."

"Okay, I guess I'll read it," Dina said.

Perry hugged her again before leaving. Dina scooted back on her bed and opened the book.

***

The book stated that first impressions mean everything. We may not like it, but that's just how the world works. This would not be Mordechai's first impression of Dina, but she wanted to start over. A clean slate. Hopefully Sam wouldn't ruin it for her this time.

Okay, she couldn't hold him responsible for ruining her date. He hadn't done anything wrong. She just wished he didn't have such a strong presence in her mind, her life, and in her heart.

Mordechai smiled when Dina walked into the kitchen. That immediately chased away some of her nerves. Since Dina didn't want to mess up this date, too, she felt an intense amount of pressure.

Mrs. Aaron sent Dina a reassuring look as her daughter and the young man left the house, telling Dina that everything would work out for the best. Mordechai grinned at his date. "This time, I made sure to find parking close to your house. My car is at the corner."

"Thanks. But don't worry, I made sure to wear flats again."

They laughed, but it sounded awkward and forced. Mordechai opened the car door for Dina and she thanked him.

"I decided to go with a hotel lounge this time," he said. "I hope that's okay."

"It is, thanks."

He gave her a smile, though it didn't quite reach his eyes. Great. Dina was worried things might be strained because of the last date, but she thought they'd get past it. *I guess not.*

He started telling her a funny story that happened this morning. Try as she might, she didn't find it very interesting. Maybe because it sounded forced. Was he forced to be here?

Perhaps just doing a favor to Mrs. Feder? Or a favor to Dina? She didn't want to be anyone's charity case.

"Do you want to be here?" she interrupted.

His mouth snapped shut and he stared at her.

Oh gosh. How could she just blatantly ask that question? Maybe it was because of what Perry had told her, and maybe because of the powers of the book. It discussed how one had to be assertive sometimes. Other people's feelings matter, but sometimes yours matter more.

"Um." He coughed, avoiding her eyes. "Of course I want to be here."

"As a favor to me?" Dina asked. "A favor to your mom? To Mrs. Feder?"

He tapped his fingers on the steering wheel, still avoiding her. "I guess a little of all the above."

"You shouldn't have agreed to go out with me if you didn't want to."

He finally looked at her. "It's not that I don't want to be here. It feels like *you're* the one who doesn't want to be here. Just like the last date."

Now Dina was the one to stare at him. "I *do* want to be here. I know I messed up last time and wanted to give this another chance."

He puffed out some air. "Okay, let's forget about the past and the conversation we just had and start over. Hello, my name is Mordechai Lowy."

Dina forced herself to give him a wry smile. "I know. I saw your name on the profile Mrs. Feder sent me."

He laughed, but it once again felt strained. They were bathed in silence again.

"Um, do you want to hear about my job?" Dina asked.

"Sure," he said, a little too enthusiastically. As though he was so happy to have a topic to discuss.

Dina spoke of her job, but it was obvious he only listened with half an ear. Dina was ready to admit that there was no salvaging this date. He may be a good guy, but it was just not working.

They drank some water at the lounge and talked about a few more things, but it appeared they both couldn't wait to get the date over with. Finally, an hour later, he drove Dina back home.

After he walked her to her door, she said, "Mordechai."

"Yeah?"

"I'm sorry things didn't work out between us. You're a

good guy, and I hope you meet the right one soon."

For the first time tonight, he gave her a sincere smile. "Thanks. I wish you the same."

As soon as Dina finished telling her mother how her date went, she called Perry. Her instructions were to call ASAP. Dina was glad she didn't feel sad as she told her best friend, in more detail, how bad the date had been. She felt at peace, because she knew that she'd made the right decision, with no hard feelings.

"Sorry it didn't work out," Perry said.

"It's fine."

"But, um, it seems we were twins tonight."

"What do you mean?" Dina asked.

Perry was quiet for a few seconds before she said in a shaky voice, "It turns out Naftali Josowitz doesn't think I'm crazy after all."

"Perry...?" Dina asked, feeling the excitement leap off her.

"We went out tonight! I didn't tell you because we literally decided an hour before we met."

"Perry!"

"And guess what?"

"What?"

"We had an AWESOME time!"

"I'm so happy for you."

"Wow," she said. "I can't believe I actually had the nerve to say that to him. He told me how he really liked how assertive I was. He, too, couldn't stop thinking about the way we broke up, and he admitted I was right. He was scared to commit and to be open with another person. I guess you can say I inspired him. I'm telling you, Dina, that book is magic."

Dina laughed. "I doubt it. I'm halfway through and didn't have luck with my date."

"Maybe you just haven't met the right guy yet," she pointed out.

"Maybe."

"So are you going to take a break from dating?"

"Nah. I want to try at least one more time. Mordechai was a good guy, it just didn't work."

"Okay, but if you do take a break, make sure it's a short one. It's hard to get back into it after taking such a long break."

"Wise words from a more experienced dater?" Dina teased.

"I may be younger than you, but I have ten years on you with dating experience."

"Don't I know it," Dina muttered.

"But it's nice to have little experience," her friend said. "You have more hope. Less disappointment."

"True. I think I'm starting to have less hope and more disappointment."

"Aw, don't say that. Things will work out for you soon. I can feel it."

"That's okay. I'm not in a hurry to get married. It'll come at the right time."

"Sooner than you think," Perry promised. "I just know it."

Chapter Ten

Why did Dina agree to go out on a date tonight? It had only been two days since she went out with Mordechai Lowy. The woman who suggested her new date was someone who went to high school with Dina's mother. The guy, Pinny Yarmish, was her nephew.

It would be nice if Dina and Perry got engaged around the same time. The next stage in life is so hard, and it would be nice to have someone by your side as you go through it. But of course Dina couldn't make decisions based on a silly dream. If Perry got married years before Dina, that was how it'd be.

Pinny Yarmish talked a lot. On the way to the hotel lounge, he enlightened Dina on every single member of his immediate family and distant relatives. The only words Dina had muttered since they got in the car were, "That's nice," "Very cool,

"That's interesting."

"I know this hotel is all the way on Long Island, quite a distance from our neighborhood," the young man said, "but isn't it so awkward when you're on a date and see someone you know? I know that's how it is, but it makes me so uncomfortable. Doesn't it make you uncomfortable?"

"I guess, but—"

"And everyone knows everyone, right? The world is so small, and it seems to grow smaller every day."

He looked at Dina, waiting for her to respond. "I'm not very social," she explained. "I don't really know that many people."

He stopped by a red light. "You're not social? Oh, I thought my aunt...well anyway, you have many friends, don't you?"

She shrugged. "I have as many friends as I need."

He squinted. "Is that a fancy way of saying you have no friends?"

"No. I'm saying the friends I do have are true and loyal. That's all a person needs."

"Whoa, calm down. I was just asking a question. Why are girls always so emotional?" he muttered under his breath.

Dina's Choice

"Excuse me?"

"What?"

"Did you not mean for me to hear that?"

"No. I did want you to hear that."

Was this guy for real?

"Look, Devorah—"

"My name is Dina."

"Right, sorry. Dina. Look, I didn't mean to offend you. My mom and sisters always tell me I need to be more careful with my choice of words because girls are much more sensitive and yada yada. But why can't you girls just be less emotional? Like I was at a wedding last week and the girls kept shrieking. It was so annoying. Why the need to shriek?"

Dina turned away from him. "I don't shriek."

"I didn't mean you, obviously. I just meant girls in general."

"You can't clump us all into one group. We're all different."

He parked in the parking lot. "But you're not. You all talk the same, dress the same. Your mannerisms are all the same."

"Right, which is why you think we all have the same name, too."

"I'm sorry I called you Dina. I remember your name now. Devorah." He grinned.

Dina rolled her eyes and opened the door. "Let's just get inside."

The hotel was breathtaking. Dina had never seen anything like it before. "Wow," she said. "This is beautiful."

"Like you," he said with a laugh.

Her face warmed.

"You can't say thank you?" he demanded.

"You didn't exactly make me feel comfortable."

"Why not?" he asked as he found an empty table in the lounge. "I told you you're beautiful. It's a compliment."

"Religious girls aren't used to getting those kinds of compliments from guys. Don't you know that?"

He waved his hand. "Please. All girls want to get compliments. You pretend you're offended and embarrassed, but I know you're secretly thrilled."

Dina glared at him.

He chuckled. "You know I'm right."

"How many dates have you been on?"

His eyebrows shot up. "You want me to count?"

I guess I got my answer.

"Do you want something to drink?" he asked.

She was about to answer, when he said, "Nah, don't bother

telling me what you want. All you girls order the same thing. Diet Coke."

"Excuse me? I don't drink diet Coke."

"Right." He winked. "And I suppose you don't only eat salads."

Dina got to her feet. "I don't want to be here."

His jaw dropped. "What? I just drove us all the way here. It's the prettiest hotel in all of Long Island. Sit down, Devorah."

"Dude, my name is Dina."

"Then why did you tell me to call you Devorah?"

She threw her hands up. "Good night, Pinny Yarmish." She walked away.

"Wait a second." He caught up. "I can't just leave you here. I need to bring you home."

"I don't want to go anywhere with you. I'll be fine."

"No way. I'm taking you home."

"Did you not hear me? I said I don't want to go anywhere with you."

His eyebrows creased. Then he pursed his lips. "Fine. I don't know what's wrong with you girls. Maybe I'm better off staying single for the rest of my life." He marched out of the room.

Dina leaned against the wall, breathing heavily. *Oh my gosh.* She couldn't believe that guy. She felt as though she'd just been in a strange movie. And now she was stranded in the middle of Long Island.

Taking out her phone, she was about to call her mom, but she didn't want to worry her. Besides, they didn't have a car. She could call a cab, but that would cost a lot of money. Perry! She was ready to call her, when she remembered her friend was also out on a date tonight, with Naftali. There was no one else to call.

Except, that was not true. Someone had put his number in Dina's phone only a few days ago. She scrolled through her contacts and found his name. Sam Weiss.

Her palms grew clammy. It was either call him or a cab. The truth was, after the night she'd had, the last thing she wanted was to ride with a strange man. She wished she could call Dovid, but she didn't have his number.

Sighing, she dialed Sam.

"Hello?" he spoke into the phone.

"Um, hi. It's Dina."

A pause. "Dina Aaron?"

Dina's Choice

"Yes."

"Hi, Dina."

"Um, hi."

Quiet.

"Is there something I can help you with, Dina?"

Why did he keep saying her name? It was almost as though he enjoyed saying it. "Yeah. I'm on Long Island."

"What are you doing there?" he asked. "At ten at night."

"A date."

He sucked in a breath. "I see."

"I'm stranded here."

"*What*? He just left you there?"

"No, he wanted to take me home, but I didn't want to be in the same space as him a minute longer."

"That bad?" he asked.

"You have no idea."

"I'll pick you up, Dina. Just tell me where you are."

"Are you sure you don't mind? I could take a cab, but I—"

"No, Dina. Don't take a cab. I'm coming to get you. Are you in a safe place?"

"Yeah. In a hotel lounge."

"Is the place full?"

She scanned around. "More or less."

"Okay. I'll come as fast as I can. But don't leave the lounge. Stay in a place that has a lot of people. Don't go anywhere alone."

"Okay," she said, feeling warm by his concern and protection.

"I'll call you on the way. Bye for now, Dina."

"Thanks, Sam. I really appreciate it."

She sat down at a table in the middle of the lounge, where it was heavily populated, mostly by couples. Her eyes kept wandering to the entrance, as though worried Pinny Yarmish would march right through and demand he take her home.

Her phone rang. "Hello?"

"Hey, Dina. I'm on the way. Are you okay?"

"I'm fine."

"Okay. I wanted to keep you on the phone throughout the whole ride, but my battery's going to die soon and I can't find my car charger. Just stay where you are and I'll be over as soon as possible."

"Thanks, but you don't have to worry about me. I can take care of myself."

"I know you can, Dina. But sometimes I want to take care

of you, too."

He hung up before she could respond.

It should take an hour for him to get here, maybe a little less if there was no traffic. Dina spent the time on social media, seeing how her friends back in Miami were doing. She really missed them.

Her phone rang. It was Sam. "Hi," she said

"Hey. I just parked. The hotel is huge. Can you tell me where you are?"

Dina had no idea where she was, since that was the first time she'd been there, but she managed to direct him to the right lounge. Relief washed over her when she saw him walk inside, and he seemed to hold the same relief when he spotted her. They met halfway.

Sam stopped for a second and looked Dina over. "You look really nice."

"Thanks," she said. "And thanks for coming to get me. I feel like such a loser."

"No, the guy is a loser for making you so uncomfortable."

She nodded. They stood there.

"Can I buy you something to drink?" he offered.

Now that he mentioned it, Dina was parched. She wished

she ordered herself a glass of Coke while she waited. "Thanks. I'll buy myself a Coke."

"I don't mind." He walked to the bar.

Dina sat at a table. He returned with two glasses of Coke. "You look a little shaken," he noted.

"Just upset."

"I'm sorry you went out with such a jerk," he said.

"Me, too."

Quiet.

He finished his glass. Dina finished hers. Then he stood. "It's getting late. Your mom will probably start to worry."

"Thanks for coming," Dina said as they headed to the parking lot.

"You don't have to keep thanking me."

"Yes, I do."

He shook his head. "I'd do anything for you."

Dina glanced at him before tearing her gaze away. "No, you wouldn't."

He didn't say anything as he opened the passenger door for her.

They rode in silence, mostly. Sam tried to broach a few topics, but Dina was intent on staring out the window. The date replayed in her head. She knew all guys weren't like that, but how many Pinny Yarmishes would she have to go through before she met the right one?

Even though her focus was on the window, Dina felt Sam's eyes trekking in her direction every so often. Every cell in her body begged her to face him, to look into his eyes, to show him how much his actions meant to her. How much *he* meant to her. But she couldn't.

He parked the car in the Weiss's driveway and killed the engine. The car was completely silent. Dina finally turned to him. He was looking at her. It appeared as though he wanted to say something. He even moved his hand a few inches toward her before dropping it on his knee.

"Thanks," Dina said.

He nodded. "Hopefully the next date you'll have will be with a better guy."

"Thanks. Good night. And thanks again for picking me up."

"You're welcome."

He waited until she was at her door before driving off. Dina didn't enter her house, though. She wasn't ready to make sense of what had happened tonight. First with that loser guy and then with Sam dropping everything and going out of his way to "save" her.

"Dina?"

She turned around and found Dovid standing there.

He took a step closer. "I saw Sam drop you off. You seem upset. Is everything okay?"

Dina didn't know why, but tears came to her eyes. She quickly wiped them away.

Dovid's eyes widened. "Let's sit." He gestured to the bench in front of his house.

"Sorry," Dina said as she sat next to him. "I don't really cry. I guess I'm just feeling stressed."

"About what?"

She puffed out some air. "I don't know. Dating, the future. Life." She shrugged. "So many uncertainties."

He nodded slowly. "What happened tonight?"

"I went out with a jerk. He took me to Long Island. I got so mad at him that I refused to let him take me home. I called Sam to pick me up. I would have called you, but I don't have your number."

He leaned back. "Sorry you went out with a jerk. I would have picked you up."

"I know. Thanks."

"Is that the same guy you went out with the other day? Mordechai something?"

Dina shook her head. "He was pretty decent, but I totally blew it with him."

He nodded again. "It happens. I've had my share of bad dates."

"You have to tell me some."

He raised an eyebrow, smiling in a teasing manner. "Oh, I have to?"

"Do you want to make me feel better?"

"Definitely." Dovid coughed. "It's embarrassing, so please don't tell anyone. Especially Perry. She'll tease me until I die."

"I promise."

"Okay, so I took out a girl for the first time. The matchmaker told me she came from a rich family and had expensive taste, so I took her to a fancy restaurant. I thought things were going well. She seemed very interested in our conversations, she laughed a lot. I definitely did not see this coming."

Dina leaned a little closer, curious what happened next.

"She excused herself to the bathroom," he continued. "No

problem. I paid for the check in the meantime. I waited. And waited. And waited. After twenty minutes, I started to grow concerned, but I didn't want to embarrass her by sending someone to check on her, you know? So I continued to wait." He hung his head. "I waited a whole hour before asking one of the waitresses to check on her." He sighed. "She wasn't there."

Dina's eyebrows shot up. "What happened to her?"

His gaze moved to his shoes. "She either climbed out of the bathroom window or slipped out the front door of the restaurant. I've been on quite a few dates, but I never imagined I'm such a boring person that she'd actually run away. If I would have known that, I wouldn't have spent so much money on dinner, which wasn't very good, by the way. And the worst part? When I got home, the matchmaker had already called. Can you believe it? There I was, waiting patiently for her, and she went home and called the matchmaker. Apparently, I was very rude to her. I have no idea what she was talking about. I know for a fact that I try my hardest to make my dates as comfortable as possible. Some have even complained that I'm *too* nice and accommodating." He shrugged again. "Whatever."

"Sorry, Dovid," she said. "People can be so cruel sometimes."

"Yeah. Some people."

"And you're not boring."

His smile was tight. "Thanks for saying that, but I kind of am."

"Why do you think that?"

"Feedback from some of my dates. And Perry says it all the time."

"Please, little sisters are supposed to say those kinds of things."

"Even as kids, Sam was always the more fun twin."

Dina shook her head. "You know I never compared."

"Is still doesn't change the truth."

"That was a million years ago. People change."

"Maybe." He looked out in the distance.

They were quiet for a few seconds.

Dovid looked at her. "Can I ask what had you so upset? Because of the jerk or something else? You mentioned feeling stressed? Are you referring to dating in general?"

Dina puffed out her cheeks again. "Dating and everything else. There are millions of people in the world, right? We're told we have one soulmate. How on Earth are we supposed to find them? It's like finding a needle in a haystack."

"That's why we have Hashem. And the power of prayer."

"Even with all that, we can still marry the wrong person."

He kept his eyes on her for a moment. "Are you talking about your parents?"

She turned her head away. "No. Maybe. I don't know."

"You won't have the same fate as them. And besides, isn't your father happily married now?"

"My mom isn't. And we're not exactly a family."

"Have you spoken to your dad since you got here?" he asked.

"A little. But I know he's busy with his new family, so I don't call often."

"That's not fair, Dina. You're his daughter, too. He'll always make time for you."

Dina didn't say anything.

"I'm worried about the future, too."

She looked at him. "You are?"

"Everyone is. It's normal."

"But they're not afraid to take the plunge and get married."

He glanced down at his knees. "Maybe it's not so scary once you meet the right one."

"Which goes back to that same question: how do you know

when you meet the right one?"

Dovid raised his eyes to her. "Maybe you just do."

"Maybe there's an arrow only I can see over the guy's head that says, 'Pick me!'"

He chuckled. "Maybe."

Her phone beeped. Dina slipped it out of her pocket. "My mom's worried. I'd better get in and show her I'm alive."

"That might be a good idea."

They stood, and Dina smiled. "Thanks for the talk. It was nice."

He returned the smile. "Thanks to you as well. I hope the next date you'll have will be with a better guy."

Dina gaped at him.

"What?" he asked.

She couldn't help but laugh. "Sam said the same thing before he left."

He grinned. "Haven't you noticed we're twins?"

"Oh my gosh, really? No wonder you look so similar. It totally boggled my mind."

His smile widened. "Good night, Dina."

"Good night."

She decided to spare her mother the details of what kind of

guy she sent her out with and just told her they had lost track of time. And no, Dina didn't think she wanted to go out with him again. Why? Their personalities didn't mesh well.

Chapter Eleven

Dina's life had become a very boring routine. She woke up, prepared herself for work, went to work, returned home from work, ate dinner, and then relaxed by either reading a book or watching TV or a movie before going to sleep. Some nights, she went on dates, but they weren't headed anywhere.

She called a few friends from Miami and caught up with the events going on in their lives. They may have lived miles apart, but they were all going through the same thing. Dating. The truth was, Dina was sick of talking about it and hearing about it. It was all she talked about with Perry. Seriously, it was as though the men they spent only a few hours with had taken over their lives. *I need a hobby.*

Her mother walked into the living room where Dina was watching a mystery movie, took the remote, and paused the

TV.

"What?" Dina asked.

Her mom settled down near her. "I just had a very interesting call."

Dina groaned. "No more dates, Mom. No more men. No more profiles. *Please.*"

"I think you'd like to hear about this one."

Dina raised an eyebrow.

"What do you think about Dovid Weiss?"

"Dovid Weiss our neighbor?"

Mrs. Aaron laughed. "No, the Dovid Weiss who lives on the moon."

"Who suggested him?"

"See, that's the interesting thing. It was his idea. I just hung up with his mother."

Dina glanced at her lap. "Dovid Weiss? He's like a brother."

"Do you mean that?"

She raised her eyes to her mother.

"I saw the two of you talking on the bench the other night."

Dina had tried to not think about that night because then

she would have to make sense of her feelings. She never had the same feelings for him as she did for his brother. But they had been so comfortable with each other that night. He tried so hard to make her feel better. And if she wanted to be honest with herself, she knew he felt something for her. It was obvious, even though she didn't want to face it.

"I don't know," Dina said.

"He's such a nice boy. So kind."

"I know."

But he also had the same face as his twin brother. The guy Dina had been in love with since she was twelve. Wasn't that unethical?

"You guys were practically inseparable when you were kids. Maybe you'll get along as adults, too."

"Well, it was me and Sam," Dina muttered.

"Shmuel's not *frum*," her mom said, her tone a little crisp.

Dina's eyes snapped to hers. "You think I don't know that?"

She rubbed Dina's arm. "I just don't want you to make any mistakes."

The younger woman shook her head. "Sam's not who he used to be. But Dovid…"

Her mother nodded. "Dovid is a real catch. Look, just think it over and tell me what you want to do. You want my advice? Just got out with him once. See how you feel."

"I'll think about it."

Her mom rubbed her arm again. "Okay."

As soon as she left the room, Dina grabbed a pillow and squeezed it to her chest. Dovid Weiss. Could the two of them actually work out? One thing Dina knew for sure was that he wouldn't be a jerk. He had always been so sweet, even as a kid. He was definitely the kind of guy you marry.

But if she ended up marrying Dovid, Sam would be in her life. Would her feelings for him ever vanish? It wouldn't be fair to marry Dovid when she secretly harbored deep feelings for his brother. But then again, should she throw away a possible good guy all because of a crush she had as a pre-teen?

No one was talking about marriage. One date couldn't hurt, could it? Who knew, maybe she'd fall madly in love with Dovid and lose all the feelings she had for his brother. That really would be the ideal situation.

Dina fell on her back, still clutching the pillow to her chest. Dovid Weiss. She smiled.

***

Dina's Choice

Dina had been on a few dates before, but she'd never been *this* nervous.

Dovid Weiss lived right next door. She probably glanced out her window over a hundred times. He wasn't supposed to pick her up for another half hour, but she couldn't stop looking out the window.

Last night, she had told her mother she wanted to give Dovid a shot. She hadn't expected to have the date the night after. Falling down on her bed, she hugged the same pillow and stared at the space in front of her.

"Dina, Dovid's here," her mother called.

She jet to her feet. How did she miss him? After taking a deep breath and letting it out, Dina made her way downstairs. Her mom was in the middle of offering Dovid something to eat and drink. It looked like the cookies Dina had tried baking last night, after telling her mom she wanted to go out with Dovid. She had needed to blow off some steam. But gosh, they came out horrible. Why did her mom offer him some?

Mrs. Aaron's eyes moved past him, to her daughter, which caused Dovid to turn around. As soon as his eyes met Dina's, he gave her the sweetest smile in the world. It lit up his entire face.

"Hi, Dina," he greeted.

"Hi." She wished she wouldn't sound shy.

"These are delicious." He took another bite of his cookie.

Dina laughed lightly. "You don't have to lie."

"I'm serious. I love them."

Studying his face, she realized he was sincere. *I guess if he likes my failed cookies, he's a keeper?*

"Thanks," she said, even more shy. "You can take some with you."

"Really? Because I totally will."

Mrs. Aaron packed some cookies in a bag and handed them to him. His smile couldn't be wider. "Thanks."

Dina's mother opened the front door for them and they walked out. Dovid threw Dina another smile. "Isn't this convenient? My car is parked right next door."

She laughed.

He hurried to open the passenger door for her. "Thanks," she said.

"No problem."

He stashed the cookies in the backseat before settling down in the driver's seat. Dina couldn't help but feel good by his excitement. There was nervousness packed in there, too, but he really looked very excited. That caused Dina to be excited as well.

"How was your day?" he asked as he pulled out of the driveway.

"Uneventful."

He glanced at her for a second and chuckled. "Well, at least nothing bad happened, then?"

She shook her head.

"You look really nice, by the way," he complimented.

"Thanks. You do, too."

"Yeah, I actually combed my hair tonight."

Dina just looked at him. Then she laughed. "It was a joke."

"Well, I'm *trying* to be funny. The key word here is *trying*."

That caused Dina to laugh again. "Please don't try so hard. Just be yourself."

"Am I overdoing it? Sorry. I just don't want to mess this up, you know? Gathering the courage to even ask my mom about it was nerve-wracking enough. I could have sworn you'd say no."

"Why?" she wanted to know.

He focused on the road for a bit, then shrugged. "I don't know. We knew each other before we could write. Some people would find it weird."

"We're not the same people, though. And anyway, some people say friends make the best spouses." As soon as the words left her mouth, her face grew hot. "I m-mean, not that we're going to be spouses or anything. I just meant—"

"It's okay. I know what you meant."

Awkward silence.

He cleared his throat. "My mom actually suggested we go out the Shabbos after you and your mom came over."

Dina remembered how Mrs. Weiss kept glancing at them. "But?" she asked.

He shook his head. "No buts. I was a little hesitant at first because you just got here and I was a little upset because my mom tries to set me up with *everyone*. It gets frustrating sometimes. But I guess…"

"Can I ask how long you've wanted to, um, I mean…"

"It's okay. I don't mind." He puffed out some air. "Don't laugh, but I kind of wanted to go out with you when I overheard you and Perry talking on the phone. When you were going out with that guy. What was his name? Mordechai or something."

"Oh yeah. I totally messed up that date."

Dina's Choice

He glanced at Dina for a second before focusing on his driving. "Why?"

Her mouth snapped shut. There was no way she'd tell him she ruined the date because his twin brother walked into the coffee shop with that pretty girl hanging onto him.

He must have sensed her discomfort because he said, "Sorry. That's none of my business."

"I asked you a personal question. It's only fair I answer."

"No, Dina. You don't have to tell me anything. Only what you're comfortable with."

"Thanks. You're a really nice person."

Even in the darkness of the car, Dina saw him blush. "Thanks. You're a really nice person, too."

Dina banged her head against the back of the seat. "No, I'm not."

"Yes, you are."

She shook her head. "I'm really not."

"Until you prove it, you are extremely nice in my books. Believe me, I've been out with some horrible girls. One of which you've heard of."

"Right. The one who climbed out the bathroom window."

They both laughed.

"I can write a book on bad dates."

"Have you been on that many?" Dina asked.

"Kind of," he replied, thinking. "I know, I'm young, but some days I went out nearly every night. But not more than one girl at a time. Don't worry, I'm not like that."

"That's good to know."

He smiled.

Dina looked out the window and didn't recognize where they were. "Can I ask where we're going?"

"It's a surprise."

Staring down at her outfit, she asked, "Am I dressed right for the occasion?"

She wasn't wearing anything too fancy, just a white top with a flower design and a matching black skirt. Dovid's eyes moved to hers for a second before returning to his driving. "You are dressed perfectly."

Dina wasn't sure how right he was because he stopped before a bowling alley.

"Are we going bowling?" she asked.

He grinned. "I know how much you loved it when we were kids."

She hadn't bowled in years and didn't realize how much she

missed it. "This is awesome. Thanks. I'm not sure I'm dressed right, though."

He waved his hand. "Don't worry about it. You're perfect."

He opened the door for her, and as she walked past him, her arm brushed against his. She remembered how it felt when Sam touched her. Uncomfortable because she wasn't used to touching a guy, but good too. She didn't feel anything like that now.

She shook her head. It wasn't right to compare them. Dina had promised herself last night that she wouldn't think about Sam when she was out with Dovid. She really wanted to see if they could make this work.

This bowling alley was different from the ones she remembered as a child. There were a few arcade games near the entrance, with kids crowded around them. It was so noisy Dina could barely hear herself think. Dovid motioned toward the front counter.

"Sorry," he said once they were somewhat away from the racket. "I didn't want to go to a bowling alley near our homes because this is the time where family and friends go bowling. But I didn't know it would be so noisy."

"It's okay," Dina reassured him, though she had to shout.

They paid for two games and received their bowling shoes. As they walked toward their lane, Dovid said, "And now we will look like clowns. The best part of bowling."

"Ugh, who knows what kind of diseases are in these shoes? I'd rather not think about it."

"Oh, you'll forget about that fast once you see my mean bowling skills."

"Oh, really?"

He laughed, shaking his head. "You know how bad I am."

Dina laughed, too. "I remember how upset you got when you lost. Which was like every time."

"And guess who won every time?" Dovid rolled his eyes. "I swear Sam one-upped me in everything."

"Not everything," Dina's mouth said before she could stop it.

Dovid sat down on one of the chairs at their lane and looked up at her. "What do you mean?"

She lowered herself in the chair next to his and focused on getting her shoes on. "I was referring to him no longer being *frum*. Sorry. I shouldn't have said that."

He was quiet for a few seconds as he put on his right shoe. "That's okay. It's not a secret. It's just the way it is. It's hard on all of us."

"Do you…never mind."

"You want to know if I know why he went off."

"It's none of my business. I have no right asking."

"You care about him."

She froze for a second, her heart rate speeding up. Slowly, she looked at him.

"I mean, we were best friends when we were kids. Of course you care."

"Right," she quickly said.

"He's my twin brother. It really hurts to see him choosing to live a different life." He tied his shoes and leaned back with a sigh. "But I don't know why. I've tried asking him, but he shuts down. I don't want to push him away."

"Perry told me the same thing."

He nodded. "But I know something happened at school."

Dina's heart beat even faster. "You don't mean…like something terrible, do you?"

He shrugged. "I don't think it's as bad as you think. But he changed so much in ninth grade. By the time any of us really noticed, it was too late."

She sat in silence for a few seconds, absorbing all this

information. She really hoped he hadn't gone through something horrible.

Dovid slapped his thighs, standing up. "Ready to lose?" He grinned.

Dina got to her feet. "No. I'm ready to win."

It turned out Dina was rustier than she had thought. Dovid beat her in the first two rounds.

She folded her arms over her chest. "You tricked me. You made me lower my guard so you could swoop in and take the wins."

He laughed. "Dina, I'm really not good at bowling. I came here last week with a date and I did horrendously."

She frowned. "Great. That means I really am doing horribly."

"No. I think it means I'm having so much fun that I'm pumped with all this adrenaline."

Dina gazed into his eyes, seeing just how true his words were. He really *was* having a wonderful time. The truth was, so was she. And the best part? She hadn't thought about Sam at all, except for when she and Dovid spoke about him.

She held up a finger. "I think your luck is about to change." She grabbed a ball from the ball return machine and marched to the lane. She used everything she had to swing her arm backward before pushing the ball forward. It shot at the pins, knocking them all down.

Spinning around, she raised her arms. "Strike!"

Dovid grabbed another ball. "It's on now."

Dina didn't know Dovid was so competitive. Or maybe it wasn't competiveness—maybe he was trying to impress her? Whatever the case, he beat her by ten points.

She pouted. "Not fair."

He chuckled. "How about a Coke and candy as a consolation prize?"

"I never say no to candy."

He nodded. "Be right back."

"Thanks!" she called after him.

Falling onto one of the chairs, Dina realized her cheeks hurt. She'd been smiling this whole time, really smiling. She didn't remember when was the last time she had smiled this much.

Dovid returned with two bottles of Coke and four packs of candy. "All for you." He handed her the chocolate.

"You're trying to get me fat?"

"No. I just remember how much you used to love all these

brands."

"I still do. Thanks. But I'm sharing with you."

"I hoped you would."

They chatted as they ate the chocolate—about what? Dina had no idea. But they didn't run out of things to discuss. She never felt so comfortable with a guy before. It was as though she was talking to a best friend.

Then they played the second game. Dina performed much better this time, beating Dovid by over fifty points. She narrowed her eyes. "You didn't lose on purpose, did you?"

He placed his hand on his heart. "Me cheat? Never. You did awesome this round. Do you want to play another?"

"I'm kind of burned out. Unless you want to play?"

"I'm fine with whatever you want. How about food? Are you hungry?"

"I'm not sure," she said with a laugh.

He laughed, too. "All that adrenaline has left me a bit hungry."

"Okay, then food it is."

"I know the perfect place."

They returned their shoes and headed for the car. Once again, they didn't run out of things to talk about. Dovid found everything she said fascinating, though she couldn't help but wonder if he was overdoing it just a little. It was actually pretty adorable how badly he wanted to impress her. She only wished he wouldn't try so hard. She liked him just the way he was.

"She just picked up the phone and said, 'Who is this?' Right in the middle of my phone interview. I for sure thought I wouldn't get the job." He shook his head and smiled. "That Simi is something else."

"She sure is. But you did get the job, didn't you?"

"Luckily the man doing the interview had a daughter around the same age as Simi, so he understood. Next time, I'll make sure not to have any phone interviews while I babysit."

They reached a Chinese restaurant. It was in their neighborhood, though Dina had never seen it before. "Is this new?" she asked as he opened the passenger door for her.

"Yeah. I think it opened like three years ago. It's the best."

"Cool. I can't wait to taste the food. I'm starving now."

The maître de found them a table near the window. It wasn't the greatest view because there were basically just a lot of buildings, but it was still nice to have something to look at. Dovid opened his menu and scanned the items. "There are so many things to choose from. I still haven't tried them all." He glanced at Dina. "Aren't you going to look?"

"I already know what I want."

"Chicken lo mein?" he asked.

Her eyebrows shot up. "How do you know?"

"It's the only Chinese food you ate years ago."

"Not the only one I ate. But my favorite."

He smiled. "Same thing. You're in for a treat. The chicken lo mein here is delicious."

"Yay," she said with a laugh.

His eyes remained on hers for a few seconds before returning to his menu.

"What?" she asked.

"Hmm?" He looked up at her.

"Why did you look at me like that?"

His cheeks turned bright red. "Sorry. It's just that…you haven't been smiling a lot since you got back from Miami. You have a really pretty smile. I wish I could see it more often. Maybe that's why I keep making these lame jokes."

Her cheeks burned. "You're so sweet for trying to make me smile. And your jokes are not lame."

He brought his thumb and index finger together, leaving an inch between them. "Maybe a teensy weensy?"

Dina's Choice

She laughed. "Definitely a teensy weensy."

"And I have managed to make the fair maiden laugh again. I should keep score."

Dina laughed again. "You'd better not."

He actually made her laugh ten more times for the rest of the night. Yes, he had indeed kept score.

It started to pour as soon as Dovid parked in the driveway. "Punishment for having too much fun," Dina said.

"No way. There never can be any punishment for having too much fun with you."

That caused her to blush again.

"I'm willing to sacrifice my jacket for you."

"I already have a jacket," she pointed out.

"For your head," he said.

"Are you sure?"

"Yes. Just return it to me on our next date. If there will be one, I mean," he quickly added.

She gave him a sincere smile. "There definitely will be another date."

His face washed with relief and joy. "Thanks. I'm glad." He shrugged out of his jacket and handed it to her. "I really don't mind. Your head is more important than mine."

"Thanks. Good night, Dovid."

"Good night, Dina."

She couldn't believe she hadn't realized this before. Dovid and Dina. It went perfectly well together.

The race to her house seemed longer than usual. There was no protection over the stairs, and Dina got wet as she fished out her key and stabbed it into the lock. She leaned against the door, the water dripping into a puddle at her feet.

Dovid Weiss. Her cheeks were so sore she was forced to rub them. But she could definitely get used to this.

***

Dina loved being huddled under the blanket as heavy rain slammed into her window and air conditioner. She couldn't sleep because all she thought about was her date with Dovid. Could he be the one? She had no idea—it was too early to tell. But don't they say that when you know, you know? Did she know? The marriage book stated that one shouldn't expect to be smitten after the first date. Was she smitten?

Something hit her window. She ignored it, assuming it was a branch, and returned to obsessing over the date and her feelings. She wondered if Dovid was obsessing over it as much as she was. Do guys even obsess like this?

Dina's Choice

Another hit at her window. That didn't sound like a branch. It sounded like someone throwing something at her window. She bolted up in bed. Was someone trying to get into her room?

"Dina!"

Her heart hammered in my chest. Someone was calling her name. Slowly, she climbed out of bed and trekked to the window. She was scared to look out—what if it was a criminal? A criminal who knew her name?

"Dina!"

Moving closer, she pressed her forehead against the glass. She didn't see anything at first, just the heavy rain and leaves. But then something moved on one of the branches and she stumbled back. When she pressed her head against the glass again, she saw someone balancing on the branch. It was hard to make him out in the rain. Maybe she should call the police.

"Dina, it's me! Sam Weiss."

Sam? What on Earth? She quickly opened the window. "What are you doing out there?" He was beyond soaked. And beyond shivering.

"Can I come in?" he asked, his teeth chattering.

"What?" He wanted to come into her *bedroom*? "No, you

can't come into *my room*."

He hugged himself, shivering even more. "You'd rather me die of pneumonia?"

"No. I'd rather you get down from the tree and go back home."

"I'm not leaving until I talk to you."

"Now?" she asked, incredulous. "At two o'clock in the morning, in this pouring rain?"

He nodded.

She looked at her closed door. Orthodox Jewish men and women are not allowed to be alone in a room together with the door locked. She shut her eyes for a second before saying, "One second," and opening the door a crack. She hoped her mother wouldn't wake up. Having a man in her room was *not* okay.

She was about to return to the window when she realized she was dressed in pajamas. She quickly threw on a robe and rested her hands on the windowsill, leaning out, the top of her head getting a little wet. Sam was shivering so badly it looked as though he was about to fall off the branch. "Come in." She opened the window wider. "But only for a few minutes. You're crazy."

Dina's Choice

She stepped back as he stretched his arms and grabbed onto one of the bars by the window. He pulled himself through.

"Stay by the window," she warned, backing away until she hit the door. Maybe this wouldn't be as inappropriate if there was a big distance between them.

She was about to tell him she couldn't offer him a towel because she'd have to leave the room and might wake her mom up, when he said, "Why did you go out with him?"

"What? Who?"

"Who do you think who?"

She stared at him for a moment. "Who, Dovid?"

"Yes, Dovid. My twin brother, Dovid."

"Why shouldn't I go out with him? Dovid's the sweetest guy I know. So kind and considerate. And surprisingly funny. We share the same values and want to build similar futures. He's such an amazing guy. Any girl would be lucky to go out with him."

Sam stood there, no expression on his face. "You think I don't know that?" he said in such a low voice Dina nearly missed it. "You think I don't know what an amazing person my brother is?"

"What's the problem then?" she asked.

He didn't say anything, just stared at Dina. She still couldn't read the expression on his face.

Dina's gaze dropped to his shoes. "You're making a puddle in the middle of my room."

He looked at the floor, seeming to be in a daze. "You're right. Sorry." He turned around and headed to the window. "And I'm sorry for barging into your room and putting you in an uncomfortable situation." He climbed through the window and leaped onto the branch.

She dashed to the window. "Sam!"

He looked back at her.

Dina's breath caught in her throat. There was so much she wanted to say, but no words came out of her mouth.

He turned away and climbed down the tree. She watched as he reached the ground and raced off into the dark night.

Chapter Twelve

Dina's boss, Mr. Hershkowitz, called her into his office an hour before her lunch break. She sat down in the chair across his desk.

"Hi, Dina. I just wanted to check in and see how everything is going."

"Everything is fine."

He nodded slowly. "I was hoping you'd say that. But unfortunately, it doesn't reflect in your work."

"What?"

"You did amazing work for us the first weeks you were here. But lately, your performance has been declining."

Panic seized every part of her. "I'm sorry. I'm just going through some personal things. It's hard to concentrate at times."

She hadn't been able to do much of anything since the night Sam visited her room. She could hardly eat, barely sleep, and she couldn't concentrate on anything. Dovid had called multiple times to know when she would like to go on their next date, but she kept making excuses.

Sam had stood outside her room in the heavy rain because he'd discovered she went out with his brother. And then they had the most bizarre conversation and he had run off. What did that guy *want* from her? He had left her world and he had no intention of returning. Why didn't he allow her to move on with her life?

Mr. Hershkowitz locked his fingers together. "We all are dealing with personal things. But we are in a work environment. I would rather you not bring your personal problems into your work, just as I hope you don't bring work problems into your personal life."

Dina nodded. "I'm sorry. I won't let it happen again."

He nodded and leaned back in his chair. "Great. Please continue working on whatever you're working on."

She was numb as she returned to her desk. But after a few minutes, she straightened up and woke her computer from its sleep. *No, not anymore Sam Weiss. No longer will I let you control my*

Dina's Choice

heart, my mind, my life. You have chosen your path, now it's my turn to choose mine. And you know something? It may very well be with the person who shares your DNA.

***

"You're *what?*" Dina nearly shouted into the phone.

Perry squealed. "Yep, you heard me. I'm engaged!"

"*Mazel tov!* But I'm not surprised."

Perry giggled. "And to think none of this would have happened if not for the book you leant me."

Dina was glad the book had helped her friend, because it sure hadn't helped her.

"You okay?" she asked.

"Of course I am. My best friend just got engaged."

Perry laughed again, then stopped abruptly. "Okay, but that doesn't mean you're not upset about something else."

"I'm honestly okay." And she would be. Because Sam Weiss no longer had a presence in her heart.

"Listen." Perry lowered her voice. "I don't want to get involved, but I kind of feel like I need to because I love you both."

Dina knew where this conversation was headed.

"Dovid's kind of down, Dina. He was so happy the

morning after your date. Seriously, it was so annoying. But good, too. Now he walks around like you tore out his heart."

"Perry…"

"You're my best friend, Dina, but Dovid's my brother. I won't let you play with his heart like this."

"I'm not playing with his heart."

"Then why are you doing this to him? If you don't want to go out with him, just tell him."

How could Dina tell her what she was feeling? Sam was her brother, too. She needed to talk to someone who was unbiased. But she didn't feel so close to her Miami friends anymore. And while her relationship with her mother had gotten better, she didn't feel comfortable talking to her about this.

But was there even something to talk about? She'd pushed Sam out of her life. She didn't want to ever see him, speak to him, or even *think* about him.

"You're right," she told Perry. "Please put Dovid on the phone."

Some shuffling noises were heard before Dovid said, "Hi, Dina." Even though he must have been hurt, he still sounded very excited to talk to Dina.

"Hi, Dovid. *Mazel tov.* I'm sorry I've been avoiding you. I guess…" Dina puffed out some air. "I guess I'm just scared. I'm sorry. I didn't mean to hurt you."

"Dina, you don't have to apologize. I'm so glad you're being open with me. I understand how scary all this can be. But I'll be with you every step of the way. You don't have to go through anything alone."

His words brought tears to her eyes. Maybe because he was so sweet. What did Dina do to deserve him? Nothing. That was the thing—she didn't deserve him.

"You're going to make a woman so happy one day," she said.

He was quiet for a bit before, "Is there any chance that woman could be you?"

"I want it to be."

"Then let's try to make this work. Just be honest with me, okay? Tell me what you're feeling. You don't have to be embarrassed about anything."

"Thanks, Dovid. I'll see you by the engagement party tomorrow night. And we can talk about our next date."

"Okay, but no pressure, Dina. Whenever you're ready."

***

Perry looked gorgeous at her engagement party. She wore a

black outfit with many designs and colors. Her smile captured her entire face and she was glowing. Her groom, Naftali Josowitz, stood beside her, looking at her as though he had hearts in his eyes. They made the cutest couple.

"Dina!" Perry rushed over and yanked her friend in for a big hug. "You're here!"

"*Mazel tov*."

"Thanks. I'm going to be annoying now and say God willing by you."

God willing by you. The four dreaded words uttered to singles. It's a blessing sure, but one every unmarried person hates.

Dina playfully slapped her arm. "Don't you dare." She stepped aside, giving her mother a chance to hug the bride.

"You look beautiful, Perry." Mrs. Aaron kissed her cheek. "An absolute beauty."

Perry flushed. "Thanks. I'm so happy."

Mrs. Weiss hurried over to exchange hugs and kisses. She looked out-of-this-world ecstatic. This would be her first child getting married. She was glowing, too.

She was about to say something when her eyes flitted to the area on the right. "Simi! Please be careful with your dress.

Dina's Choice

Excuse me." She dashed to Simi, who was about to spill Coke over her beautiful light blue floral dress.

As Dina and her mother headed to the food table, Dina said, "Mom, I've been wondering about something…"

"Hmm?"

"Do you ever think about getting married again?"

Mrs. Aaron took a plate and filled it with cookies. "Why the sudden question?"

"I don't know. Perry got me thinking. And you *did* go on that date the night I arrived here."

"I told you I want to focus on you."

"C'mon, Mom. I know this has nothing to do with me."

Her mother focused on moving some of the cookies around on her plate before sighing. "I don't think marriage is for me." She lifted her eyes to Dina's. "But that doesn't mean it's not for you. You should meet the right one, God willing soon, and have many healthy and happy years together."

"Amen," Dina said, not sure how she felt about this. She didn't want to get in the way of her mom's happiness. But maybe she was content with the way her life was. One can still live a fulfilled life without having a husband. Still, Dina hated for her mother to be alone.

The two of them sat at one of the tables. "Can I ask why don't you want to get married?" Dina wanted to know.

"It doesn't matter, Dina."

"Please?"

Her eyes searched her daughter's. Then she sighed again. "All right, sweetie. It's hard for me to have relationships with people. Why do you think my marriage failed? I couldn't connect with your father. He eventually left me."

Dina fell back on her chair, staring at her plate.

Her mother rested her hand on Dina's. "What's the matter, Dina'la?"

"Maybe I'm not the greatest at having relationships either."

"No, you're like your father. You don't have many friends, but you are extremely loyal to the ones you do have. You'd do anything for them. That's a good quality to have in a spouse."

Dina shrugged.

"Look at me, sweetie. I have a plethora of friends. But am I extremely close to any of them?"

"I have no idea."

"Exactly," she agreed. "I have no idea, either." She looked at something behind Dina. When Dina turned around, she found Dovid standing there, talking to a few guys. She also spotted Sam at the food table with Simi, choosing cookies for himself and his sister.

"Excuse me," Dina told her mother and made her way to Dovid. When he saw her approaching, he stepped away from the guys and met her halfway. He smiled. "Hi."

She returned the smile. "Hi."

"Can we talk outside?"

"Sure."

Dina made sure not to look at Sam as they passed, but she felt his eyes boring into her back.

She and Dovid sat on the couch in the small lounge. They both didn't face each other at first, nor did they say anything. Then Dina started, "Perry looks so happy."

His smile couldn't be any wider. "She is. I'm so happy for her."

"God willing by you," Dina teased.

He chuckled. "God willing by you."

They both laughed, and then they laughed some more because this was awkward and strange and because they didn't know what else to do.

Then someone lowered himself next to Dina on the couch. Sam.

"What's up, bro?" he said. "What's up, little lady?"

"Who are you calling little lady?" she demanded.

It seemed Dovid hadn't yet finished his laughing fit. "You *are* a little lady, Dina. You're like a foot shorter than us."

"No, you two are giants."

Dovid burst out laughing again.

"Dude, how much did you drink?" Sam asked.

"I don't think he did," Dina explained. "I think he's just nervous."

Dovid's fit finally ended. They were all quiet.

"I should have brought Glinda," Sam said.

"Glinda?" Dovid asked. "What, that witch from the *Wizard of Oz*? What are you talking about?"

Sam nodded to Dina. "Ask Dina. She knows who I'm talking about."

Dovid's eyes flitted to hers. Then they moved to Sam's. He looked confused and a little hurt.

Dina stood up. "I think my mom's looking for me."

"Wait, Dina. You said we were going to discuss our next date," Dovid said.

"Oh, your next date. Isn't that so adorable."

"Cut it out, Sam," Dovid said.

"Why? Maybe you guys can double date with me and Gloria."

"I really have no interest in hanging out with your girlfriend," Dina told him.

"Why not? She might be your sister-in-law."

Dina felt like the air was knocked out of her. She stared at Sam for a few seconds, searching his eyes, trying to determine if he was just messing with her. But she couldn't read his expression.

It didn't matter. Let him date whoever he wanted. Let him marry whoever he wanted. Dina had the perfect guy sitting right next to her.

"Let's go back in, Dovid," she said.

Once they were inside, he said, "Sorry about Sam. He gets very uncomfortable by family gatherings or *simchos*. Relatives and neighbors are always so judgmental. He'd rather not come, but he didn't want to hurt Perry's feelings."

"That's sweet, I guess."

"He's a good guy, Dina. I hope you don't think low of him."

"Why does it matter what I think of him?"

He rubbed the back of his head. "Because he's my twin

brother and my best friend."

"I don't judge him. I just wish things were different."

He nodded slowly. "Yeah, me too." But Dina noticed something else in his eyes. A sort of relief. And she knew why he felt that way. Because if Sam hadn't gone off the *derech*, Dina would be dating him and not Dovid. Which made her feel like the biggest jerk in the world.

"I'm going to look for my mom. Call me later tonight so we can discuss our next date."

He nodded and smiled. "I will."

Mrs. Aaron sat at a table with three women. Something Dina had always envied her as a kid was how easy it was for her to make friends. Even if many of them didn't last, at least she had the ability to make them.

"Dina!" Her mother waved her over. "This is my Dina." She introduced her daughter to the women, but their names passed over Dina's head.

"Wow, what a beautiful girl," one of them said. "Is she seeing anyone right now? I know so many good boys."

Not wanting to deal with this right now, Dina turned around and walked away. And nearly collided with Sam.

"Miss me?" he said.

Dina's Choice

She pushed past him.

"Don't break Dovid's heart."

She whirled around. "Why do you think I will?"

He took a step closer. "Do you think you'll marry him?"

"Why shouldn't I?"

He didn't say anything.

"Because I'm definitely not going to marry you."

His eyes flashed to hers. "Who said I want to marry you?"

Dina rolled her eyes. "Real mature, Sam." She turned away.

"Just don't hurt him, okay? Do whatever you want to my heart, but don't break his."

Dina threw her hands up. "What do you want from me? Just leave me alone."

He lowered his head. "As you wish." And he slid away.

Scanning the area, Dina was relieved to learn that no one had paid attention to their little altercation. Good. But she couldn't stand being here a second longer. She forced herself back to the table her mom was at, still with those women.

"Dina, where did you run off to?" Mrs. Aaron wanted to know.

"I'm not feeling well. Can we go home?"

"Of course, sweetie."

They wished the women good night and exited the hall. "There are so many matchmakers," her mother noted. "If things don't work out with Dovid Weiss, I want to give that woman a chance. The boys she has sound very promising."

"Okay," Dina said absentmindedly.

Her mother touched her forehead. "I think you really might be coming down with something. Let's go home."

Chapter Thirteen

Dina had been on a total of three dates with Dovid. And she was glad to report that things had been going very well. Slow, but well. They hadn't yet dipped into serious discussions, but things were looking great.

Perry called her just as she was about to video chat with her dad and his family for the first time.

"Hey, my mom and I are going gown shopping today. Want to join?"

"Already? You just got engaged."

"I know," she said. "But we're having a short engagement. Less than two months."

"Wow."

"I know. Naftali's going to start law school soon and wants the wedding out of the way."

"Sure, I'd love to come gown shopping with you."

"Thanks. I know my mom's going to make me pick something so traditional and boring. But she loves you. I know the two of us can change her mind."

"Okay, you're putting a lot of hope in me. I don't know if I can deliver."

"Please. So did I catch you at a bad time? You sound a little preoccupied."

"I'm about to video chat with my dad and his family," Dina told her.

"Ohhh."

"He's been asking for weeks, but I kept pushing it off. I think it's time."

"Okay. My appointment is in two hours. We'll pick you up. Bye."

After hanging up, Dina took a deep breath and let it out. She'd spoken to her dad several times since she moved here, but she hadn't seen him face to face, or spoken to his wife and kids. She no longer wanted to run away.

She called them. A few seconds later, they appeared on the screen. "Hi, Dina!" they all greeted.

His wife, Rachel, moved her face closer to the screen.

Dina's Choice

"Look at you. A few weeks away from the sun and your tan is gone. I think that means it's time you paid us a visit."

Some of the kids said, "Yeah! Come visit us, Dina."

She smiled. She didn't know they missed her so much. And if she wanted to be honest with herself, she missed them as well.

The older boy, Chananya, pushed his face to the camera. "I called dibs on your room, but Mom says we can't dismantle it because you're going to visit. But even if you do visit, you're fine with sleeping on the couch, right? Or on the floor?"

Dina's dad pulled him back. "Excuse me. Your sister will not sleep on the couch or the floor when she visits. She'll be sleeping in her own bed."

"But she'll be married soon, won't she?" the younger daughter, Rina, asked. "Daddy told us you have a boyfriend."

"*Frum* people don't have boyfriends, Rina," Shaina corrected. "They date for marriage."

"How do you know what's going on in my life when you're all the way down there?" I demanded.

Her father laughed softly. "Let's just say your mother likes to talk a lot."

Dina gave him a face. "And I gather you like to talk a lot,

too?"

He held up his hand. "What can I say? The kids will make great spies one day."

His daughter folded her arms across her chest and pretended to be upset.

"So who's the lucky boy?" Rachel asked.

"Will you guys slow down? You're acting as though I'm engaged."

"We're being hopeful." Dad grinned.

"Fine. It's Dovid Weiss."

Her dad raised an eyebrow. "The boy from next door? Isn't he the one who…?"

"No, that's Shmuel."

"Ah. Well, we wish you the best. The kids have to leave for school soon. Please visit us, Dina. We'd love to have you."

"Okay. Bye, everyone."

Once they were disconnected, Dina couldn't help but smile. The last time she had been with them she needed to escape. Now she couldn't remember what was so terrible. Maybe she had been the problem. It was so hard for her to let people in. But she didn't want to be like her mother. She didn't want to constantly have a shield around her heart.

Dina's Choice

An hour later, she waited outside for Perry and Mrs. Weiss. She could hear them arguing before they walked out the door.

"I just know we won't agree." Perry shoved the door open and marched out. "It's my wedding, Mom."

"How about we wait and see once we get there?" Mrs. Weiss's face brightened when she took Dina in. "Dina! Thanks so much for tagging along. We need a referee." She laughed to Perry, who rolled her eyes. "Come on, sweetie. Don't be so tense. It's your wedding."

"I'm sorry. I just want it to be perfect."

Her mom kissed her cheek. "It will be."

They climbed in the car and Mrs. Weiss drove to the gown store. The first half of the shop was for regular gowns, usually worn by close family members. The bridal gowns were in the back. There was such a huge selection it caused Dina's head to spin.

"Hello," a woman greeted. "My name is Yael. Do you have an appointment?"

"Yes. Bracha Weiss, here with my daughter Perry."

Yael looked from Dina to Perry. "Who is the beautiful *kallah*?"

Perry raised her hand.

"A beautiful *kallah* indeed. And this is your sister?"

"My best friend." Perry threw her arm around Dina, pulling her in for a hug.

Yael took Perry by the hands and scanned her from top to bottom. "You are so thin. Turn around for me." Perry complied. "Okay, I think I have just the thing."

"Nothing too out there," Mrs. Weiss said. "I want her to look classy but beautiful."

"I don't mind looking a bit modern," Perry said. Her mother gave her a disapproving look.

"Don't worry. I'm sure we'll find something that will please you both," the woman tried to make peace. "And you don't have to worry, Mrs. Weiss. Every one of our gowns is made to look very modest."

She picked one off the rack and handed it to Perry, telling her to try it on in one of the changing rooms. Dina and Mrs. Weiss sat on the chairs in the waiting area. Now that Dina was alone with Mrs. Weiss, she felt awkward. She was dating her son. He probably discussed their dates with her.

"So how are you, Dina my angel?" she asked.

"I'm good, thanks."

She took the young woman's hand. "Maybe it won't be

long until it's you trying on the gowns."

"I appreciate that, Mrs. Weiss, but I'd like to think there's more going on in my life other than dating, marriage, and weddings gowns."

"Of course, of course," she said. "But it doesn't hurt to get married during all that other stuff."

Perry emerged from the dressing room. Mrs. Weiss's lower lip quivered and her eyes filled with tears. "Oh, Perry. You look beautiful."

She really did. For the first time since she got engaged, it finally hit Dina. Her best friend was going to get married in less than two months.

Perry laughed. "Dina, you look more scared than me."

"I just can't believe you're getting married."

She pressed her hands to her cheeks. "I know." Then she did a small twirl. "How do I look?" She examined herself in the mirror and twisted her nose. "I don't know…"

"If you don't like it, there are many more to choose from," the shop owner said, sorting through the many gowns on the rack. "You look, too, Perry and Mrs. Weiss. See if you can find any you like."

The next twenty minutes consisted of Perry and her mother

debating and arguing, and occasionally asking Dina for advice. But finally, they find two that looked promising and Perry disappeared into the dressing room.

Mrs. Weiss sat down near Dina with an exasperated sigh. "I can't wait until this is over and she's happy with her gown."

Dina was about to respond, when Mrs. Weiss's phone rang. She fished it out of her bag and answered. "Yes, this is Bracha Weiss..." Her eyes widened. "The appointment is for *today*? Are you sure? I thought it was scheduled for tomorrow..." She nodded. "I see. I must have written down the wrong date. I'll come as soon as I can."

Perry stepped out of the dressing room. She appeared even more beautiful than the last time. "Oh, sweetie." Her mother hugged her. "I can't get over how beautiful you look." She wiped the corner of her left eye. "But I need to run. I didn't know I had an appointment."

"What? Can't you reschedule?"

She shook her head. "I waited for weeks for that appointment. I need to get there as soon as possible. Listen, you know what you want and you have Dina for advice, and of course the help of Yael. Can she choose a few and put them aside?" She asked Yael. "We'll come back tomorrow."

214

Dina's Choice

The woman thought for a few seconds. "Okay, but only if you come back tomorrow. I can't reserve it for more than that. It's not fair to other customers."

"I understand. I'm sorry for the inconvenience. I just can't miss this appointment." Mrs. Weiss grabbed Perry by the chin and kissed her cheek. "I'll see you later. Oh, ask Dovid to drive you home."

"He's at work."

"Oh. See if Shmuel's available. If not, take the bus." She left.

"This is weird," Perry whispered to Dina. "Just an hour ago, I wanted my mom to leave me alone so I could choose the dress I want. Now that she's not here, I'm totally lost."

"Do you like the one you're wearing?" Yael asked Perry.

She examined herself in the mirror again. "I like the way it looks at the front, but the profile looks weird."

Yael stood behind her and pulled down the dress. "I don't know what you mean."

"I don't know. I can't explain it. Let me try on the other one."

Yael and Dina were left alone. In awkward silence. Dina hated such situations.

"So how long have you and Perry been friends?" Yael asked.

"Since we were babies."

Her eyebrows rose. "Really?"

"Yeah, we're neighbors."

"And you stayed close all these years. That's so nice."

"Well, we kind of lost touch for nine years when I moved to Miami. I just got back a few weeks ago. It's like I never left."

"That's really beautiful. Don't lose touch again. I know it's sometimes hard to keep close friendships when you are at different stages in life, but hopefully you'll get married soon, too."

"Thanks," Dina said.

Perry came out. Both Yael and Dina stared at her. "That..." she breathed.

"Is the dress," Dina finished for her.

Perry's face lit up. "Really?"

She stood in front of the mirror and stared at herself. The dress wasn't terribly poofy and it had a swirly design on the bodice. Perry took in a deep breath. "I found my dress."

As she and Yael discussed what needed to be taken it or let out, and so on, Dina wandered to the wedding dresses hanging on the racks. She pushed aside dress after dress, imagining which she would pick if she were the bride. Or *when* she'd be the bride? Who knew, maybe things would work out with Dovid. But gosh, she couldn't fathom it.

"See anything you like?" a voice said from behind her.

Dina whirled around so fast she knocked one of the dresses off the rack, catching it in time. "Oh, sorry," she said.

"There's nothing to be sorry about. Do you want to try any on?"

"But I'm not getting married."

"Yet," the woman emphasized. "You're not getting married *yet*. But *im yirtzeh Hashem*, God willing, you will one day, hopefully soon. It would be nice if you had an idea what you're looking for."

"I guess…" Dina knew Yael hoped she'd return there when the time came.

"Really, Devorah—is your name Devorah?"

"Dina." Why did everyone think that? Did she look like a Devorah?

"Sorry. Dina. I don't mind. Try as many as you like."

"Um…" Dina took one off the rack. "I think I'll just try on one. Just to see what I look like."

"Sure. Don't worry, you'll look beautiful."

As Dina headed to the other dressing room, Perry came out of hers and gave her friend a surprised look. "She made me do it," Dina hissed, which caused her to laugh. Then she was in the dressing room, clutching a *wedding dress*.

Dina stared at her reflection in the mirror, her heart pounding. Why was she stressing out like that? It wasn't like she was the one getting married. But in a few months' time…could it be her?

Not wanting to dwell on it for too long, she put it on and, purposely not looking at her reflection, left the room. Both Perry and Yael's jaws dropped.

"Oh. My. Gosh," Perry gasped.

Yael leaped off the chair she was sitting on and hurried behind Dina to zip up the dress. "What did I tell you? Absolutely stunning. Now all we need to do is find you a man to marry."

Um, *we*? Since when had she become part of Dina's life?

Perry burst into giggles. "Look at her face. She's about to faint."

Yael led Dina to the mirror and rested her hands on her shoulders. "What do you think?"

Dina's Choice

I think I need to get out this dress ASAP before I really do faint.

Yael pulled off Dina's hair tie, allowing her hair to roll down her shoulders in soft waves. Then she gathered the strands and styled Dina's hair.

"I've always wanted a daughter," the woman said as she continued styling her hair. "Thank God, Hashem blessed me with five boys, but for years I dreamed of putting my daughter in a wedding dress and making her looking breathtaking." She sighed in a wistful way. Then she tapped Dina's shoulders. "Do you like what you see?"

"I guess."

She laughed. "If you're so nervous now, I wonder how you'll be when you actually are getting married. Don't worry—it's not as scary as it seems. Just look at your friend. She's totally calm."

Perry didn't get anxious about these things like Dina did, but Dina knew her friend wasn't as calm as she made people think. Inside, Dina bet her knees were shaking and her hands were clammy. Every single person gets nervous. The only difference is that they don't let the anxiety hold them back from moving on to something wonderful.

"I heard Mom ditched you?" a male voice said from

behind.

Dina turned around and found Sam standing there.

His eyes held nothing but humor, but they took on a completely different look as they swept over Dina. From the top of her head—still with that hairstyle Yale had made—down her dress, to the bottom where it brushed the floor.

And he just stared.

Dina's face burned.

"May I help you?" Yael asked.

"Oh, sorry. Am I not allowed in here? My mom asked me to pick up my sister. And Dina." His voice had a different pitch when he said her name. Almost as though he was holding his breath.

"I was just about to text you," Perry told him. "Thanks for coming."

Sam acknowledged his sister with a nod, but his gaze was dead-locked on Dina's.

Forcing herself to move, she muttered, "I'm going to change," and vanished into the dressing room. She quickly got out of the dress, put it back on the hanger, and left, handing it to Yael.

The older woman smiled brightly. "Do you want to take a

picture of this dress? It'll make things easier when, *im yirtzeh Hashem*, you come by to pick your real wedding dress."

For reasons beyond Dina's understanding, her eyes trekked to Sam. Once again, his gaze was pasted on her.

"I don't...I mean..."

"I'm sorry," Yael said. "I'm making you uncomfortable. No worries. Have a good day. And Perry, remember that you and your mother must come by tomorrow or else you'll lose the reservation on your dress."

Perry nodded. "Thanks for your help."

They left the shop. Sam scanned the area before rubbing his forehead. "Well, aren't I the fool. I forgot where I parked my car."

Perry groaned. "Are you serious? You parked like five minutes ago."

"Just wait here." He walked up the block.

"Sorry about that," Perry said. "That Yael woman was way too pushy. But if it'll make you feel better, you looked amazing! If I were you, I'd want to get married just so I could wear a wedding dress."

Dina gave her a look. "I'd hope not, or else I'd feel bad for your future husband."

She laughed, bumping her shoulder into Dina's. "You know what I mean. But hey, if my brother plays his cards right…"

Dina's cheeks burned again. "Perry!"

"What? We could be sisters-in-law! Wouldn't that be awesome?"

"You're only getting excited about it now? We've been going out for a few weeks already."

"I know." She squealed. "I didn't want to jinx anything, so I kept quiet. But I'm *so* excited. And Dovid's awesome. I'm not just saying that because he's my brother. He really is special."

Dina glanced down at the bottom of her skirt. "I don't know what he sees in me."

"What are you talking about? You're so loyal and you try to make everyone around you happy. You can talk about anything with anyone and you won't be judgmental. And of course it doesn't hurt that you're, like, gorgeous."

Dina gently slapped her arm. "Stop it. Dovid doesn't care about looks."

"Please. All guys do."

"All guys what?" Sam's voice asked.

"Why are you here without the car?" Perry demanded.

Dina's Choice

"Because it seems I parked it that way." He nodded toward the opposite direction.

Perry groaned again. Dina couldn't help but laugh.

"So what is this stereotype about guys?" he asked, looking at Dina.

"Just that you're all pigs and the only thing you care about is looks," Perry enlightened him. "Now go find your car. I have other things to do, you know! I *am* a bride." She gently smacked his back.

He planted his feet on the ground and folded his arms across his chest. "Do you share the same opinion, Dina?"

"Shmuel, c'mon!"

"Sh, Perry." He pinned his eyes on Dina. "I'd like to hear what Dina has to say."

"I kind of agree with Perry. Guys might say they don't care about looks, but the truth is that they secretly do. Girls aren't that much better, though."

He scrutinized Dina's face. "Hmm, maybe you're right. But let's say a man loved a woman for her personality. Maybe he's loved her for years, even. In his eyes, the woman would be beautiful on the inside and outside, no matter what."

Dina just stood there, staring at him as he stared at her.

Was he talking about…her? Then it dawned on her that he must be referring to Glinda.

"My brother." Perry laughed. "Ever the romantic."

He stepped closer to Dina. "For the record, I think you're the most beautiful girl in the world. Both inside and out. My brother's a lucky man." He stepped back. "The car is this way." He walked away.

Dina swallowed a few times, and when she looked at Perry, she found her eyes narrowed at her best friend.

"What?" Dina asked, her voice shaky.

She shook her head. "Nothing."

"It's not nothing."

She sighed. "Just don't…look, I know it's easy to fall for him. He's cool and stuff and yeah, he's very good looking, but…"

"Perry—"

"He's not coming back, Dina. He's not."

Dina turned away. "I know. And I'm with Dovid. You have nothing to worry about."

Perry slung her arm through Dina's. "Good, because hopefully in a few weeks I'll no longer be calling you my best friend but my sister."

Chapter Fourteen

"I heard the woman at the store convinced you to try on a wedding dress," Dovid said as he drove them to the restaurant.

Dina hit her head against the back of the seat. "Are there no secrets in your family?"

He chuckled. "Perry just mentioned last night how pushy the woman was. But the good news is that she found a dress, so the world is no longer coming to an end."

"Don't be mean. Finding the right dress is very important. Not that I would know anything about that."

"I'm not trying to be mean. I think it's cute how nervous Perry is. She's usually not like that."

"That's true."

"So how did it feel putting on the dress?" he asked.

Dina's eyes scanned his face closely. Was that an innocent

question, or was there a hidden meaning?

"It caused me anxiety," she said.

He was silent for a moment, then burst out laughing. "Only Dina Aaron would claim a wedding dress caused her anxiety." Then he glanced at her with a more serious expression. "Why did it cause you anxiety?"

"Um…"

"Can we pick this up in the restaurant? We're here."

She would rather not pick it up at all. She knew this was something she needed to face, but she didn't want to face it right now.

They were led to a table and sat down with their menus. Dina used her menu to shield her face. Maybe Dovid would forget about his question.

"Hmm," he said. "I have no idea what to pick."

"Me, either."

They were at a dairy restaurant, so there were basically fish and pasta dishes. Dina wasn't the greatest fan of fish, so she skipped that section and focused on the pasta.

"I don't think I've ever contemplated something for this long," Dovid admitted.

"Cleary you've never shopped with Perry," Dina said with a

chuckle.

"Oh, I've shopped with her plenty. She and my mom together drive me up the wall." He shook his head with a smile. "I'm really going to miss her when she moves out. It'll just be Simi and me. The house will be so quiet."

"That's life, right?"

He nodded. "That's life." He leaned back and closed the menu. "I'm just going to go with today's special."

After a few more minutes of contemplation, Dina chose a pasta dish with two different kinds of sauces and cheeses. "I'm going to gain like a thousand pounds," she said.

Dovid waved his hand. "We don't think about calories when we're at a fancy restaurant and having a good time."

She smiled wryly. "Remember that the next time you see me and I've blown up."

He laughed. "No matter what you look like, you'll always look good in my eyes." As soon as the words left his mouth, his eyes widened and his gaze dropped to his closed menu. "Sorry. Did that make you uncomfortable?"

"No. I think we've been seeing each other long enough where those compliments don't make me feel uncomfortable."

"Oh, okay. Good to know."

"At least you're sweet about it. That other guy I went out with? The one who took me all the way to Long Island? We were only together for like an hour and he was all, 'The hotel is so beautiful, just like you.' I felt so uncomfortable."

"Sorry about that," he said. "Some guys honestly have no idea how to talk to girls while others are just jerks."

Dina raised an eyebrow. "And you know how to talk to girls?"

He shifted in his seat. "I might have been coached by a certain strong-willed sister of mine. And well…Sam gave me lots of advice."

"He did?"

"Yeah. Um. He has more experience with girls, so I asked him for some pointers. Surprisingly, he knew what would make religious girls uncomfortable, even though he hasn't been religious for a while."

"Did his advice work?" she asked.

He grinned. "I would say no, because of all of my past dates, but I *am* sitting here with you."

Dina played with her cloth napkin. "Did you talk about me?"

His eyes lifted to hers.

Dina's Choice

"I mean, that's none of my business. Sorry for asking."

"It's okay. I know how curious you are," he said with a smile. "We didn't talk that much about you. I just asked him advice on where to take you, if certain things I say to you would be wrong, that sort of thing. It's a little easier with you because the three of us have known each other for so many years. Still, I didn't want to mess things up with you like I did with the other dates. I would kick myself if I did."

"I'm not the kind of person who would break up with you if you said the wrong thing. Unless the thing you said was inappropriate, of course."

He nodded. "I hope I've never said anything inappropriate to you."

"I don't think so. I hope I haven't either."

He shook his head. "I don't think you ever could."

All the talk about Sam reminded Dina of what he had said at the gown shop. How intense his eyes had been. But she shoved all that away. For once in her life, she was putting an end to Sam Weiss. He was no longer Sam Weiss, but Shmuel Weiss. A stranger. An old neighbor. A man who was no longer part of the world she lived in. It was the only way she could have a real shot at a future with Dovid.

229

The waiter took their orders and returned a few minutes later with their drinks—orange soda for Dovid and Coke for Dina. "Orange soda is nostalgic," he told her. "I used to drink it all the time as a kid."

"I remember that."

"And you always liked...Cherry Coke."

She smiled. "Yeah, I did."

They talked about various topics until their food arrived. As soon as Dina saw how large her portion was, she said, "There's no way I'll finish all of this."

"Eat as much as you want. Please don't feel obligated to eat it all because I paid for it. I'd like to think it's more about the company than the food. We can always take home the leftovers."

"Thanks, that's so sweet of you. The first date I went on back in Miami, the portions were even larger than these and I only managed to eat half. Actually, it was less than half. I couldn't get it down. The guy said, 'Don't stop now. There's still a lot of food left.' I took a few more small bites, but that was it. So the guy said, 'This is so inconsiderate of you. I paid good money for the meal.' And silly me, instead of standing up for myself, actually apologized. Apologized for what? For being a normal human with a normal sized stomach? So anyway, he said he was taking home the leftovers because he paid for it."

Dovid shook his head. "That's so wrong. You didn't deserve to go out with such jerks. Why is it that the nice people always go out with the jerks?"

"Thanks for calling me a jerk," Dina teased.

For a second, he looked alarmed. Then he laughed. "I actually thought you were serious."

"You're not the only one with a sense of humor."

"I like your sense of humor very much."

"Thanks. But we don't have to worry about going out with jerks now, right?"

He grew silent and played around with the vegetables on his plate. "Dina?"

"Yeah?"

"Can I ask a serious question?"

"Uh oh."

He gave her a tight smile. "I love going out with you and getting to know you, but I can't help but feel like…"

Dread nestled in her stomach. "What?"

"I guess I don't feel like we're progressing. I mean, it's been quite a few weeks since we've been going out."

She swallowed. "So…what are you saying?"

"Nothing bad! Please don't worry. I was just wondering if we can take things to the next level."

More dread nestled inside her, along with anxiety. "What do you mean by the next level?"

"It's not what you're thinking. I don't want to ever pressure you or make you feel like you need to rush into anything. I just wonder if we can discuss more serious topics, like what we want for the future, the kind of homes we want to build, what kind of kids we want to raise. And maybe we can share more personal stories or even traumatizing ones, if that's okay. I just want to feel closer to you. What do you think?"

This time, she was the one playing with her food. "I kind of thought that was happening naturally."

"It is," he assured her. "But at a very slow pace. If we keep this up, we'll be dating for years," he added with an awkward laugh. "Does what I'm saying make sense?"

"I guess."

"Do you remember when you shared with me how nervous you are about marriage and all of that? I told you that you can talk to me, right?"

She nodded.

"But we never did talk about those kinds of things. I think it's important to be open about it. I want to be there for you."

It felt like the walls of the restaurant were closing in on her.

"Don't say anything, Dina, okay? Just think it over and let me know how you feel. If you're fine with keeping the pace we're at, we can. If you're open to trying to form a deeper connection, that's fine, too. I just want to make sure you're comfortable and okay with how things are going."

She puffed out her cheeks. "This is all so serious."

"I know. That's why I want you to take as much time as you need. We don't have to rush to go out the next time. We can wait a few days, weeks. However long you need."

She looked him in the eyes. "Thanks, Dovid. You really are a great guy."

His cheeks reddened. "Thanks. You really are a great girl."

The truth was that Dina was not as good of a person as he was. But if she were to commit to him for the rest of her life, she knew she'd grow to be a much better person than she was today. As scary as the thought of marriage sounded, having the right guy by her side would make it not as scary. The way things were looking, maybe Dovid Weiss was the right guy.

***

As soon as Dina came home, she sat with her mom at the kitchen table and a cup of hot cocoa. Her mother might not have been the best cook when she was growing up, but she knew how to make a mean hot coca, marshmallows and all.

"How did it go?" Mrs. Aaron asked.

"He wants to move things to the next level."

She nodded slowly. "Okay.'"

"What does that mean?"

"What do you think it means?"

"At first I thought he was referring to getting married, but then he assured me he wasn't. He just wants to get closer."

"Okay. So what's the problem?"

"But what does that even mean? When two people hang out, they get to know each other better and grow closer."

Her mother took a sip of her hot cocoa. "Maybe. Or some people just stay at the same level, never progressing to where things need to progress to."

Dina moaned, banging her head on the table.

"You just have to let him in. Open your heart. Expose yourself. Allow yourself to be vulnerable to him. Dina." She gently lifted Dina's head. "I didn't allow myself to open up to your father. I didn't allow myself to be vulnerable. It wasn't good for our marriage."

Dina banged her head on the table again. "I know. We spoke about this already."

"Dina." Her mother raised her head again and looked into her eyes. "I know how scary it is, giving someone the opportunity to stab you in the heart. But if you don't open your heart, how can you let anyone in? How can you let someone love you the way you deserve to be loved?"

Dina covered her face. "I don't think I'm mature enough for this. Maybe I'm not ready to get married until I'm like forty. Or maybe not at all. I must be defective."

"Everyone feels this way. We just need to be brave."

She wished she was as fearless as Perry. She had been brave enough to confront Naftali Josowitz and tell him how she felt, and now look at them—they were engaged.

"Step out of your comfort zone, sweetie," her mom said. "Or you'll never be ready."

She sounded like Dina's book. It also discussed exposing your heart and letting another person in. Maybe it was time for Dina to read it again. It didn't apply when she had dated Mordechai Lowy, but maybe it applied now. Dovid had told her he didn't want to mess things up with her and lose a shot with her. She didn't want to mess things up and lose a shot with him, either.

She wanted to call Perry and discuss this with her, but she had told her she would be busy all day with wedding preparations. Dina went up to her room and settled down with the book. Maybe it'd be as useful to her as it had been to her friend.

Chapter Fifteen

My coworker slammed the door and hurried back into the office. "Does anyone know what it's like out there? It's like the sky is falling apart."

As soon as the words left her mouth, lightning crackled in the sky. *This is just great.* Dina loved the rain when she was inside her house, but when she needed to get home from work? Not so much.

She took out her phone and texted Dovid. **Hey, what time are you out?**

He responded a few minutes later. **Hey, Dina, how are you? I plan on going to learn after work.**

Okay, have a good time.

She frowned as she put her phone aside. She had hoped he would pick her up, but the last thing she wanted was to take time away from his learning. He told her he didn't have a lot of time to learn the Talmud because of his job, and that he grabbed whatever chance he could get. It appeared Dina had no choice but to take the bus like usual.

Some of her coworkers and Dina remained an extra half an hour, hoping the rain would let up. Although there was no longer lightning or thunder, the rain beat down just as strongly as it did thirty minutes ago. Dina buttoned up her coat as she left the office. Because she was the most unprepared person on the planet, she had neglected to bring an umbrella today.

Some New York City buses have a booth you can stand in, but some don't. The stop Dina waiting at was part of the latter. She and a few others at the stop stood there with rain dropping down on them like buckets of ice-cold water. She managed to tie a shopping bag around her bag to protect it from the onslaught, but the rest of her was exposed to the attack.

Of course the bus took forever to come. It wouldn't be a bad day if it didn't.

"Dina!"

Was someone calling her name or was that the wind?

"Dina Aaron!"

Spinning toward the direction of the sound, Dina noticed a

dark car at the curb, a few feet away from the bus stop. The passenger window rolled down and a head peeked out. Sam.

"Come in, Dina!" he called.

Why was he there? He wasn't supposed to exist anymore. Not to Dina.

"I'm okay," she called back.

He motioned for her to come.

"I said, I'm okay."

He rolled back up the window. The young woman sighed in relief. But then the driver's door opened and he climbed out with an umbrella. He headed over to Dina. She stepped back. *No, he can't be within twenty feet of me.* She didn't want to see him, speak to him, think about him. She promised herself she was going to put everything behind her, including her fears and insecurities, and try to establish a deep connection with Dovid. That couldn't happen if Sam existed.

He stood before her, holding the umbrella over her head. "Dina, you're soaked."

"Of course I am. It's pouring. Don't you see how soaked everyone else is?"

"They have umbrellas."

"The bus should come any minute."

"I just came from that direction. There won't be a bus for at least another fifteen minutes."

Then she'd just have to wait. She'd been in worse conditions before, none she could think of at that moment.

"Dina—"

"I'm fine."

"You'll get sick."

"I said I'm fine. I'm not even cold."

Her body betrayed her by causing her teeth to chatter.

"Dina." He closed his hand over her arm. "Please come into my car."

She yanked her arm free. "Don't touch me. What are you doing here anyway? Did you purposely come here looking for me?"

He tightened his grip, though not hard enough to hurt her. "Yes, I did. I saw how horrendous the weather was and the first thing I thought about was you. How you just ended work and are probably standing at the bus stop completely soaked."

She stared at him for a moment. Then she tried pulling her arm free.

"I'm not letting go until you come into my car."

She gaped at him. "You're threatening me now?"

"No. I just can't stand seeing you here like this. Please, get in the car."

It was almost as if he was begging. Like he was actually in pain to see her in that state.

Lightning crackled in the sky. Sam's hold tightened even more. "Please, Dina."

Pulling her arm free, she walked to the car and got in the passenger seat.

"Thanks," he said once he got in.

He was thanking her? He was the one who just rescued Dina from uncertain death.

The car was completely quiet, the only sound coming from the rain splattering the windshield. Sam stopped the car. Dina glanced out the window. She couldn't see anything because of the heavy rain, but this couldn't be her house. The ride was too short.

Sam got out and opened the door for her. "Where are we?" she asked.

"Somewhere where I can get you warm clothes."

"No, just take me home."

"My apartment is right here. Let me at least get you a towel so you can dry off."

Dina scanned the area. They were in a parking lot. Of his apartment building? "Sam, can you please just take me home?"

"I will, I promise. As soon as you're dried off. If you don't come with me, I'll go up myself and grab you a towel. But I don't want to leave you here alone in the parking lot."

She crossed her arms. "I'm perfectly capable of taking care of myself."

"It's not worth the risk. This isn't like your neighborhood. Some people who live here aren't good people."

"All the more reason to take me home."

Her teeth were chattering. Her knees were shaking. And of course, her body decided to release three sneezes in a row.

"You're so stubborn, Dina. You'd do anything just to stop me from helping you."

"I don't need your help. I don't need—I don't want." She puffed. "I just want to go home."

He frowned. "Fine. If that's what you want. God forbid you actually let me care for you." He slammed the door shut and opened the driver's side.

Dina grabbed the handle of her door and pushed it open. "Fine. But only a towel."

The young man and woman stepped into the elevator,

which was *freezing*, and took it up to the sixth floor. Sam led her to an apartment called 6D. The place was tiny. There was a small living room that was attached to a tiny kitchen and a bedroom and bathroom in the back. That was all.

"This is where you live?" Dina asked, making sure to keep the door slightly ajar.

"It's the only thing I can afford on a musician's salary." He disappeared into the bathroom and returned with a dark green towel, tossing it to her. It smelled like him, just like the apartment did. Dina wrapped it around herself.

"Can I make you hot tea or something?" he asked.

"I'm fine. I just want to go h—" Her mouth snapped shut when she noticed something sitting on the small table near the couch. "Is that *tefillin*?"

His head whipped in that direction. He glanced back at her but didn't utter a word.

"Do you put it on?" she pressed.

"Every day since my *bar mitzvah*. I haven't missed a day."

"Why?"

Again, no words left his mouth.

Silence.

"I think I'll make you tea after all." He rummaged through

his cupboard and produced two cups and tea bags.

Dina didn't care much for tea, but she didn't inform Sam because she couldn't stop thinking about the Phylacteries. Sam was no longer religious. Why was he so careful not to miss a day?

"This thing is great," he spoke to himself. "Warms up in no time." He poured the hot water into the cups and added the tea bags and sugar. "Please sit." He gestured to one of the two chairs in the living room. Dina sat down and accepted the tea from him. Even though she didn't like tea, she swallowed it down because it warmed her up.

"Why don't you move back home?" she asked.

"My apartment's not that bad."

"Neither is your family."

His eyes met hers. "There are nosy neighbors."

"Who cares what they think?"

"My parents."

"Oh."

Silence. The only sounds were their slurping.

"I think I'm going to marry Dovid," Dina said.

His eyes met hers again. He took another sip.

"I..." she stammered. "I think I'm going to marry Dovid."

Dina's Choice

"I heard you."

"But you didn't say anything."

"You should do whatever your heart tells you."

She stared down at her cup.

"Does your heart tell you to marry him?" he wanted to know.

She looked up at him, unable to read the expression on his face. She placed her cup on the table. "Can you please take me home now?"

Nodding, he stood. Dina followed him out of the apartment and toward the elevator. Sam jabbed his finger into the button. The elevator didn't come. He jabbed it again, but that failed to cause the elevator to come quicker. They stood there in silence for minutes, though it felt like hours.

Finally, the doors pinged open. Standing in the elevator as it creaked down the floors at an antagonizing slow rate was even more awkward. When the doors opened, both Dina and Sam quickly stepped out and made their way to Sam's car.

It was no longer raining. The drive to Dina's house was silent. A few times, Sam opened his mouth, as though he wanted to say something, but then changed his mind. When they were a few blocks from Dina's house, he said, "You looked really pretty in that wedding dress."

Her cheeks heated up.

"I don't know if it's okay for me to say that, but I wanted to say it."

"Thanks," she whispered.

He stopped the car in front of her house. "If you want to marry Dovid, then marry him. But marry him for the right reasons."

She reached for the door handle.

He gently grabbed her wrist. "Do you love him?"

"It's too early for that."

"Do you think you can love him?"

"I'm sure I can. I'm sure I will."

He shook his head. "That's a ridiculous answer."

She jerked her hand away. "Maybe you've been out of my world for too long, but you know we don't marry only for love. We need common values, common goals. Love builds up in a marriage."

He scoffed. "That's what they feed us."

"Do you love Glinda?"

His eyes snapped to hers.

"Are you hopelessly and madly in love with her?"

He narrowed his eyes. "No, I'm not."

"Are you going to marry her?"

"I might."

Now she narrowed her eyes. "But you don't love her."

"How can I when my heart belongs to someone else?"

It felt as though the air got knocked out of her. She sat there, frozen, staring at him. His deep, blue eyes were glued to hers, soft, hurt, aching. Time stood still. Rain started to hit the windshield again.

Dina forced herself to open the door and get out of the car.

"Dina."

She turned around.

Sam stood outside the passenger door. "Don't make a mistake."

"Believe me, I'm not." The mistake would be throwing Dovid aside for Sam.

It appeared as though he wanted to say more, but Dina turned her back and headed into her house.

Chapter Sixteen

Dina hadn't seen Dovid in a few days. He was extremely considerate, giving her enough time to think things over. Then he called her last night and asked if she wanted to go out, which was a loaded question—he wanted to know if she thought things over. The truth was, Dina hadn't thought about anything but the night Sam picked her up from work. That was very unfair to Dovid. *I'm such a terrible person.*

Dovid picked her up and took her to a park. The weather was beautiful for early December. They walked for a bit, talking about light topics and not venturing anywhere near serious territory. After twenty minutes, Dovid suggested they take a break and rest on a bench.

"Dina…"

"I know what you're going to ask. If I thought about what

we spoke about the last time."

"I don't want to pressure you."

She held out her hand. "You're not. You've been nothing but sweet to me."

They were quiet. Dina didn't know what to say, what to feel.

"Can I ask you a question?" he asked.

"Of course."

"Do you like me?"

"Of course I do."

"Do you really like me?"

She simply looked at him.

"I read somewhere that in any relationship, one party will always love the other one more. I'm fine if it's like that for us. I just want to know how much you care about me."

"A lot," she admitted.

"But not as much as you like Sam."

She blinked at him.

He looked down at the ground. "I saw you two the other night, when there was that crazy storm. He drove you home?"

"He passed by the bus stop and saw me waiting."

He held up his hand. "I'm not accusing you of anything,

Dina. Never. It's just…" He took in a breath and exhaled. "The way Sam looked at you…"

"What?"

"He's in love with you."

"It doesn't matter. Forget about Sam. This is between you and me."

"Do you love him?" he wanted to know.

Her mouth shut.

"I'm not blind. I've seen the way you two have been looking at each other since you moved back here. I know how you two felt about each other when we were kids."

She shook her head. "The past doesn't matter. All that matters is the future. I want to try to have one with you."

"I really like you, Dina. Very much."

"I like you very much, too."

"I told myself I was okay with being second best. But when I saw the way Sam looked at you…I want someone to look at me like that. I don't want to be second best. I want to be someone's first choice."

Tears entered her eyes. She covered her face. "I'm sorry, Dovid. I've been horrible to you."

"No, you haven't. You've been kind and sweet—"

Dina's Choice

"How can you say that when you knew how I feel about Sam?"

"Because for the first time, it felt good to have something he desperately wanted."

Dina slowly lowered her hands from her face.

"I've been horrible to you as well. I've liked you since that first Shabbos you and your mother spent with us. But as we started to date and get to know each other, I knew Sam was jealous. It made me feel good to have something he didn't have. I used you."

"No, you didn't use me, Dovid. Please don't be upset with yourself. You're only human."

He shook his head. "You shouldn't be so understanding."

"You deserve to be someone's number one. I want to try to be that person."

He raised his eyebrows. "But what about Sam?"

"He's not religious."

"And if he was? You'd be dating him and not me."

Her mouth snapped shut and her eyes closed for a second. She didn't want to admit how right he was.

"So what do we do?" she asked.

"I don't know."

"It's so easy to talk to you," she informed him. "It feels like I'm talking to my best friend."

His eyes searched hers. "Maybe that's the most we can ever be. Best friends."

The tears welled up in her eyes. "But I want to try to be more."

"Feelings never truly go away. You'll be in love with him for the rest of your life. As much as I like you, I can't compete with that."

"Don't break things off," she begged. "We can try to make it work."

"I want to, so desperately. But one of us will end up hurt. I know it."

Dina didn't want to let him go, but perhaps he was right. That deep connection he was talking about? She wondered if they could ever achieve it. Because when she imagined herself married, Dovid's face didn't float before her eyes. Sam's did. Dina couldn't have a future with Sam. *I'll probably stay single for the rest of my life.*

She stood. "I'm sorry, Dovid. I want you to be happy."

"I want you to be happy, too. I really care about you. I would hug you if I could."

Dina's Choice

"I really care about you, too. I know it won't be long before you meet the right one. Just promise me one thing."

"Yeah?"

"Make sure the girl you marry deserves to have you."

He smiled. "Thanks. I will."

***

"But I don't understand!" Perry nearly cried into the phone. "Things were going so well between you two."

"Some things aren't meant to be." Dina actually felt good about it. She and Dovid were two good people who were not soulmates. They ended things amicably, with no hard feelings.

"And my wedding is *next week*," Perry grumbled. "I can't handle all this stress."

Dina fell back on her bed and stared at the ceiling. "You don't have to stress about anything. This is my life, not yours."

Her friend sighed. "I so wanted to be sisters."

"Didn't I tell you already that we are sisters?"

She felt Perry smile. "Yeah, you did.

"Forget about me and my problems. What's going on with you?"

"Well, in case you didn't get the invitation, I'm getting married on Tuesday."

"I have indeed gotten the invitation. I'm wondering how the bride is feeling. But I want you to tell me how you're really feeling, not what you tell everyone else. You don't have to be strong in front of me."

Perry was quiet for a while, and Dina wondered if she hung up or if she offended her. Then Perry exclaimed, "I'm a nervous wreck!"

"That's understandable."

"No, it's not. Like, I'm beyond an emotional wreck. I was the one who made all this happen. What if it was the biggest mistake of my life? What if he grows to hate me? What if I never learn how to cook?"

"I'm sure he'll forgive you or try to help you out with the cooking…"

"And what if we have a horrible marriage? What if I get a divorce?"

Dina couldn't help but think about her parents and their divorce.

Perry gasped. "Oh my gosh. I didn't mean to say that to you."

"Don't worry about it, Perry. I worry about that, too. Maybe everyone does."

Dina's Choice

"Ugh! I hate myself. We should probably hang up before I say another insulting thing."

"No, don't hang up. I just want to tell you one thing. You might be getting cold feet—that's normal. At least, that's what I heard. And sure there are so many uncertainties, so many things to worry about. But push that aside for now. Pretend it's just you and Naftali on a secluded island. How does that make you feel?"

"Hold on. I have to close my eyes and picture it." Perry released a deep breath. "I feel...good. Excited."

"Okay, that's all that matters."

"Wow, Dina. You talk as if you've been married for twenty years."

She laughed. "I have no idea where that came from."

"Me, either. But it was awesome. When you do that, do you see Dovid?"

Dina's heart leaped in her throat. No, it wasn't Dovid she saw. It was Sam.

"Dina?"

"A blank face," she lied.

"Well, duh. Mr. Perfect hasn't arrived yet. One second...yeah, Mom...? Dina, my mom needs me. Thanks for the talk."

"No problem. Good night."

When Dina went downstairs, she found her mother preparing dinner. "Can I help?" she offered.

"Sure."

Mrs. Aaron instructed her daughter to cut carrots and parsnips for the vegetable soup while she worked on the ground beef mixture for the meatloaf. They worked in silence, which Dina enjoyed. There was something comforting about being there with her mom. She was worried about her future and her feelings for Sam, but working side by side with the woman who gave her life eased her nerves a bit.

Mrs. Aaron smiled at her daughter. "You seem to be in a better mood."

"I was in a bad mood when I got home?"

"A little."

"But Dovid and I ended things amicably. No feelings were hurt."

She rubbed her arm. "A breakup is still a breakup."

What her mother failed to understand was that she had been in a sour mood because of someone else. Dina had no one to talk to about the emotions whirling inside her. If she told her mother she had feelings for the non-religious twin, it would only cause her to worry. Having a future with Sam would mean no longer being religious and living a secular life. Dina couldn't throw her life away, even if Sam was the right one for her.

But how long was she going to feel this way? She tried to fight it—she even lost a great guy because of it. Would she continue losing guys because of him?

"You seem to have a lot on your mind," her mother observed.

"I guess I'm just wondering if I'll ever be emotionally ready to have a relationship with anyone."

"Of course you will, sweetie. Just continue working on yourself and making sense of your feelings. What kind of person do you want to be? What kind of life do you want to have? Everything will fall into place. You'll see."

She hugged her mother. "Thanks for everything, Mom. I know we got to a rocky start when I first moved back. I feel much closer to you now."

She patted her back. "So do I. And I'm very proud of the person you are. I love you, sweetie."

"I love you, too."

Later that night as Dina read the marriage book, her phone buzzed. She assumed it was a text from Perry, but she nearly dropped her phone when she saw the words on the screen.

You broke up with Dovid.

Sam.

She texted back, **We both kind of broke it off.**

It felt like ages before he responded. **Why?**

Sam and Dina weren't face to face. They weren't speaking on the phone. It made communicating with him so different. It was almost like she was talking to another person.

Ask him, she texted.

A few more minutes of silence. **I'm asking you.**

What did he want her to say? That she and Dovid broke up because of him?

We weren't good together, she responded.

You told me you were going to marry him.

Are you mad at me? Dina asked.

Why should I be mad?

Then why do you care?

I don't.

You're lying.

Dina, you've been lying since you got here.

Dina's Choice

She shut her phone and threw it aside, focusing back on her book. She didn't hear anything from him for the rest of the night.

Chapter Seventeen

Dina couldn't believe her best friend was getting *married* tonight.

When she went downstairs, her mom was in the middle of putting on her shoes. She smiled when she took note of her daughter, reaching for her hands and giving them a loving squeeze. "You look beautiful."

Dina wore a dark blues dress and black shoes with two inch heels. She didn't wear high heels very often, but tonight was a special occasion. "Thanks, Mom. You look beautiful, too."

Dina didn't understand why butterflies flapped around in her stomach. She wasn't the one getting married! Perhaps because it was a preview of what it would be like when her day arrived. Or maybe it was because a certain someone of the male variety would be there. Dina hadn't seen him since he picked her up from work on that stormy day. She was somewhat nervous to see Dovid as well. They had bumped into each other a few times over the past few days, and things were a little awkward.

Once mother and daughter were all set, they called for a cab and drove to the wedding hall. The first person Dina caught sight of when they walked in was Simi. The little girl wore an adorable pink dress with layers of petticoats. She ran around the place like she had been zapped with an energy booster.

"Simi!" Dina called.

The five year old ran over. "Dina! Dina! Look at my dress! Did you see my dress? Isn't it so pretty?"

Dina smiled. "You look beautiful."

Dovid came over and took his sister's hand. "Sorry. I might have given her a bit too much sugar before the wedding. Big mistake."

Dina gave him a small smile. "Hi."

He returned it. "Hi. How are you?"

"I'm good. You?"

"I'm good."

Mrs. Aaron took Simi's hand. "Do you want to show me

what's yummy to eat?"

"Yes!" They walked away.

"How are you really?" Dina asked the tall man standing before her.

"I'm okay. I'm actually seeing someone right now."

"Really? That's great."

"Yeah. What about you?"

"Oh, no. I'm not going to date for a while."

He frowned. "I hope I didn't ruin dating for you."

"No, no! Not at all." *Your brother did, though.*

"Okay. Good."

Awkward silence.

"I'm going to say *mazel tov* to your parents."

Dovid nodded, stepping aside. Doing a quick sweep of the room, Dina concluded that the bride hadn't yet arrived to the main hall. She didn't see Sam either. She found Mrs. Weiss chatting with another woman. The mother of the bride wore a gorgeous golden gown and her wig was styled beautifully. When she noticed Dina walking up to her, her face brightened and she grabbed her in for a big hug.

"*Mazel tov*, Mrs. Weiss."

"*Mazel tov, mazel tov*, Dina! Thank you so much for

coming." She pulled back and scanned Dina from top to bottom. "You look gorgeous. *Im yirtzeh Hashem* by you."

"Amen, thanks."

Other women pushed to hug and congratulate Mrs. Weiss. Dina headed to the smorgasbord table and filled up her plate. Weddings are an excuse to eat whatever you want.

After a few minutes, Mrs. Weiss and the mother of the groom brought Perry in. The bride perched herself on the bridal chair, and everyone formed a line to wish her a *mazel tov*. Dina and her mother managed to be one of the first ones.

"Dina!" Perry kissed her best friend's cheek. "Hi."

"*Mazel tov!*"

"Thanks. You look stunning!"

"I look stunning? Just look at you."

"Thanks." Her eyes shone with exhilaration. "Can I say it? You have to let me say it—a bride's blessing holds special meaning."

Dina laughed. "You can say it."

"*Im yirtzeh Hashem*, it won't be long until you're sitting on this chair. *Im yirtzeh Hashem, im yirtzeh Hashem* really soon!"

Dina hugged her tight, knowing how sincere her words were and loving her for it.

Mrs. Aaron wished the beautiful bride a *mazel tov*, then she and her daughter returned to the smorgasbord table. The funny thing about smorgasbords is that they offer a variety of food, even though the guests will be eating a huge meal after the *chuppah*. No matter how much Dina ate at the smorgasbord, she knew she would always have room for the meal. It must be the magic of the wedding.

When her plate was full, she scanned the tables for a place to sit. Of course they were all occupied, save for a random chair here and there. She noticed her mom chatting with those women she met at the engagement party, including that matchmaker. Dina wasn't very interested in joining them because she knew the woman would bring up her long list of potential boys. She didn't want to think about dating for another two hundred years.

Then a table with girls around her age caught her eyes. As she edged closer, she recognized a few faces. These girls must have been Perry's friends from elementary and high school, some of which had been in her grade.

They smiled when she sat down and introduced themselves. "I'm Dina Aaron. I'm an old friend of Perry's."

One of the girls, who had been staring at Dina intently

since she sat down, blinked a few times. "That's why you look so familiar! You were in my class."

Now it was Dina's turn to scrutinize her face. "Oh my gosh. Kayla Klein. I didn't recognize you. You changed so much."

She giggled. "How can you forget me when my name is Kayla Klein?"

Dina returned the laugh. "Good question."

They caught up on each other's lives as they ate, and Dina wasn't surprised to discover the topic of this discussion revolved around dating and marriage. True they were at a wedding, but Dina was tired of dating taking over her life. She focused on her food, occasionally adding input here and there. Never having been the social kind, she didn't mind keeping quiet.

"Is that the twin who's no longer religious?" one of the girls suddenly asked. When Dina raised her eyes to her, she saw that her gaze was pasted on the spot behind her. She turned around and found Sam talking to another man. He wore a crisp black suit, his dark hair combed behind his ears. A black, velvet *kippa* sat at the center of his head.

"Yeah, probably," Kayla said. "That's most likely the

religious twin." She nodded toward the opposite side of the room, to where Dovid conversed with another guy.

Dina's gaze returned to Sam. Now he was in the middle of helping Simi get some food. As though feeling her watching him, his head snapped in her direction. She quickly tore her eyes away. When she glanced back at him a few seconds later, she found his eyes trekking to hers.

"Hello, girls." The matchmaker dropped down in the seat next to Dina and introduced herself to the other girls, emphasizing that she was a matchmaker who, thank God, had made quite a few successful matches.

The girls immediately perked up, each one wanting to make a good impression. Dina picked at her food, hoping the woman wouldn't try to set her up right now.

"How are you, Dina?" she asked.

"Good, thanks."

"Great. I want to give all you girls my phone number. I have so many great boys."

Dina didn't know how she did it—it was definitely a superpower—but in the span of five minutes, the matchmaker learned the names of every girl at the table, a little bit about her, and what kind of guy she was looking for. She assured them all that she had a guy for each and every one of them.

She patted Dina's arm. "And I didn't forget about you, Dina. Just call me when you're ready."

Dina finally looked the woman in the eyes and realized that she had a kind expression on her face. It was obvious that her mother had told her about her breakup with Dovid. What she and her mother couldn't possibly understand, though, was that *he* wasn't the reason she was upset.

Even though the woman could be a little much at times, Dina realized she was a sweet woman who just wanted to make other people happy. Matchmakers really put a lot into this whole dating thing, most of the time gaining nothing in return.

"Thanks for all you do," Dina told her. "I know it's not easy."

She smiled. "Thanks for saying that. It's nice to feel appreciated once in a while."

Once she left the table, Kayla said, "I feel so lucky when I meet a new matchmaker. There are so many unmarried people out there that no one even thinks about. Everyone else goes on date after date while they stay at home, hoping for the phone to ring."

"Please don't tell me you stay home all day sitting near the phone," Dina said.

She laughed lightly. "Okay, I can be a little overdramatic at times. But I wish more people would think about me."

"Please, take her. As much as I appreciate her thinking of me, I can't deal with dating right now."

She seemed curious, wondering why Dina was taking a break. But instead of questioning her about it, she said, "I don't know if there's even a point. I bet my profile will get buried beneath all the other profiles. It happens all the time. I hate having to remind matchmakers about me."

"Don't," Dina said. "Be brave and call them, as many times as you need to. Sometimes you need to be assertive. Leave your comfort zone. Go after what you want."

"Hey, is that from that marriage book?" one of the girls at the table asked. "*You, Me, and the Life that Could Be?*"

"Yes," Dina replied.

Everyone at the table started gushing about the book. Once again, the topic revolved around marriage and marriage only. Dina stood with her plate and browsed the large selection of pastries.

"I'd recommend these," a voice said from behind. Dina turned around and came face to face with Sam. He plucked a vanilla cookie with a cholate center off the platter and placed it on her plate.

"Thanks."

They just stood there looking at each other. Dina bit into her cookie to keep busy, and her eyes widened. "Wow, this is the best cookie I've ever had."

"Thanks," he said.

Her eyebrows crinkled. "Why are you saying...did you make these?"

He nodded at the table. "I made them all."

"All these cakes and cookies?"

He nodded again.

"Wow."

He chuckled softly. "Don't act so surprised. A guy can learn to cook and bake."

"No, it's not that. I just didn't think you cared enough."

His eyebrows rose. "Didn't care about my sister?"

Dina shook her head. "No, about the wedding. I didn't even know if you'd show up."

He scanned around and frowned when he noticed some people staring at him. He shrugged. "This isn't about me or even my parents. This is about Perry and Naftali."

"Shmuel! Shumuel!" Simi tugged on his pants. "Can I have more of the chocolate cookies? Please, please?"

He ruffled her hair. "You need to save room for the meal."

"I'll have enough room. I have a big stomach."

He took one of the chocolate cookies and cracked it in half. "Only half, because I want you to have room for the meal."

"Thank you." She munched and zoomed away, leaving Sam and Dina in another awkward silence.

"I like the *kippa*," she found herself saying.

"My father made me wear it."

"Oh."

"It doesn't mean anything to me, Dina."

He was lying. He *had* to be lying.

He lowered his head. "*Mazel tov.*" He walked away.

Dina returned to the table and just sat there, her mind jumbled with thoughts. A few minutes later, Simi hopped onto her lap and kept her busy with her stories. After another few minutes, the music blared. Naftali was coming to pull the veil over Perry's head. It's a tradition Jews have been doing ever since their patriarch Yaakov was tricked by Lavan and given the wrong woman to marry

"Go to Mommy," Dina told Simi.

Dina's Choice

She nodded and ran off. Dina joined the other women who were crowded around the bride, pushing to get a glimpse of this important and special part of a Jewish wedding. Naftali's friends danced in front of him as his parents lead him to his bride. Dovid and Sam stood right behind them. Dina could only glimpse the back of Naftali's head, but she managed to see Perry's face. She smiled, nothing but love and joy in her eyes. As Naftali lowered the veil, he whispered something in her ear, which made her smile widen.

Dina's eyes searched for Sam's. His were locked on hers. They stared at each other for a moment, as though their gazes were glued to each other's. It wasn't until one of the dancing guys knocked into Sam that he was brought out of his reverie.

All of the guests headed for the *chuppah* room. Dina located the row her mother sat at and joined her.

The *chuppah* ceremony began. Naftali concentrated very hard as his parents walked him down the aisle. A few blessings were made. Then it was time for the bride to walk down with her parents. She, too, concentrated very hard. Then the rest of the blessings were made, the bride and groom drank from the wine cup, and Naftali slammed his foot on another cup. The music blared and everyone yelled *mazel tov*! Perry and Naftali were now officially married. They left the room, their hands clasped.

All the guests made their way to the main hall, where they would eat the meal. Dina and her mother were seated at the table with Mrs. Aaron's new friends. The first course was a salmon dish and a small salad. Not being the greatest fan of fish, Dina nibbled on the vegetables. As the women around the table chatted, Dina's eyes flitted to the partition between the men and women's sections, trying to get a glimpse of the family table on the men's side. From where she sat, it was impossible to see past the wooden partition. It didn't matter, anyway, because there was a good chance Sam was taking pictures with the new couple and the rest of the family.

It wasn't too long before the next dish was brought in. It was a choice between two soups, vegetable and mushroom. Mrs. Aaron decided on the mushroom while her daughter chose vegetable. It was delicious.

As the guests finished up their soups, many of Perry's friends stood near the entrance to the room, holding up arches decorated in white. That was a sign that the pictures had been taken and the bride and groom were preparing to join their guests in the celebration. The music began to play as the girls waved the arches. Then an announcer blared, "Introducing for the very first time, Mr. and Mrs. Naftali and Perry Josowitz!"

The door opened and the bride and groom, holding hands, rushed through the arches. Then their hands drew apart as the new couple separated, Naftali to the men's side and Perry to the women's. The first person Perry danced with was her mother. With tears in her eyes, Mrs. Weiss danced enthusiastically, with the energy of a twenty year old. The rest of the women formed a circle around them and danced. Then Mrs. Weiss and her daughter posed for the camera before the mother of the bride enveloped her in a strong hug. Close family members danced with Perry next, followed by extended family and friends.

Perry clutched Dina's hands as they spun around, both nearly tripping over Perry's dress and laughing. Perry yelled something at her, but Dina couldn't hear anything over the loud music. They posed for the camera and hugged.

"I said soon it won't be long before we dance at your wedding," Perry wished.

"Amen," Dina said.

Dina joined the outer circle as another one of Perry friends danced with her. One would think the bride would be exhausted by now, but it appeared as though Perry could dance like this for hours. But eventually, the music slowed down and the guests returned to their tables for the next course. The bride and groom settled down at their table located at the head of the room, between the men and women's sections.

The final course consisted of a choice between fried chicken cutlets or grilled chicken, with a side of baked potatoes, sweet potatoes, string beans and rice. Like the rest of the meal, this dish was delicious as well.

The remainder of the night was filled with more chatting, more dancing, and eating dessert. Toward the end of the dancing, Perry was taken into the men's section, sitting beside her new husband. The men danced before the young couple, each one attempting stunts, trying his hardest to bring a large smile to the newlyweds. Even Naftali did a crazy dance before his bride, producing some giggles from her.

Around midnight, Dina and her mother decided to go home. Many of the guests had already left.

They stepped up to the bride and groom's table, wished them *mazel tov*, many happy and healthy years together, and they exchanged hugs and kisses with Perry. She and her new husband looked beyond ecstatic. Perry kept her arms around her best friend, giving her blessing after blessing until reluctantly freeing her.

From where Dina stood, she had a clear view of the men's section. She hadn't peeked in before because she was preoccupied with the dancing, but now she took a good look at the family table, where Dovid and Sam sat with their father and close family members. Dovid was in the middle of talking with another man, but Sam just sat there, looking miserable. Dina wondered what caused him to feel that way.

"Dina, ready to go?" Mrs. Aaron asked.

She nodded, then looked at the newlyweds. "*Mazel tov* again."

"Thanks!" they both said.

Before they left, they wished Mrs. Weiss *mazel tov* as well.

"I love weddings." Mrs. Aaron sighed contently once she and her daughter got into a cab. "They always leave a good feeling inside me."

Dina nodded, but all she saw before her eyes was Sam's miserable face. He not only looked miserable, but also lost. She didn't know why she couldn't get the image out of her head. Why did she care? If he wouldn't have chosen the path he was on, his life could have been completely different. No, it *would* be completely different. And hers would be completely different as well.

"You're quiet, sweetie," her mother said.

"Weddings make me feel good, too," she told her. "But they also make me feel sad."

Mrs. Aaron nodded. "I understand. Just have faith. Everything will work out in the end."

That was what everyone claimed, and it was what Dina believed, too. But she couldn't imagine how things could work out when everything seemed so messed up.

Chapter Eighteen

Dina woke up from her sleep at the sound of something hitting her window. She ignored it at first, turning onto her side and squeezing her eyes shut. But the sound grew more incessant. Her eyes flew open. She knew that sound. Pushing her blanket aside, she hurried to the window and opened it, sticking her head out.

Sam was balancing on the tree outside her room.

"Sam, what are you doing?" she called.

"I need to talk to you."

She glanced at the clock on her nightstand. "It's four in the morning."

"I need to talk to you."

"Aren't you tired? Your sister just got married a few hours ago."

"Please, Dina."

Not this again. They weren't allowed to be alone together. She didn't *want* to be alone with him. She didn't think she could bear it.

"Go home, Sam. We'll talk tomorrow."

"I'm not leaving until we talk."

"Again with the threats?"

"Dina, please."

There was a strange expression on his face. A sort of desperation. And a loss of hope.

She sighed. "One second."

After making sure her mother was asleep in her room, she left the door slightly ajar, threw on a robe over her pajamas, and opened the window wider. Sam was slightly shaky as he climbed through the window, much more than that stormy night. Just as he was about to roll inside, his foot slipped and he lost his balance.

"Sam!" Dina grabbed onto him and pulled as hard as she could. His body was practically hanging off her window. One more inch and he'd plummet to the ground.

She didn't know where the strength came from, but it was as though she was zapped with super strength. She tightened her hold on Sam and yanked so hard they toppled into her room. Sam landed on top of her, his knee pressing into her leg.

He stared into her eyes. She stared into his.

"Dina…" His hand brushed the side of her head. He gently picked a lock of hair off her eye and pushed it to the side. He rubbed the back of his palm down her cheek.

She was completely frozen underneath him. She could hardly breathe.

He must have realized the state she was in, because he rolled off her. Dina sat up, fixing her robe that fell slightly open. They both sat on the floor of her room.

"You okay?" he asked.

She nodded. "You?"

He returned the nod.

Quiet. The only sound was the ticking of the clock.

"It's 4:30 in the morning," Dina informed him.

He lifted his eyes to hers. "I just had to see you."

"Why?"

He broke his gaze. "Because the only thing I thought about at my sister's wedding was you. How you would look in her place, wearing that wedding dress you tried on. And then I thought about your groom, standing with you under the *chuppah.*" His hands clenched. "I hate him, whoever he is."

Dina merely stared at him. He leaned his head against the wall and closed his eyes.

"It can be you," she told him. "You can be the one standing with me under the *chuppah.*"

He opened his eyes. "You'll never accept me the way I am."

She shook her head.

"Why can't you?"

"Sam, you're not religious."

"So what?"

"*So what?* How can you say that? Being an observant Jew means everything to me. It means everything to my family. And it used to mean everything to you, too."

He scoffed. "Yeah, it used to."

"What does that mean? What happened to you? What made you go off?"

He shook his head. "It doesn't matter."

"Yes, it does. I want to know. I *need* to know."

"You don't need to know anything."

"I know you secretly want to be *frum,*" she said. "But you're too scared to admit it."

"I'm not scared of anything. And you're wrong—I don't

want to be *frum*. That is part of my past."

"Then why do you keep kosher? Why do you put *tefillin* on every day?"

He turned his head away from her. Then his eyes landed on the marriage book sitting on her nightstand. He reached to sweep it off and scanned the title. "What is this garbage?" he asked.

"It's not garbage. It's actually pretty good. Very insightful."

He turned to the first page. "After reading this book, you'll have a better understanding about love and marriage, and how to develop a deep, meaningful relationship with your spouse." He scoffed. "Written by one of the greatest rabbis of our generation. I wonder how much love and romance this guy actually has in his marriage. Probably as much as the mice and cockroaches crawling in these walls."

"Sam, that's disrespectful."

He moved closer to her, so close his face was only a few inches from hers. "You think you can learn about love from a silly book? The only way you can truly learn about it is by experiencing it."

His face was too close. Dina moved a few inches back. "And I suppose you're such an expert because you're with a new woman every night?"

His eyebrows came together. "What are you talking about?"

"I don't know. I just said it."

"You think I…? I've never been with a woman *that* way. I'm not even with Gloria anymore."

"Her name is Glinda," she reminded him.

He smiled a little. "I'm not with Glinda anymore."

"Am I supposed to be happy about that?"

"Am I supposed to be happy that you broke things off with Dovid?"

"We both broke it," she told him. "It was a mutual decision."

He waved his hand. "Whatever." He tossed the book aside. "No one knows anything," he muttered. "Everyone's just trying to figure things out as they come."

Dina scooted a little closer to him. "Tell me, Sam. Tell me what happened to you."

He shook his head.

"I'll try to understand. I won't judge."

He shook his head again.

"Sam, you're unhappy."

His eyes flashed to hers. "You don't know anything about

me."

"Who's fault is that? The last I remember is you at twelve, so excited to turn *bar mitzvah*. And now look at you." She swallowed. "You've abandoned our faith. You've abandoned me."

"I haven't," he said. "Why can't you accept that this is my life now? That this is who I am?"

"Because it's not you!"

"You don't know me!"

"Tell me, Sam. Just tell me. Please."

His chest rose and fell heavily. Darkness conquered his face. Dina's chest rose and fell just as heavily. The only sounds in the room were their heavy breathing. They sat there quietly for a good few minutes.

Sam said, "You won't understand."

"I'll try. I promise."

He shut his eyes. "I don't want to relive it."

"I know, and I don't want to make you relive it. But I need to know. It's the only way we can move on. The only way we can...maybe have something."

He opened his eyes and looked at the young woman before him. She saw the doubt in them, the fear. The pain. But she also glimpsed a glimmer of hope.

She moved a little closer. "It's me, Sam," she said softly. "It's Dina. You can talk to me."

He nodded slowly, moving his gaze to the spot in front of him. He took in a deep breath and let it out slowly. "A teacher terrorized me in seventh grade."

Dina squeezed her eyes shut as her heart sank. She had hoped this wasn't the reason.

"It continued all the way into ninth grade," Sam went on.

Keeping her eyes closed, she swallowed. "Terrorized how?"

She didn't want to hear the answer. She knew she had to.

"He picked on me all the time. Called me dumb in front of the whole class. Failed me even when I did well on my tests."

Her eyes snapped open. "Wait a second. You mean, he didn't touch you?"

He shook his head.

"He just bullied you?"

He nodded.

Dina sat there, staring at him for a few seconds in total disbelief. His eyes were pinned on his shoes. She slowly stood up and looked down at him. "You're telling me you went off the *derech* because some teacher picked on you? That sort of thing happens all the time. My tenth grade teacher was so horrible to me, she made me cry in front of the whole class. And she sent me to the principal's office and told me to explain to her why *I* was crying. You don't see me going off the *derech* because of that."

Sam gaped at her, his jaw nearly touching the floor. He rose off the ground, so slowly it was as though his body was broken. As though he aged sixty years. He looked into Dina's brown eyes, his own hollow. "I…can't believe you," he uttered, so low she almost missed it.

"What?"

"You told me you'd be understanding. You said you wouldn't judge. I didn't tell a single person about this. Not even Dovid. I thought I could be open with you. I thought I finally found the one person I can talk to about this. And this is how you react?"

Betrayal conquered every inch of his face. He had nothing but pain in his eyes.

"Sorry, I didn't mean to be judgmental," she apologized. "I just don't understand why you would go off because of something a teacher did when you were a kid."

"I was only thirteen," he said.

"I know, but these things happen all the time."

"That makes it okay?" he demanded.

"No, of course not. But that doesn't mean—"

"You know something? Forget this. Silly me for thinking the girl I love would try to make an effort to understand what I've been through. Or at least not be judgmental like everyone else. Maybe it doesn't seem like a big deal to you, but it was a very big deal to me. I didn't get physically abused, but I was emotionally abused and sometimes that's worse than the physical abuse. I didn't think you of all people could make me feel worse than that teacher did." He stormed to the window.

"Sam—"

He spun around to face her. "You're not the person I thought you were. The Dina I love doesn't exist, only in my head and in my heart. I don't want to see you again. I don't want to talk to you. I want you out of my life."

Tears sprang to her eyes. "Sam, wait!"

Ignoring her, he climbed onto her window.

"Sam." She rushed over and grabbed his hand. "I'm sorry. I didn't mean to say those things. Please don't go."

He wrenched his hand away and leaped onto the closest branch.

Dina's Choice

"Sam!" she called. "Sam!"

Continuing to ignore her, he climbed down the rest of the tree, disappearing into the night.

Dina fell to her knees, tears bursting out of her eyes. *What did I just do?* She felt like such a horrible person. Sam was trying to be open with her. For the first time, he was letting someone in, sharing one of the most traumatic experiences of his life. And she threw it in his face. What was *wrong* with her?

She fell to the floor and wept. He was only a kid back then. Innocent, full of hope. And a teacher stole that from him. No one could understand what kind of effect that had on him. No one had the right to judge. What may seem trivial to one person can be an extremely traumatizing for someone else. Everyone is different. Everyone experiences things differently. Sam had always been a sensitive person. He took things more to heart than most people. Dina should have realized that. She should have understood.

Perry claimed she wasn't a judgmental person, but now Dina learned that she was probably the most judgmental person in the world.

"Sam," she sobbed into her hands. "I'm so sorry."

She didn't know if he'd ever forgive her.

Chapter Nineteen

Four days passed. Four days of calling Sam a million times. Four days of leaving him a million messages. Four days of sending him a million texts.

He hadn't responded to any.

They say you can't change a person, but Dina always believed that with the right influence, and maybe some love, a person could change. She could have been the one to shine a light at the end of the tunnel Sam was lost in. She could have been the one to fill him with love and hope, and help him return to the life he so desperately wanted to return to. But the only thing she managed to do was stomp over his already fragile heart. She had shoved him deeper into the tunnel. He might be gone for good.

"Dina, why aren't you dressed?"

She lifted her head and found her mother standing in the doorway of her room.

"Huh?"

"We have the Shabbos *sheva brachos* to go to."

Sheva brachos is a week of celebration following a wedding. Close family and friends take turns hosting a party every day of the week, inviting the newlywed couple. It's tradition for the bride's parents to host the Shabbos *sheva brachos* and invite close friends and family, plus the groom's side, of course. Dina and her mother planned to go early to the synagogue to catch some of the praying as well.

"You go ahead," she muttered. "I'll join later."

The older woman sat on her daughter's bed, pushing some hair off her face. "What's going on, sweetie? You've been down these past few days. Since the wedding."

Dina couldn't talk to her about it. She couldn't talk to anyone. All she wished was to bury it deep inside, where it would hopefully disappear forever.

"Hmm?"

"It's nothing."

"I understand how hard it can be, seeing your best friend happily married. But you'll get there soon, God willing."

Dina turned away from her, a little too sharply. "It's not about that."

"Okay," she said gently. "Then what is it about?"

"Nothing."

"You know something, Dina? You won't always be able to talk to Perry about the things you are going through. She's your best friend and will always be there for you, but she has a husband to think about now. Soon she'll have a family. You'll need someone to talk to."

She lifted her eyes to her mother. "That person is you?"

"I'd like it to be."

"But you're my mom. There are some things I can't talk to you about."

A hurt look passed over her face, but she nodded. "I understand. I need to act more like your mother and not your best friend."

"I'm sorry. I want to talk to you about stuff, but some things I need to keep to myself."

She nodded again as she played with her daughter's auburn hair. "I guess you'll have to make some new friends."

Dina frowned. "I'm not good at making friends."

Mrs. Aaron leaned forward to press a kiss on her forehead.

Dina's Choice

"Maybe you'll be married soon and will have your husband to talk to."

At the mention of marriage, of a husband, tears filled the younger woman's eyes.

Her mother hugged her. "Don't despair. You'll find a husband soon."

She didn't understand. She never would. Just like Dina couldn't understand what Sam had been through. There was only one person she wanted to talk to, cry to, laugh with, marry. That person was Sam Weiss. *I've lost him forever.*

Mom reached for the tissue box on her night stand. "Come, dry your tears. Let's go to *shul* and forget about everything. Praying will make you feel better."

Dina doubted it. She didn't think there was anything God could do for her at this point. She dug her own grave. There was no saving herself.

The entire Weiss gang was at the synagogue, little Simi playing with the other kids outside. Well, everyone besides for Sam. He'd probably arrive after prayers. Dina didn't think she could bear being in the same room as him.

Perry, who was in the middle of silent prayers, smiled to her. This was Dina's first time seeing her best friend since the wedding. She looked amazing in her wig and she was glowing, as though she was the happiest person in the world. Dina was extremely happy for her, but she'd be lying if she said she wasn't jealous as well. Perry met her soulmate. She was happy. The hardest part was over. Now she could live happily ever after.

Her mother was right—praying *did* make Dina feel better. It was comforting to know there's Someone watching over you, no matter what. Even if you make a mistake, He forgives you. Dina couldn't say the same for people.

When prayers were over, the guests made their way downstairs, to where the meal had been set up. Perry caught up to Dina and hugged her. "I've missed you so much. How are you?" She peered closely into her face. "What's wrong?"

"Who said anything is wrong?"

She squinted at her. "I know you better than you think."

She shrugged. "It's nothing."

"Dina—"

"You're a married woman now. You have more important things to worry about than my silly problems."

She took Dina's hands and looked into her eyes. "Your problems are not silly. I will always be there for you. Always. I might live twenty minutes away, but I'm only a phone call away. Call me anytime you need, okay?"

Dina hugged her. "Thanks."

When they pulled apart, Dina heard Mrs. Weiss say, "What do you mean he's not coming?"

She was in the middle of talking to Dovid. Mother and son stood off to the side and were speaking in hushed voices, but Mrs. Weiss had never been good at keeping her voice down.

Dovid shrugged. "He stopped by for a second, like an hour ago. He told me to tell you he wasn't coming to the *sheva brachos*."

A look of hurt, anger, and betrayal passed over the older woman's face. "How can he do this to us?"

Something caught in Dina's chest. *It's because of me. I know it is.* Of course the world didn't revolve around her, but in this case it did.

She didn't know he hated her so much that he'd let his own family down.

Mrs. Weiss squared her shoulders. "We'll just have to have a good time without him." She headed to where the guests were gathered near the entrance to the room that was set up. "Please, can everyone come in so we can start?"

A large part of Dina hoped she and Sam would somehow find a way to get past this. That their feelings for each other were so strong that they would find a way to make their relationship work. But she was finally starting to realize she could flush those thoughts down the toilet.

She was numb as she washed on the *challah* and sat down near her mother. She didn't taste the first course. She didn't even know what it was. While absentmindedly eating her soup, she told her mother, "I want to go back to Miami."

Mrs. Aaron, who was in the middle of talking to the woman seated near her, turned to her daughter. "You said something, Dina'la?"

Dina's gaze was locked on her half-eaten slice of *challah*. "I want go to back to Miami."

"What? Where's this coming from?"

Her mother's new friend watched them curiously.

"We'll talk about it at home," Mrs. Aaron promised her.

Throughout the rest of the meal, Dina's mother was very quiet, hardly saying a word to her or her new friend. Dina knew she was worried and hurt about the news she just shared. The truth was, she wasn't even sure how she felt about it, either. Actually, Dina didn't feel anything at all. It was as though she turned into a zombie. But she knew one thing: *I can't stay here anymore.*

***

"I don't understand," Mom said as she watched her daughter add some shirts to her suitcase. As soon as Shabbos was over, Dina had called her father and asked if she could visit. He was so happy he bought her a ticket right away. Her flight was scheduled for early tomorrow morning.

"I just need to get away for a bit," she told her mom.

A disappointed look conquered her face. "Are you not happy here?"

"No, I am," Dina quickly assured her. "You're a great mom and make me feel very at home here. But there are some things I need to sort through."

"What kind of things?"

She shook her head.

"Please be open with me, Dina. I don't like you having so many secrets from me."

Again, she shook her head. "They're not secrets. Just feelings. About Dovid and everything," she lied. "I just need to get away and clear my head."

Mrs. Aaron frowned. "But I thought you said things ended

amicably with Dovid."

Dina folded a skirt and added it to the suitcase. "They did. But that doesn't mean I'm not messed up inside. I just need to assess my emotions."

"You can't assess them here?"

The young woman shut her eyes for a second. "Please accept my decision, Mom. I'll return. I promise."

Tears filled her mother's eyes. "I hope so. Because I really love having you here."

That caused tears to enter the daughter's eyes as well. She walked over to hug her mother. "Thanks, Mom. I love living here, too."

She wiped her eyes. "Let me help you pack."

Dina didn't pack much, just enough clothes for two weeks. She wasn't planning on staying long, but just in case. She left a message on her boss's phone, letting him know she was taking a personal leave. She couldn't care less if she lost her job because of this. She just needed to get away, and she'd deal with the consequences later.

Mother and daughter spent an hour watching a romance movie on TV. They didn't talk much, just munched on popcorn and enjoyed each other's company. Then Dina took a shower and went to bed. She'd have to wake up at four in the morning.

She didn't know why she thought she'd actually get some sleep. She managed to sleep for maybe twenty minutes. Her mother woke up early with her and called a cab to take her daughter to the airport. It was so dark outside.

Mrs. Arron hugged Dina. "Call me as often as you need. Or maybe as often as I need."

Dina smiled. "I will. Don't have any fun without me."

She grinned. "Never." She hugged her daughter again and kissed her.

They bid each other goodbye one last time before Dina got into the cab. She gazed out the window, watching her neighborhood vanish before her eyes. Hopefully, she'd be a different person when she returned. One who was more confident, knew what she wanted, and able to have a deep connection with another person. One who no longer was hung up on a man she could never have.

Chapter Twenty

"Dina! Over here, Dina!"

The young woman clutching the handle of a black suitcase scanned the throngs of people bustling around the airport. She spotted a man waving his arms around and smiled. "Dad."

He wasn't alone. Rachel and the whole crew were with him, too. Dina hurried over and allowed her father to gather her in his arms.

"Hi, Dina. Welcome back to Miami." Rachel hugged her tightly.

The kids jumped in their spots, each waiting for a hug.

"I'll take your bag," Dad offered.

"Thanks." She passed him the handle.

The two girls grabbed hold of each of her hands and pulled her toward the parking lot. Rachel strapped the younger kids in

Dina's Choice

the back seats of the minivan while Dad placed her suitcase in the trunk. Then they were on their way to the house.

"You have to tell us all about New York," Rachel said.

Dina shrugged. "It hasn't changed much since nine years ago."

"Did you bring us any presents?" the younger boy, Yisrael, asked.

Shoot. Dina was in such a hurry that she didn't even think about presents. She could have found some kosher candy at the airport.

"Yisrael, you can't ask that," Dad scolded.

"Why not? That's how it is. When a grownup visits, they always bring the kids presents. It's the law."

Mr. Aaron and Rachel laughed.

Dina felt terrible.

"So did you?" he asked.

"Sorry. I was in such a rush that I didn't have time. But I'll buy you whatever you want when I go to the grocery store."

"Mommy, does that mean Dina doesn't get her present because she didn't get one for us?" the older daughter, Shaina, wanted to know.

"Shaina," Rachel said.

ortrt

"What? Oops. It was supposed to be a surprise."

"You didn't have to, Dad and Rachel…"

Rachel waved her hand. "Don't worry about it. It's not a big deal."

"Then why did you rush to the store after Shabbos to get it when you found out Dina was coming?" Rina asked.

"Kids, enough about the present. Let's hear what life is like in New York."

Dina spent the rest of the ride comparing and contrasting life in New York versus life in Miami. The kids asked a million questions, of course, and before she knew it, they were parked in the Aaron's driveway.

Getting out of the car, Dina stared at the house. It had only been two and a half months since she was there, but it felt much longer. Like she had been gone for ten years.

Chananya grabbed his older sister's hand and pulled her up the stairs. As soon as Rachel opened the door, he tugged her inside. The house appeared exactly the same. It kind of felt as though Dina were coming home, because she lived here for nine years, spent most of her awkward years here, but it also felt like she stood in a strange home.

"Open your present!" Yisrael jumped onto the couch and

pointed to a wrapped box sitting on the coffee table.

"Yisrael, don't bother your sister," Rachel said. "Dina, would you like something to eat or drink? I baked cookies for Shabbos."

"They are so yummy," Rina informed her. "You *have* to eat one."

"Okay, thanks," Dina told Rachel.

They gathered in the living room, with Dina on the couch and Yisrael and Rina next to her. Rachel carried in a tray filled with cookies and soda. She instructed the kids to wait until Dina took first before they could take. It was as though they waited on pins and needles until Dina reached for a cookie. Then they jumped on the cookies and gobbled them down.

Rachel laughed, embarrassed. "Kids, you act as though we don't feed you."

"Oh, we feed them all right," her husband muttered. "You should see our grocery bill."

"Don't you wanna open your present?" Yisrael asked with a full mouth.

The curiosity was bursting out of Dina. But at the same time, she couldn't accept the gift. She didn't know why. Maybe because they were trying so hard to make her feel welcome. It caused her to feel guilty for leaving them in the first place.

"Let your sister enjoy her cookie, Yisrael," Rachel said. "Honestly, maybe we should have gotten the present for you instead."

His face lit up. "Can I have it?"

"No," both his parents stressed. He sulked.

Dina wiped her face with a napkin. "These cookies are amazing, Rachel."

"Thanks."

"I'll make you happy, Yisrael, and open the present."

He was about to reach for it, when his father reprimanded him not to touch it. He pouted.

"You can help me open it," Dina told him.

The other kids complained that they wanted to open it, too. Dina passed it around. It seemed heavy and was a rectangular shape. At first, Dina thought it might be clothes, but they wouldn't have weighed that much. Finally, the last of the wrapping was ripped off and the young woman was left with a box. She put it on her knees and opened it. A laptop sat before her.

With her mouth wide, she gaped at her father and stepmother. "You bought me a laptop?"

Dina's Choice

Mr. Aaron nodded with a smile. "Your mother mentioned that the one you're currently using is old and slow."

"You didn't have to. I don't need a new laptop."

"Every young adult your age needs a laptop," Rachel pointed out.

"Thanks, this is really nice of you."

"Can I play with it?" Yisrael asked. "The box says it comes with a trial of a game all my friends play."

"Yisrael," Dad warned.

"What? You said I won't get my own laptop until I'm *bar mitzvah*. That's in like four years."

"We want to play, too!" Chananya and the girls chimed in.

"Sure you can play on it," Dina promised them.

They cheered.

The kids got ready for school while Dina unpacked in her old room. Like the house, it felt comforting to be back in her room but a little strange, too.

While she unpacked, the kids stopped by to wish her a good day before their school buses picked them up. Dad walked in a little while later to wish her the same. When she finished unpacking and went downstairs, she realized how quiet the house was. Too quiet.

Sounds came from the kitchen. When Dina entered, she found Rachel standing at the counter with a mixer. She looked up. "Hi. I'm making a cake."

"Looks delicious."

Awkward silence. Why was there always an awkward silence?

"Any plans?" Rachel asked as she poured sugar into the bowl.

"Not really. I'll probably get together with my friend soon."

Her stepmother nodded. "That'd be nice."

More awkward silence.

"I think I'm going to go for a walk. See the neighborhood."

"Okay. Have fun."

The place hadn't changed, not that Dina expected it to. Walking around, seeing the familiar places, it was as though she went back in time. She didn't feel like the same person she was three months ago.

Dina passed the park she used to play at all the time when she and her father had first moved there. There were some kids and their parents inside, but it was mostly empty because everyone was at school. Dina sat down on one of the swings and swung, staring into space and thinking. About nothing.

About everything. Sam. The hurt and betrayal on his face. The horrible words she had said to him. The ache in her chest. The ache in his chest.

Needing to chase away the thoughts and images, she called one of her closest friends, Miri. She might be at work, but Dina needed to distract herself.

"Dina?" Miri asked when she picked up.

"Where are you?" Dina wanted to know.

"Um, at home. Why?"

"You're not at work?"

Her friend was quiet for a bit. "Uh, no. Not today."

Dina told her to come to the park. Miri was confused and asked why, but Dina reassured her to trust her. Miri sounded overly suspicious, but she agreed. Dina pumped harder on the swing, enjoying the feeling of the wind blowing against her cheeks. For the first time since that night with Sam, she felt a sense of peace come over her. Only a small one, though.

About ten minutes later, a young woman walked down the block. By her gait, Dina recognized her as Miri. Miri stepped into the park and glanced around, puzzled. Then she caught sight of the young woman on the swing. A look of surprise passed over her face, followed by excitement. Waving both hands, she rushed toward the swings.

Dina hopped off and ran to her friend, wrapping her arms around her.

"Oh my gosh! What are you doing here?"

Dina squeezed her tighter. "Surprise. I missed you."

They pulled apart and Miri smiled. "I don't think you came all the way down here just because you missed me."

Dina sat back on her swing and motioned for Miri to take the one near her. "I wanted to visit my dad and his family."

She looked Dina up and down. "You look so good."

"Thanks. You, too. You have a day off or something?"

Darkness passed over Miri's face. "Oh. Um…yeah."

Miri had always been honest and open with Dina. She wasn't really the kind of girl who got insecure. Dina suspected she was lying, but decided to drop the subject.

Dina kicked off the floor. "Do you remember how we used to beg your mom to take us to this park?"

"I know! Even when we were too old. The little kids would get so mad at us."

"Yep. We are horrible people."

And one of us is still a very horrible person. Without meaning to, Dina sighed heavily.

Dina's Choice

Miri looked at her. "You okay?"

Her friend forced a smile. "Sure."

She forced a smile, too.

Silence. Ugh, again.

"So...how's New York?" Miri asked.

"Fine."

Miri pressed the tip of her shoes into the soft ground beneath the swings. "I've really missed you, Dina. Things aren't the same without you. Do you plan to stay in New York for good?"

That was a good question, one Dina had been wondering about since she got on the plane. She couldn't imagine going back to New York and facing everything...facing him. It was a good thing he didn't live next door, but he was over there pretty often. Dina wouldn't be able to bear it. But how could she just leave her mother like that? Her dad was happy here with Rachel and her stepsiblings. Mom had no one. And the truth was, Dina liked living with her. She'd miss her terribly.

"I don't know," Dina told Miri. "I just needed to get away."

She looked into her friend's eyes. "You're running from something?"

Dina shook her head.

"Someone?"

She nodded.

Dina wasn't sure why she was being open with her. Maybe because she missed her so much, or maybe because she needed to talk to someone about her feelings. Miri was the best candidate because she didn't know Sam.

"From who?" Miri asked.

"A guy, who else?"

She nodded. "Who else indeed. Believe me, I can relate."

Now Dina dug her shoes into the ground. "Why do they do this to us? Our whole life we didn't care about boys. We played with them when were we kids, got as far away from them as possible when we were teens, and now we actually have to *deal* with them. With our *feelings.*" She tightened her hands on the chains of the swings. "It's not fair. My life was much less complicated when I didn't date. Why do I have to date? Why do I have to get married?"

Miri kicked a bit off the ground, causing her swing to lift slightly. "That's a good question." She looked at Dina. "What happened with that guy?"

A part of Dina begged her not to tell. To keep it inside so it wouldn't exist in the real world. But it *did* exist in the real world—inside her. If Dina kept it all inside, she'd never make sense of her feelings. She wouldn't be able to move on. If she even could move on.

"I knew a guy when I was younger," Dina told her. "I used to play with him, his twin brother, and his sister all the time. They were my neighbors."

Miri nodded for her to continue.

"Anyway, I liked him. A lot."

She nodded again. That was why Dina loved Miri. She never judged her. Someone else might think low of Dina for liking a boy when she wasn't allowed to, but not Miri. Maybe Dina needed to take a page out of her book.

"We lost touch when I moved. I found out a few years later that he went off the *derech*. I met him in New York. Actually, we bumped into each other many times. Sometimes it felt like he was doing it on purpose. To make a long story short, we basically told each other that we liked each other. But I couldn't be with him when he's off the *derech*."

"Right," Miri agreed.

"Now this is where I ruined everything. I convinced him to tell me why he went off. He finally opened his heart to me, and you know what I did? I threw it back in his face."

"Dina, I'm sorry."

"And now he won't talk to me." Dina lowered her head. "I don't know why it matters. He has no intention of coming back. Why am I agonizing over a guy who left our faith? I deserve to be with someone better than that."

Miri took her hand. "I'm sorry you're going through this."

"Thanks."

"I got fired from my job."

Dina looked at her. "I'm sorry."

"I'm not. The guy was a jerk. I'm just upset because he refuses to give me a recommendation letter. I've been trying to find a job for weeks."

Squeezing her hand, Dina said, "I'm sure you'll find something soon. Just have faith."

She nodded. "Thanks. And have faith that everything will work out with your situation."

"Thanks, but I doubt it. I bet I'll be single for the rest of my life."

Miri dragged her swing closer, resting her head on Dina's. "You won't be. I'm glad you're back. It's nice talking to you again."

"Same with you."

Dina's Choice

***

Miri and Dina spent the day shopping, talking about old memories, and eating at Dina's favorite pizza shop. It was nice to take a break from life and just live in the moment. They steered clear of any topics that would remind them of work or guys. When Dina arrived at her dad's house, the kids were not yet home from school and Rachel was working on dinner.

"How was your day?" she asked the younger woman.

"Good. I met up with my friend."

After telling her in more detail about her day, Dina excused herself to her room and checked out her new laptop. It was an advanced one, with a great processor and graphics card. Perfect for practicing her designs. She browsed the internet for a few minutes, and before she realized what she was doing, she searched Samuel Weiss on Google.

She found a flyer for his band. They were performing at a club. She found another site that rated undiscovered musicians and bands. The person gave Sam's band a ten out of ten.

Dina shut the laptop. She didn't want to think about him. She couldn't. The whole reason for coming to Miami in the first place was to forget about all of this. To give her heart a break.

Making her way downstairs, she found a book in the bookshelf and settled down on the couch, near the window. But she managed to only read half a page before thoughts of Sam conquered her mind. *Get out. Get out, get out, get out.*

"Dina, I didn't know you were here," Rachel said, sitting down near her.

"Oh, sorry."

She looked into Dina's face. "Are you okay?"

Dina nodded.

"Would you like a slice of cake?"

"No, thanks."

Rachel nodded.

Quiet.

Dina glanced down at her book.

"Are you sure you're okay?"

"I am," Dina replied, a little too forcefully. Her stepmother's face fell. "Sorry."

"That's okay. I'll leave you to your book."

Dina felt terrible. Rachel was just trying to make conversation, maybe even trying to get to know her better. And she pushed her away. That was what she did to everyone—she pushed them away. She hurt them. She didn't deserve to have any form of relationship.

Perhaps she was blowing things way out of proportion. But this thing with Sam was driving her insane. Would she ever get over it and be normal again?

Luckily, the kids came home from school and Dina's evening was jammed. She played various games with the kids, including watching over Yisrael as he played his game on her laptop. He was a good kid, but he tended to break whatever he touched. Dina also helped the kids with their homework, got them ready for bed, and read them a bedtime story. It was the same sort of things she used to do when she had lived here, but she didn't feel as annoyed now. Had she changed that much in New York?

Chapter Twenty-One

Dina had been in Miami for a week. Her days consisted of hanging out with Miri, running errands for Rachel, playing with the kids and helping them with school. She'd grown so accustomed to her schedule that she almost forgot how things had been in New York. There was one thing she didn't forget, though. Sam.

She tossed and turned in bed, thoughts of the events of that night clouding her brain. She tried different methods to help her fall asleep, counting sheep, reading a boring book, trying to solve difficult math equations in her head to overwork her brain. But nothing worked.

Sam's face didn't leave her head. Dina wished there was a way to suck him out like a vacuum.

Eventually, she did fall asleep.

Dina's Choice

"Dina," a voice said. "Dina…"

She opened her eyes. Someone was in her room. She quickly sat up and found Sam standing in front of her.

She clutched the blanket closer to my body. "What are you doing here?"

"I had to see you."

"You came all the way to Florida?" Dina looked around. "How did you get in here?"

He sat near her on the bed. "Marry me, Dina."

Her eyes nearly popped out of their sockets. "What?"

"Marry me. I love you."

"I can't. You're off the *derech*."

"I don't care. You're the girl for me. There's no one else. And I know I'm the only guy for you."

"It's impossible. You're off."

"I want to be back *frum*, though. I've just been through a hard time."

Dina scoffed. "Hard time? You call what you've been through a hard time? My parents got divorced when I was a kid. It killed me. I cried myself to sleep every night. I even blamed myself. Somedays, I didn't even want to live. Did I go off the *derech*? No. You know what you are, Sam? You're a

315

coward."

A pained look passed over his face. "What…what did you just say to me?"

Standing up, she looked down at him. "You heard me. You're weak. You're pathetic. People go through worse things every day. People get hurt, they see their loved ones get hurt before their eyes. But you? Your little ego got hurt."

"Dina…how can you say this to me?"

"You're weak," she said. "Weak. I can never love someone like you."

"Dina…"

His voice faded away.

Dina's body sprang up in bed. She blinked a few times. The room was pitch black. She sighed in relief. It was just a dream.

A few tears slipped down her cheeks. It might have only been a dream, but the way she hurt Sam wasn't. She hated herself for doing that to him. All she yearned was for him to forgive her, but she didn't forgive herself. She didn't know if she ever would.

Getting out of bed, Dina made her way downstairs and poured herself a glass of water. She headed to the living room and sat down on the windowsill, staring out at the dark night.

Dina's Choice

The image of Sam's hurt face the night he opened his heart to her refused to leave her head. She tried to replace it with something, anything, but the image was just too strong.

"Dina?"

She spun around and found her father standing in the entrance. "Hi, Dad."

"What are you doing up?" He walked inside, he too with a glass of water, and lowered himself on the couch. "Trouble sleeping?"

Dina nodded.

"Me, too."

"Are you stressed about something?" she asked.

He waved his hand. "Just the usual things. Job stress, family stress. It happens to a man every now and then."

"Oh. Sorry about that."

He waved his hand again. "That's just life. What about you? You're stressed about something?"

She shrugged. "Just the everyday stresses of a twenty-one year old."

He nodded, taking a sip of his drink.

Dina should have been used to the awkward silences by now, but she wasn't.

Her dad moved closer to her. "Dina, Rachel and I couldn't help but notice that you seem…sad."

She didn't look at him.

"Is everything okay, honey?"

She nodded.

"From the way you've been behaving, I find it hard to believe."

Dina still didn't look at him. "It's just some stuff I'm dealing with."

"Guy stuff?"

Her gaze flicked to his. "Is it that obvious?"

He laughed lightly. "Not to me. I'm a man, what do I know? But Rachel suspected it."

Dina closed her eyes for a second. She didn't like the fact that they'd been talking about her behind her back.

He moved even closer and reached to stroke her arm. "Are you sure you don't want to talk about it? I'm your father. You know how much I care about you."

"I know, and that means a lot to me. But this thing with the guy…" She sighed. "It doesn't matter. I messed it up and there's no way I can fix it. I need to just forget about him."

"I believe everything can be fixed, if a person wants it badly enough. What went wrong with this boy?"

"He told me something very personal, something that happened to him when he was younger. Instead of trying to be understanding and supportive, I was judgmental. I was so horrible to him, Dad. I'm a horrible person."

"No, you're not, Dina. You are far from a horrible person."

Teared filled her eyes. "But I made him feel so badly. I hate myself."

"Please don't hate yourself. It's hard to put yourself in someone else's shoes and try to see things from their point of view. Sometimes, the only thing you can do is just accept things the way they are, no questions asked, no opinions shared. If the boy told you he went through a terrible time, you should have taken it at face value. He trusted you enough to share his personal story with you. That means something, Dina."

Dina covered her face. "I told you I'm a terrible person."

"You're not, honey. Please stop saying that you are."

She lowered her hands from her face. "It doesn't matter. It's over."

"It's never over. Not if you want to make it work. Don't give up on him. Don't give up on yourself."

She shook her head. "He'll never forgive me."

He stood to press a kiss on the top of his daughter's head. "Things have their way of working themselves out. Whatever happens, it's for the best. I really believe that, honey."

Dina gave him a thankful smile. "Thanks for the talk. It feels nice talking about it."

He returned the smile. "No problem. I'm here whenever you need me." He turned to go.

"Dad?"

He turned back around. "Yeah?"

"I'm sorry."

His eyebrows came together. "For what?"

"I couldn't stand being here three months ago. I just had to leave. But I don't know why I felt that way. I know I was a jerk to you and Rachel, and to the kids. I realize now that I love being here. I'm sorry for the way I treated all of you. Rachel is so sweet and nice, and the kids are adorable and lots of fun. And you are an amazing father. You've always been. I was just so blind."

He sat back down and took her hand. "You don't need to apologize for anything. You're a young woman now. This is the time for you to get out there and figure things out. Learn things about yourself and the world around you." He smiled wryly.

Dina's Choice

"It's hard to do that with a house full of annoying kids."

She laughed. "Your kids are annoying, but we love them anyway."

"We sure do."

Dina stood to hug him. "Thanks for everything, Dad. And please thank Rachel, too"

He wrapped his arms around her. "Thank you for everything, Dina."

***

"I can't believe you beat my score!" Yisrael complained.

Dina grinned. "That's because I rule."

He and the other kids were crowded around the TV in the living room, where Dina had hooked it up to her laptop, enabling them all to watch the game.

"My turn, my turn!" Rina jumped up and down.

"No, I come first," Chananya argued.

Rachel walked into the room. "It's time for bed."

"Aww, Mommy!"

"Ten more minutes!"

"But we have to see if Dina will pass the next level!"

Rachel clapped her hands. "No more questions. You can continue playing the game tomorrow."

They grumbled some more, but Rachel stood her ground. One by one, with backward glances at the TV screen, they filed out of the room.

"I'll go up to read their bedtime story." Dina was about to get up when Rachel held up her hand.

"One second. Something came for you in the mail."

"What? For me?"

She handed the younger woman an envelope. The handwriting seemed very familiar, but Dina couldn't place it. When she scanned for the return address, the letter slipped out of her hand. It was from Sam.

"Dina?" Rachel asked. "Is everything okay?"

Dina clutched the envelope to her chest. "I'm going to read this upstairs. Can you tell the kids I'll continue the story tomorrow?"

"That's okay. I'll read for them tonight."

"Thanks."

She raced to her room, nearly running over one of the kids who was on his way to the bathroom. She closed the door of her room before leaping onto her bed and staring at the letter. Why had he written to her?

The way he wrote her name on the envelope...perhaps

Dina's Choice

Dina was being overly sentimental, but it appeared as though every letter he had printed onto the envelope held a world of meaning. Loss, betrayal, hope, love.

Carefully, Dina opened the envelope, stuck her fingers inside, and pulled out the letter. After taking a few deep breaths and regulating her breathing, she unfolded it.

Dear Dina,

Hi, how are you? This letter is from Sam Weiss. I heard you were back in Miami…I hope you're not planning on staying there for good. I've been contemplating contacting you for a while now, debating whether I should wait until you got back to New York. But I decided to write you a letter…for old time's sake.

First of all, I want to start this by offering you my sincere apologies. I shouldn't have treated you the way I did. I was upset and hurt…but that's no excuse. I've been grilling my brain for days now, trying to figure things out, figure me out. The only explanation I can come up with is that I love you. I love you so much, Dina. I think I love you more than a man has ever loved a woman before. When someone you love hurts you, it's one of the most painful things you'll ever experience in your life. It's like someone taking a knife to your chest, stabbing and stabbing until every last breath is knocked out of you.

Chaya T. Hirsch

I know I said it already, but I'll say it again. I'm sorry, Dina. So very sorry. You tried to apologize, but I shut you out. I hope you can find it in your heart to forgive me. I hope you'll return to New York. I'm not that so self-centered to think that I'm the reason you left, but because of the timing, it's a good bet.

I want to explain more of the experience I had in seventh grade. I know you were expecting something much more extreme, but sometimes it's the little things that can change a person's life forever.

I don't know why this teacher was out to get me, but he was. He did everything possible to make my life a living nightmare. He would purposely ask me to answer the difficult questions, knowing I didn't know them. He would mark my answers wrong when I clearly got them right. When I complained to my parents, he would give an excuse that the points were taken off for my bad behavior in class. But I didn't cause any trouble. Just the opposite, I made sure to behave so that he wouldn't dock my points. No matter what I did, he found ways to make things hard for me. He even turned my parents against me. You know very well how much trouble I caused as a kid. My parents assumed I was acting out again. They didn't believe me, and that hurt. A lot. The teacher caused my friends to stray from me, telling them I was a bad influence and would end up in prison one day. I used to cry to God all the time, beg Him to make that teacher leave me alone. I tried so hard to be a good kid, helping my parents when they didn't ask, behaving in class even when the teacher didn't deserve it. I even made him look good in front of the principal one time. It didn't matter.

One of the worst things I had to deal with was getting accepted into high school. I don't know what he said to the principals of the schools, but no one wanted to accept me. I tried to explain to my parents that it wasn't my fault, that the teacher was giving me a bad name. They believed me at first, but the teacher twisted everything around to make me look like the bad guy. I have no idea how he did it, but it's a talent. My dad had to beg one of the schools to accept me. I think he knew the assistant principal. All this was even affecting Dovid. One of the top schools he got accepted to called out of the blue and revoked his acceptance. Dovid had no idea what was going on—he just assumed I was causing trouble again. I didn't want to tell him about it. I guess I didn't want to involve him and let that teacher ruin his life, too. I had to deal with this for another two years, since the teacher decided to take a job at my high school.

At the end of ninth grade, I met a group of kids who lived outside our neighborhood. They were kids like me, who were having problems. I hung out with them only a few times at first, nervous to be around them. But the more time I spent with them, the better I felt. I actually started having fun. I started feeling good about myself again. When I was with them, I didn't feel like the loser no one wanted to be around. I felt like people liked me, that I mattered. I didn't realize it at first, but I started to change. I stopped wearing my white shirts and black hat. I let my hair grow a few inches too long. I started using language I wasn't allowed to use. I went to places I wasn't supposed to go to. Soon I no longer wore my kippa *or my* tzitzis. *I was no longer praying. I didn't give any thought to God anymore. The truth is, I didn't care much about anything anymore. There were a few things I did care about, though. Music for one. My family for another. And you. Throughout all this, I never forgot about you. I'd be unable to sleep because of everything that was going on, and I'd think about you. I wondered what you looked like. I wondered if you were happy. I wondered if I would ever see you again. And then I did. I understand that you were hurt when you saw what happened to me. The last you remember was me being a* frum *kid who knew what was important in life. But I'm sorry to say that kid doesn't exist anymore. He died the day that teacher walked into the classroom.*

Dina, I hope you now have a better understanding of what I went through in my early teen years. I'm sorry I didn't tell you sooner or tell you in a way where you'd understand. I've kept this bottled inside me for so long, I didn't even know how to talk about it. But I'm glad to be sharing this with you. I wish I could share even more with you. I wish you could share what's in your heart. I know all you want is for me to return, but I don't know if I can.

Dina's Choice

If I'm the reason you are now in Miami, please come back. Not for me. Come back because this is where you want to be, with your mom. You don't have to respond to this letter. You don't even have to look at me. I just wanted to apologize for my behavior and explain what I've been through. I sincerely wish you only the best. I will love you for the rest of my life and I doubt I'll love anyone as much as I love you. That doesn't mean I expect you to return the feelings. I just want you to be happy.

All the best,

Sam Weiss

A few drops of tears splattered onto the letter. Dina read it over another three times, adding more tears. To go through what he went through…it must have been terrible. Dina should have been more understanding and accepting. *My poor Sam.* She wished she could go back in time and save him. To stop that teacher from ruining the life of an innocent sweet boy. Wherever he was, Dina hoped he'd suffer for what he did to Sam. She didn't care if that made her a bad person. He deserved it.

Someone knocked on her door. She wiped her eyes just as her dad walked in. "Hi. I just wanted to make sure everything is okay."

Dina hugged the letter to her chest. "I need to go back to New York."

"Is everything okay?"

She gave him a small smile. "Hopefully they will be."

His eyes moved from her face, to the letter, then back to her face. He smiled softly. "I told you things have their own way of working out." He bent to kiss the top of her head. "Go get him, Dina."

Chapter Twenty-Two

Mrs. Aaron waved the second Dina stepped out of the airport. A large smile took over Dina's face. "Mom!" She ran into her arms.

"I missed you so much!"

Dina's mother led her to where the taxi was waiting for them. They climbed in and Mrs. Aaron told the driver to take them back home. Her mom hugged her again. "Look at you, you're all tanned. Did you have a good time?"

"I think so." It had definitely been enlightening. "Mom?"

"Yeah?"

"I think I want to visit my father more often."

She smiled. "I'm glad to hear that."

Mother and daughter chatted about various things, until the older woman's eyes widened. "I forgot to tell you the good news."

"What good news?"

"The Weiss's get a *mazel tov*. Dovid is engaged."

Dina gaped at her. "What? Already? He and I…"

She nodded. "I guess when it's the right one, it's the right one. The engagement party is tonight."

Wow, this certainly was shocking news. But good news. Dina was genuinely happy for Dovid. She wanted him to have his happily ever after.

Every part of her filled with nerves. She'd probably see Sam at the engagement party. She thought she'd have at least a day or two to get her bearings. As nervous as she was, she was excited. She wasn't sure why. Sam was still not religious. If he refused to return, there couldn't be anything between them. But at least they were no longer mad at each other.

They arrived home and Dina's mother helped her unpack. She'd only had a two hour flight, but she was exhausted. She took a nap, asking her mom to wake her up later so she could take a shower before the engagement party.

Dina lay in bed, trying to fall asleep, but her mind was too active. She thought about Dovid and how happy she was for him. She thought about Sam and what would happen when they saw each other tonight. She told herself not to hope for anything. Maybe the best she and Sam could be was friends, as painful as it was. She would never force him to return to Orthodoxy. He needed to do that on his own, if that was what he wanted. Dina needed to learn to respect his decision, as much as she didn't want to.

She slept for maybe ten minutes before her mother woke her up. After taking a quick shower, trying to block out the thoughts that refused to leave her mind, Dina dressed into one of her best outfits and went down to the kitchen. Her mother offered her something to eat, but she assured her she'd eat something at the engagement party.

Out of nowhere, her mother wrapped her arms around Dina and squeezed her so tightly she couldn't breathe. "Mom," she gasped.

"I'm sorry." She loosened her hold a bit. "I'm just so happy you're back."

"Did you think I wouldn't come back?"

"I was worried. You were so distraught when you left. But you seem better now."

"Yeah, I am. I wonder if I lost my job…"

Mrs. Aaron patted her daughter's arm. "I'm sure your boss

will understand." She peered at her watch. "Okay, let's go."

Dina's heart pounded as they made their way to the synagogue, where the engagement party was being held downstairs. Many people were already there, crowded around the bride and groom.

Mrs. Weiss was the first to see Dina and her mother. She hurried over and enveloped both the mother and daughter in a hug. "*Mazel tov*! Thank you so much for coming."

"*Mazel tov*, Bracha," Dina's mother wished. "How wonderful, two *simchos* in such a short amount of time."

"*Baruch Hashem*. And *im yirtzeh Hashem* by your beautiful Dina."

"Amen, thanks."

Mrs. Weiss hugged Dina. "So good to have you back. Did you enjoy your time in Miami? Wow, look at your tan!"

"Thanks. I had a great time," Dina told her.

Once Mrs. Weiss released the young woman, Dina found herself in Perry's arms, with her skirt being tugged by Simi. "I'm so glad you're back! I missed you."

"We texted like every day."

"It's not the same."

Dina pulled back and looked at Perry. "You look great."

Dina's Choice

"Thanks. You look great, too."

Simi tugged on Dina's skirt again. Dina smiled to the little girl. "You look beautiful. Is that a new dress?"

She nodded. "It's from my grandmother. I love how it looks when it spins. I turn into a cupcake." She demonstrated by spinning around faster and faster.

"So pretty!" Dina complimented.

She and her mother headed to Dovid and his bride to wish them *mazel tov*. Dovid appeared beyond ecstatic, and his *kallah*, Tzippy, looked radiant.

"Thanks for coming, Dina," Dovid said. "You just got back from Miami, right?"

"Yeah. I landed this afternoon."

"It means a lot to my *kallah* and me. Thank you."

"It's my pleasure. I'm very happy for you, Dovid. Really. You deserve the best."

He blushed. "Thanks. You deserve the best, too. I hope you find the right one soon."

"Thanks."

Dina and her mother browsed the table that had been laid out with a few pastries and salads. Dina didn't realize how hungry she was. Her mom updated her on the events that

3333

occurred in the community while she had been gone, and Dina couldn't stop her eyes from periodically scanning the room, hoping to find Sam. Why wasn't he there?

When her plate was clear, Dina went back to the table to grab a few more spoonfuls of salad.

"Hi, Dina."

She nearly dropped the serving spoon. Slowly, she turned around and came face to face with Sam Weiss. He wore a dark blue dress shirt and black pants, a small *kippa* on his head. For a second, Dina was hopeful, but then she remembered he was just doing it for his family, like by Perry's wedding.

"Hi," she greeted.

"I didn't know you were back."

"I just got in."

He nodded. "Thanks for coming. My family really appreciates it."

She returned the nod.

And there they were again, standing in awkward silence. One woman squeezed herself to take some salad, forcing Dina to move closer to Sam. A little too close. When she lifted her head, she found him staring down at her, an unreadable expression in his eyes.

Dina's Choice

When the woman finally left, Dina stepped back. "I got your letter."

His face lit up. "You did? When I saw that you were back already, I worried you didn't get it."

"No, I did."

"Good."

Silence.

More silence.

He shifted in his plate. "Do you want to talk outside? Oh, you're eating."

"It's fine. I ate too much anyway." She laughed lightly.

"Please, don't let me stop you from eating. I'll meet you outside in ten minutes?"

"Okay."

He nodded and walked away, then chased after Simi and swept her off the floor, producing giggles from her. Dina smiled as she watched him. He seemed to be in a better mood than he had been months ago. She didn't want to attribute it to her, especially because they would never be...anything. But it was nice to see him happier. Maybe that meant...no, she needed to stop hoping he'd return. This was the life he'd chosen for himself. Dina needed to accept it.

She had no idea what he wanted to talk about, but she had the biggest lump in her throat. She doubted she'd be able to get any food down. Why was she dreading this? Maybe because they might discuss something she didn't want to talk about. She sat back down near her mom and forced herself to finish what was on her plate.

Just as she finished eating, she caught Sam heading outside, glancing back at her. She nodded to him, letting him know she'd be out there soon.

After telling herself to relax, she stood up and left the room. Sam sat outside on one of the chairs, scrolling through his phone. He glanced up when Dina drew near and smiled, nodding to the chair next to him. She sat down, trying to regulate her breathing.

Dovid and Tzippy walked out and headed to the exit, smiling as they chatted, not paying attention to anything or anyone around them. It was as though they were in their own private world. It was very sweet to watch.

"Dovid looks so happy," Dina told Sam.

Sam kept his eyes on his brother and future sister-in-law until they were out of sight. "They do. I'm so happy for him."

"Me, too."

Dina's Choice

Silence.

"I got your letter," Dina told him, then mentally smacked herself when she realized she had already told him that.

But he was nice about it and said, "I'm glad you got it before you left."

"Well." She played with her hair. "I came back because of it."

Surprise registered on his face. "You did? Oh." He laughed to himself. "Then naturally you got it before you left."

"Thanks for writing it. I really needed to read it."

"I really needed to write it."

Dina turned to look into his face. "I'm sorry for saying those things. I—"

He held up his hand. "Dina, it's okay. You don't have to—"

"No. I need to. I just want you to know that I'm truly sorry. You're right—no one can understand what a person goes through, what kind of affect it could have on him. I shouldn't have been so judgmental."

"I understand why it was hard for you accept it. It happened gradually for me, but it was bam, in your face. It must have been shocking."

"And hurtful. Very hurtful."

He looked away. "I'm sorry."

She shook her head and looked at her lap. "Don't be. It's your life. Only you can decide how to live it. I need to accept that."

"But you don't want to."

"It's not about what I want."

"Isn't it?"

She slowly lifted her eyes to his. "I can't help but feel that deep down you want to be *frum*."

He tore his gaze from hers.

Dina was about to reach for his hand, but dropped hers to her side. "Don't tell me it's all in my head. You only eat kosher. You wear *tefillin* every day. You probably do a lot more that I don't know about. Be honest with yourself, Sam. You don't have to be scared anymore."

"I'm not—"

"I'm here. Your family is here. You don't have to go through anything alone. Not anymore."

He refused to meet her eyes. Dina suspected it was because he was battling tears.

Finally, but still not looking her way, he said, "I can't make you any promises. I'm messed up. I won't be good for you. You deserve to have someone who will give you the life you want."

"Why can't it be you?"

He slowly turned to her and she noticed he was indeed crying. She wanted to take his hand, to comfort him, but she couldn't. "Dina…"

"Don't do it for me, Sam. Do it for yourself. Because you want to be a better person. A better son. A better brother."

"I…" He swallowed hard. "I can't…it's too much…"

"You don't have to jump into anything. Take as much time as you need. I'm not going anywhere."

He shook his head. "I'm not going to ask you to wait for me. I can't promise I'll be back *frum*."

"That's not up to you. That's my decision."

"Dina—"

"Just promise me you'll think about it. That's all I want."

He was quiet for a moment, his eyes searching hers. Dina saw so much inside his, all the pain he'd endured the past few years, the betrayal, the loss of hope. And then a sliver of hope. Of the possibility of a good life. Of a life filled with happiness and love.

He nodded.

"Thanks."

They sat in silence again, but Dina didn't mind it. It was enough just to sit with him, it was enough that there was hope that he would change his life around.

"Can I ask you something?" he said after a few minutes.

"Yeah."

"Can you come hear me play tomorrow night?"

"At a, um, club?"

"It's not a bad one. I promise. I just…want you to hear me play."

Dina thought about it for a few seconds, noting the hope in his eyes. "Okay, if you're sure it'll be okay."

"I promise. I'll never let anything happen to you, Dina. Ever."

"Thanks. I'm looking forward to hearing you play."

Chapter Twenty-Three

Sam picked Dina up at seven o'clock and they drove to the club he was singing at. Dina was nervous and excited to hear him play. Nervous because she'd never been to a club and excited because she loved hearing him sing. Sam appeared nervous, too. He kept tapping his fingers on the steering wheel.

Once they arrived, he parked nearby and led her inside. She'd been expecting loud music and many people, but there was a woman singing a light song and the place wasn't crowded.

"Can I introduce you to some people?" Sam asked.

"Okay."

He brought her to where three men were in the middle of talking. "Hey, Sam," they greeted.

He introduced two of the men as his bandmates and the

third one as the band's manager. They were all very nice to Dina, and one of them made a comment about her being the girl behind the inspiration. Dina wasn't sure what he meant by that. She knew the song she had listened to was about her—did that mean all of Sam's songs were based on her?

Dina sat down at the table with a glass of water while Sam and the guys went backstage. She glanced around at the place and at the people. It was not a bad place—Dina didn't know why she had always thought clubs were a place for people to get drunk and make trouble.

About twenty minutes later, the female singer finished, producing claps from the audience, including Dina. One of Sam's bandmates went on the stage and introduced them. Then they started to play.

Immediately, Dina was swept away by the song. It was beautiful, magical, out of this world. And it was about her. Sam sang about a wonderful girl he had in his life, a girl who was beautiful inside and out, a pure soul, a heart made out of gold. He sang about how he fell for her, how she made him feel whenever she was nearby. But he was too afraid to tell her how he felt. Then he talked about how he lost her, how he was scared he'd never see her again. The song ended with him tracking her down and opening his heart to her. They lived happily ever after.

It was a very heartfelt song, and very romantic. His eyes had been locked on Dina throughout the entire song. The audience went wild, begging for an encore. Dina stood and clapped as well, beyond proud of him.

When they were done, they thanked the audience and got off stage. Sam sat down near Dina. "What did you think?"

"It was amazing. I loved it. You have such an amazing voice and your band is great."

"Thanks. It was about you."

"I know."

"Music is such a big part of my life. I can't imagine giving it up."

"Why would you have to?"

His eyes met hers. "If I were to come back *frum*, I wouldn't be able to sing."

"What do you mean? With your voice, you'd be amazing."

"I'm not talking about singing at weddings and selling some CDs. I mean singing these songs. About love. I can't do that if I was *frum*."

He was right about that—singing about love is a big no no

in the community. Those things are kept between a husband and wife in the privacy of their home.

"You can sing them in private," she told him. "You can sing them to me."

His eyebrows shot up. "To you?"

"I mean, your wife. You can sing them to your wife."

He smiled. "That means you want to be my wife."

Dina moved a little closer to him, gazing into his eyes. "If you were *frum*, we would have been married by now."

He looked away. "I know." He sighed. "You're right about what you said. I *am* afraid to come back. I'm worried I'll get hurt again."

"I'll never understand what you've been through, Sam, but I would hate for you to let one person ruin your life. If you continue down the path you're on, you'll show him that he won. You're much stronger than that. I know you are. And I'm here. I mean, if you want me to be."

"I do. You know I do."

"I've looked up to you my whole childhood. I knew deep in my heart that you're the only one for me. That's why it hurts so much to see you off. I hate that that jerk of a teacher did this to you. I wish I could go back in time and stop him somehow."

Dina's Choice

He was quiet. When Dina glanced at him, she saw him battling tears. "You're so sweet, Dina. I want to spend the rest of my life with you. I need time. I don't want to make you wait."

"I told you I'll wait. However long you need. Because there's no one else I want to spend the rest of my life with. I only hope that you want to change for yourself and not for me."

"It is for myself, but it's because of you. I don't know if I could do it without you."

She gave him a warm smile. "You have no idea how glad I am to hear you say that."

He returned the smile. "Can I say I love you?"

She laughed. "Yes. And can I say I love you?"

"I can hear you say it all day."

Chapter Twenty-Four

Six months later.

"*Mazel tov!*" everyone shouted.

The veil was lifted off Dina's face. Her mother pulled her into her arms and kissed her cheek. She didn't let her go for what felt like hours. "*Mazel tov*, sweetie. I'm so proud of you. I love you."

Dina's eyes locked with Sam's, who was in the middle of being squeezed to death by his mother. Mrs. Weiss had so much energy that Sam's *kippa* nearly flew off his head.

He sent her a warm and loving smile. She returned it. *My husband.*

She couldn't believe how things turned out. Only seven months ago, she had no idea what her future would be like. She had no idea if she'd ever find happiness. And now? She was the happiest person in the world.

Her mother finally let go and Dina was able to breathe again. But only for a second—Mrs. Weiss grabbed the bride in for an even tighter hug. "I'm so happy to have you for a daughter-in-law." She kissed both Dina's cheeks. "You're my little angel."

"Thanks, Mom."

Next Dina was in Perry's arms, though she was careful not to squeeze too hard. Perry's baby was due in three months.

"We're sisters!" she squealed. "I'm so happy I can die right here."

Dina smiled as she glanced at her husband. "I can die a happy woman now, too."

Sam held out his hand. "Ready, my beautiful wife?"

She took hold of his hand. "Ready, my wonderful husband."

They embarked on their walk down the aisle as husband and wife, with all of their friends and family here to rejoice with them. Dina spotted her dad, Rachel, and the kids in the first few rows. They each sent heartfelt smiles, Yisrael trying to whistle with two fingers. Dovid waved from the men's section, his eyes sneaking to his wife in the row across, in the women's section. They'd been married for four months, but from the way they looked at each other, one could think they had just gotten married last night.

Miri, Yehudis, and some of Dina's other Miami friends sat in the back rows, each one smiling brightly as Dina and Sam passed. A few of Dina's coworkers came as well. Mr. Hershkowitz had been very understanding six months ago when Dina asked him for her job back. He'd even agreed to pay for some of her schooling if she chose to go for her Master's. It seemed every part of her life was falling into place.

Sam squeezed Dina's hand as they entered a private room, where they would be alone together for the first time. As husband and wife. They sat down at the table and Sam poured them each a glass of water.

"I can't believe my life right now," he said, sending her another loving smile. "Sometimes I want to pinch myself because there's no way this can be real."

She grinned. "Oh, it definitely is real. I wouldn't be wearing this dress if it wasn't."

He laughed softly. "And you look just as beautiful in it as the day you tried it on when you went gown shopping with

Perry for her wedding. No, you look even more beautiful."

"Thanks." She drank from her glass. "I never imagined I'd be sitting here with you eight months later."

He shook his head. "Never in my wildest dreams."

"All my dreams are coming true," Dina said. "All my prayers have been answered."

He took her hands in his and squeezed them gently. "All my prayers have been answered as well, and I am living my dream. I can't wait to start my new life with you, Dina. Mrs. Weiss. My amazing wife."

She returned the squeeze. "And I can't wait to start my new life with you, Sam Weiss. My amazing husband."

Chapter Twenty-Five

Ten Years Later

Dina Weiss entered her house, set her groceries on the kitchen table, and pulled off her long winter coat. It was mid-December and freezing outside. How pleasant was it to walk into a nice, cozy house? She knew there were many others out there with no heat and she silently thanked God for providing her with this wonderful, perfect life.

After putting away the groceries, Dina noticed the answering machine blinking, flashing the number two. She pressed the "play" button.

"Good afternoon, my lovelies," the familiar, exuberant voice of her mother-in-law permeated through the room. "The weather's a bit crazy out there, don't you think? I bet we're going to have snow this Chanukah." She chuckled. "I remember how you kids used to play in the snow all the time, and no matter how many times I or Dina's mother asked you to come in, you refused." Another laugh. "And now, Baruch Hashem, my precious little gems of granddaughters are the same. Anyway, I'd better stop before I start crying. You didn't forget the Chanukah party I'm hosting tomorrow, right? It's been months since the whole family got together. Dina, sweetie, don't worry about making anything—though I'm sure you will. You're such an angel. The party starts at eight o'clock *sharp*. I say sharp because I know no one will get here on time." A third chuckle. "Your father and I are looking forward to having everyone over, so please, please, please come. And on time. Also, Dina, make sure your mother and her new husband drop by, too. I've told her over and over again that she's family. See you all tomorrow!"

Dina laughed. Mrs. Weiss hadn't changed one bit in ten years. Always calling her an angel, always putting her family first. It was something Dina herself strove to do, to emulate her, to be the best wife and mother she could be.

The next message played, and as soon as Dina heard the voice, her stomach dropped. Not again.

"Hello, Mrs. Weiss. This is Miss Bernstein, Esty's teacher. I hate to call you again like this, but I'm afraid your daughter has once again disrupted the class. If her behavior doesn't change soon, I don't know…"

Dina shut her eyes, unable to listen further. This was not the first or second voicemail she had received from her daughter's Hebrew teacher in the last three months. She didn't understand why. Nine-year-old Esty was a good, well-behaved child. Her English teacher had no complaints, claiming it was a pleasure to have the girl in her class. What was the problem, then? She'd have to have a long talk with her daughter.

As if on cue, her watched beeped. Was it four thirty already? Donning on her coat, she zipped it up and opened the door. Her daughters' school bus should be here any minute.

The ice-cold wind bit her cheeks. Perhaps her mother-in-law was right—it *did* feel like it was going to snow any minute. The meteorologists hadn't predicted snow in the near future, but they've been known to be wrong sometimes.

In the distance, she caught sight of the familiar yellow bus heading down the block. A few seconds later, it pulled up before the house and identical girls dressed in navy winter coats hopped off. They ran toward Dina, who knelt a bit and held out her arms. Her twin girls rushed into her arms and she enclosed them tightly.

"Hi, Mommy," Chani, the older twin said, her cheeks flushed from the cold wind. "How was your day?"

Dina kissed each girl on the cheek, running her hand down their auburn hair. It was a darker shade than her hair, due to her husband's black locks. "It was great. Hurry, come inside. It's freezing out here." With her arms still around her girls, she led them into the house. As they took off their coats and dropped their backpacks on the floor, Dina prepared some hot cocoa for them.

When all three were sitting at the kitchen table, their fingers wrapped around their steaming mugs of hot cocoa, Dina asked the girls how their day was.

"It was so much fun," Chani gushed. "I helped my teacher with the bulletin board. Our class was a little late with the Chanukah decorations on the board, and I helped her. My best friend Malky helped, too."

Dina smiled. "That's great, Chani." She turned to the younger twin, whose gaze was focused on her rainbow-colored mug. "How was your day, Esty?"

The little girl shrugged.

"Care to elaborate?" her mother asked.

Esty shrugged again.

"Her teacher yelled at her again," Chani pipped up. "It was in front of the whole class."

Esty didn't utter a word.

Dina turned to the older twin. "Chani, how about you let Esty and I talk?"

She nodded and stood up, taking her hot cocoa with her to the room she shared with her sister.

Mother and daughter sat in silence. Dina watched her daughter carefully, trying to determine what she could do to ease the situation, to coax her child to open up.

She bent forward. "Sweetie, tell me exactly what happened."

The little girl threw her hands up. "I don't know. My teacher always picks on me for no reason. I didn't *do* anything."

Dina nodded slowly. "I believe you, but this isn't the first phone call I received from her. It's the fifth. Clearly something's wrong and we need to get to the bottom of this. Are you absolutely sure you've been on your best behavior?" The younger twin had been known to be a bit of a trouble maker at home.

Dina's Choice

Like her father.

Esty nodded earnestly. "I'm well-behaved. Especially at school. I don't make trouble. I don't want the teachers to hate me. I want to do as good as Chani does. She's, like, the smartest girl in her class."

She was, and the pride melted Dina's heart. But she was just as proud of her other daughter. She would never compare the two, just like her mother-in-law hadn't compared her twin sons. She treated each twin like an individual.

"Okay, I'll discuss this with Daddy when he comes home and we'll decide what to do. For now, get started on your homework while I make dinner."

Light finally brightened the little girls eyes. "What are we having?"

Dina laughed. She knew just how much her enter family loved her cooking. "Potato soup and stuffed chicken."

Smiling widely, Esty stood up and ran up to her room. Dina looked after her, glad to see the sad expression had vanished from her daughter's face.

She finished her drink, then got started on dinner. Even though her daughter seemed to be in a better mood now, she couldn't get that gloomy expression out of her head. Something was nagging at the back of her head. She wasn't sure what, but she knew she had to do something about it.

The child was unhappy. This reminded her of…

The door opened and in walked a tall man, wearing a black winter coat, his bangs blowing in the wind. Shmuel Weiss shut the door behind him. And, with a large smile on his face, he greeted his wife.

He breathed in the heavenly aroma as he shrugged out of his coat and adjusted his *kippa*. "Dina, it smells wonderful in here. But I thought we decided I'd make dinner tonight."

"I know, but you've been busy rehearsing with your band for the Strauss-Weinberg wedding and I know you just want to come home and rest."

Racing toward her, he gently took her by the waist and spun her around. "Did I ever tell you how much I love you?"

She laughed. "Only every day. Did I tell you how much I love you?"

"Only every second of every day. When I'm home, I mean." He gently pressed his lips to her forehead. "You're my world," he whispered. "You and our girls." He rested his forehead against hers. "I never imagined my life would turn out like this. I'm the happiest man in the…" His mouth snapped shut when he took in the worried expression on her face. "What's wrong?"

She lowered the fire on the stove and gestured to the kitchen table, where husband and wife sat down. "It's Esty," Dina told him. "Her teacher called. *Again*. When I spoke to Esty, she insisted she doesn't make trouble during class. How could we choose one's words over the other? How can we believe a teacher over our child?"

Shmuel sighed. "She's been known to…"

"Act out. I know. But that's only at home. And I can't help but feel like there's more to this. Esty looked so unhappy. If she was indeed making trouble, wouldn't she brag about it? Or at least not care? Esty cared. She was *hurt*. What if…" She hesitated.

He reached for her hand across the table and gave it a squeeze. "What if what?"

She hated to bring up this subject, but she felt as though she had to. "What if her teacher is picking on her?"

A cloud of darkness passed over his face. He seemed to know exactly where her thoughts were headed. "Like my teacher picked on me. He terrorized me."

Dina nodded slowly. "We haven't been getting complaints

from her English teacher. Chani told me Miss Bernstein embarrassed Esty in front of the whole class. Sam, I can't help but worry…"

"I know. Let's talk to her. Esty?" he called. "Can you come down here for a minute, sweetie?"

Footsteps were heard on the stairs before a head peeked into the room. "Are you mad at me?" Esty asked.

Shaking his head, Shmuel motioned for his daughter to take a seat at the table. "I heard your teacher called."

Esty slumped down in her seat. "I didn't do anything."

Her father nodded. "We believe you, which is why we want to talk to you." He hesitated. "Has this teacher been giving you a hard time? Does it seem like she purposely does this?"

Esty shrugged.

Dina took her hand. "This is important, Esty."

"I guess. She always calls on me in class, even when I don't know the answer. And she makes me feel dumb sometimes."

Dina and Shmuel exchanged a glance. Dina pushed a smile on her face. "Why don't you and Daddy finish up your homework while I call your teacher?"

Once father and daughter were out of the room, Dina called back Miss Bernstein. She didn't manage to get a word out before the younger woman started complaining about Dina's daughter.

"I'm sorry, but I'm going to need to interrupt you," Dina said. "Esty is a good kid, and the child you're describing is not my daughter. She would never be disrespectful. She would never talk during morning prayers. And she always does her homework. She's very upset and we need to do something about this."

The teacher was quiet for a moment. "Mrs. Weiss, I know you'd like to think your daughter is perfect, but..." Her voice trailed off.

"She denies everything you said."

"Of course she would. She's just a child after all and she's scared to get in trouble."

Dina didn't like the tone of the teacher's voice. "Maybe we should call her in here."

"Sure, why not?"

Dina called for Esty and Shmuel to come downstairs. Chani remained on the last step, listening closely. Dina told her to come inside, too, since this was affecting all of them as a family.

Once they were seated, Dina turned to the younger twin. "Miss Bernstein told me some things and I want to verify them with you. She claimed you talked during morning prayers last week. Is that true?"

Esty's lower lip quivered as though she was seconds away from crying. Shmuel pulled her onto his lap, holding her tightly. "I was just showing Sara where we were holding," the little girl said. "She gets lost a lot, so I showed her. I didn't talk."

When Dina relayed those words to the teacher, she was quiet. "My daughter was helping out a friend," Dina said. "And you thought the worst in her." She tried to keep her voice calm. There was no sense in getting upset. It would get them nowhere.

"I'm...I'm sorry," the teacher sputtered. "I didn't know."

"Why do you call on her in class when it's obvious she doesn't know the answer? She's only nine. Why embarrass her?"

Esty buried her face in her father's shoulder. Giving his wife a concerned look, her stroked her head, telling her it was okay.

"I only call on her during class because I know she knows the answer." The teacher sighed. "She's a very bright girl, but I feel like all she needs is a little push and she could be the top student in her class. I never meant to embarrass her."

Dina's Choice

Dina shut her eyes. Miss Bernstein had good intentions, but she was going about it the wrong way. "Esty is a very sensitive child."

"I see that now. Maybe we can work something out. We all want what's best for Esty. And I'm sorry I put her through that. I guess I never realized my actions were having a negative effect on her."

Dina and the teacher spent a few minutes discussing the best way to move forward. Once she hung up, Shmuel pulled Chani into his arms and held onto his daughters. "What I'm going to tell you is very important. Are you listening?"

Both girls nodded.

"If you ever feel like someone isn't treating you right, whether it be a teacher or another student, or even the principal, you tell either me or your mother right away. Okay?"

The girls nodded again. Shmuel kissed each one on the cheek.

Esty looked at her mother. "Does that mean Miss Bernstein won't be mean to me anymore?"

Dina gave her a smile. "You're going to have a great school year. I promise."

As both parents hugged their girls, they sent smiles to each other. It appeared as though everything was going to be okay.

***

Dina, Shmuel, and their daughters gathered around the menorah. It was the first night of Chanukah, something Dina looked forward to since she was a little girl.

After lighting the *shamash* candle, used to light the menorah candles, Shmuel recited the prayer and lit the first Chanukah candle. The flame reflected in the twin girls' excited eyes. The family sang *Maoz Tzur* together and stepped back to admire the sight.

Though he knew his girls expected it, since he did the same thing every year, Shmuel made a big show of handing both daughters candy-filled dreidels and money. His wife caught it all on camera, like the previous years. As the girls fussed over their candy, Dina set up the laptop so the family could video chat with the gang from Miami. Dina sat with one daughter on her lap while her husband held the second daughter.

"Hello!" Dina's father and family greeted.

They spent the next half hour catching up on each other's lives. The one person missing from this virtual get-together was the eldest boy, Chananya. He was studying at a yeshiva in Israel. The rest of the kids were still in high school. Though Dina spoke with her family a few times a month, it never seemed enough.

After ending the video chat, the Weiss family worked on the Chanukah cookies for the party Shmuel's mom was throwing. Even though she insisted they not bring anything, husband and wife wanted to offer something in return. The girls had a great time cutting the dough with special Chanukah shapes, such as menorahs, dreidels, and candles.

The cookies finished baking just in time. At ten to eight, they placed the cookies into a container and made their way to Shmuel's parents' house. They lived a few blocks away. As soon as they walked in, they were greeted by Perry and her family.

"Yay, you guys are here!" Perry rushed to fling her arms around her sister-in-law and best friend. Dina returned the hug, though she was mindful of Perry's large stomach. The soon-to-be mother of five was due any day now.

"And who is this handsome man?" Perry laughed as she wrapped her arms around her brother. "You guys look so good."

"You know we just saw each other last week when we invited your family for Shabbos," Dina reminded her.

Perry waved her hand as she hugged Chani and Esty.

"Can't I just compliment what a beautiful family you have?"

Dina gave Perry a warm smile. "Thanks. You have a beautiful family as well."

"Yeah, we are the little munchkins?" She craned her neck toward the interior of the house. "Kids, your aunt, uncle, and cousins are here!"

No more than ten seconds passed before a stampede of footsteps entered the living room. Perry's eldest, Tova, a year older than the twins, ran over to the girls so they could discuss who received the better candy dreidel. Shmuel flipped the next child, a boy named Zacharia, over his shoulder. He did the same to his younger brother, Akiva.

Perry's husband, Naftali, walked into the room, balancing their two-year-old son on his hip. "*Shalom Aleicheim*, hello."

"My gosh, Yonatan has gotten so big," Dina said to Perry.

Perry rubbed her stomach. "And getting quite the handful. As much as I love my three boys, it feels like forever since I had Tova. I can't wait until this one is born."

Dina raised her eyebrows. "So it's a girl, then?"

Perry lowered her voice. "We weren't supposed to find out, but the doctor accidently let it slip. Don't tell Naftali, though. I want him to be excited when she's born. He's also hoping for another girl."

Dina wrapped her arms around her. "*Mazel tov*, that's amazing news."

"I agree," Shmuel said. "Daughters bring nothing but joy." He smiled lovingly at his girls who were munching on some of the candy his mother had laid out.

The door opened and in walked a man, woman, twin boys, and a four-year-old girl.

"Look who's here!" Perry rushed to throw her arms around her other sister-in-law, Tzippy. "When was the last time we saw each other? Like a month. You guys have to stop being invited to other people for Shabbos so you can spend Shabbos with us."

Tzippy shrugged helplessly. "That's what happens when you come from a family of eight."

"Okay, but we get priority next time." She pinched little Dassie's cheek. "You are such a cutie! I've missed you. And your brothers." Perry pinned her eyes on the nine-year-old twin boys, Eliezer and Binyamin. "My gosh, it's like I've been tossed back in time. You look exactly like Dovid and Shmuel did when they were your age."

"I know, right?" Tzippy agreed. "Dovid doesn't see it,

though. He thinks I'm crazy."

Dovid laughed. "I do."

Perry grabbed Shmuel's arm and yanked him to the twins. "What do you think?"

"I think you two are crazy," he replied.

Perry rolled her eyes. "You guys are blind. What do you think, Dina?"

Dina scrutinized the boys' faces. While there certainly were similarities to their father and uncle, they did not share the exact face. No one could have the same face as her Sam.

"I'm scared to answer." Dina chuckled.

Perry was about to respond when Simi entered the room. At once, the little kids crowded around her, each vying for the attention of their favorite aunt.

"I can't get over what a beautiful young woman Simi's growing up to be," Dina exclaimed. "She's stunning."

"I can't get over the fact that she's fifteen," Shmuel muttered. "My little Sim-Sim."

"Soon it won't be long before she's married and has a family of her own," Perry said.

"Don't even think that." Dovid shook his head. "I don't know if I can ever accept that."

Dina's Choice

"You two are going to give a hard time to her future husband, won't you?" Perry teased.

Shmuel grinned. "What else are big brothers for?"

Simi managed to free herself from the clutches of her nieces and nephews and made her way to her siblings and siblings-in-law. She made a face as she caught them staring at her. "Were you guys talking about me?"

Perry nodded. "We sure were. We can't believe how much you've grown."

She groaned. "Not you, too. Every day, Dad tells me that he won't let me date until I'm thirty. And Mom cries sometimes. It's *so* annoying."

Shmuel playfully slapped her arm. "Mom told me you're the top student in your class."

Simi blushed and muttered, "Mom talks too much."

"Ooh, congrats," Perry wished. "You will go on to do great things one day. I know it."

"Go on, tell them." Shmuel nodded.

Simi blushed again. "I want to be a pediatrician."

"That's amazing," Dina, Dovid, and Perry said.

Simi kicked the floor with shoe. "That's the dream anyway. I don't know if it'll come true."

Dina wrapped her arm around her sister-in-law. "It will come true, if you're determined enough to make it happen. Trust in Hashem—He'll help you along the way."

She smiled. "Thanks, Dina. You always know the right thing to say."

"It's why I married her," Shmuel joked.

Dina laughed as she playfully slapped his chest. "Oh, be quiet, Sam."

Mrs. Weiss walked into the living room, followed by her husband. She clasped her hands as her eyes roamed over the room. "Finally, all my favorite people are gathered together under one roof." Her eyebrows dipped. "Except, some people are missing. Where's your mother, Dina?"

The young woman slipped her phone out of her pocket and scanned the screen. "I don't know. I texted her before we left—"

At the moment, the doorbell rang. Dovid's twins, Benny and Eli, raced each other to the door and opened it. Mrs. Aaron—or rather, the newly Mrs. Gould—stood there with her husband. She pulled her daughter and granddaughters into her arms, then hugged all the other women. "It's so great to see all of you." She squeezed Dina's hand.

Dina's Choice

"Thanks for coming. Now we're all here!" Mrs. Weiss smiled widely, then frowned when she caught sight of the container in Shmuel's hands. "Didn't I tell you not to bring anything?"

Shmuel shrugged. "I have been known to disregard some of your orders," he admitted.

Everyone in the room laughed.

Mrs. Weiss shook her head with a proud smile. "I know my cookies could never compete with yours and Dina's. I'll add them to the platter."

Each one of the guests gathered at the large table in the dining room. Mrs. Weiss had outdone herself—the table was gorgeous. She used her Shabbos tablecloth, dishes, and utensils. Everything sparkled as though they had been polished an hour ago.

The meal began. Mrs. Weiss had prepared delicious dishes of *latkes*—potato pancakes—and *sufganiyot*, special donuts typically eaten on Chanukah, and a variety of soups. There was a plethora of salads and desserts to choose from, including the cookies baked by the young Weiss family, which were an instant hit.

As soon as the meal concluded, aunts, uncles, and

grandparents gave out their presents to their nieces, nephews and grandchildren. Once the kids opened their toys, some exchanging them with their cousins, they ran off to play *dreidels* on the living room floor. The adults conversed on the couches and recliners, catching up with each other's lives and discussing the latest news going on in the community and the world.

Mrs. Weiss sat back with tears raining down her cheeks.

"Mom." Shmuel touched her arm. "Are you okay?"

She smiled as she dabbed her eyes with a tissue. "I am, Shmuel. I am very happy. I feel so blessed. It makes me feel so good inside to have the whole family here with me."

Mr. Weiss smiled as he held his wife's hand. "I feel extremely blessed as well."

"Is that snow?" one of the kids called from where she gazed out the window. "It's snowing!"

The kids ran outside, not listening to their parents who told them to put on their coats. Dina and Shmuel stood at the doorway with the other couples, surprised at the light coating of snow that had already gathered on the ground.

"Your mother was right," Dina said as she snuggled against her husband as the wind blew against them. "She said it was going to snow today. She's always right about everything," she added with a chuckle.

"True. But you were right about a lot of things as well," Shmuel told her.

She raised her face to her husband's, her eyes searching his.

"When you were twelve, you knew you and I would be together. You held onto that dream as hard as you could. You didn't give up on me. If not for you, I wouldn't be the person I am today. I wouldn't have this beautiful family. I wouldn't be happy."

Dina smiled as she watched her daughters playing in the snow. "It's not me, Sam. It's Hashem. He's the one who guides us in life. He was the one who brought the two of us together. I am thankful to Him every day, for giving me you, our girls, our family. I couldn't have asked for a more perfect life."

Shmuel gave his wife a loving smile. "I couldn't have asked for a more perfect life, either."

Hebrew/Yiddish Glossary:

- Bais Yaakov (Hebrew)—Jewish day school for girls
- Bar mitzvah (Hebrew)—when a Jewish boy turns thirteen years old and is required to observe all commandments of the Torah
- Bas mitzvah (Hebrew)—when a Jewish girl turns twelve years old and is required to observe all commandments of the Torah
- Challah (Hebrew)—braided bread, eaten on the Sabbath
- Cholent (Yiddish)—Traditional Jewish stew, eaten on the Sabbath
- Chuppah (Hebrew)—wedding canopy
- Daven/davening (Yiddish)—pray/praying
- Dreidel (Yiddish)—a spinning top, played on Chanukah
- Frum (Yiddish)—observant Jew
- Gefilte fish (Yiddish)—fish dish, eaten on the Sabbath
- Hashem (Hebrew)—God
- Im yirtzeh Hashem (Hebrew)—God willing
- Kabbalas Shabbos (Hebrew)—Friday evening prayer

to welcome in the Sabbath

- Kallah (Hebrew)—bride
- Kippa (Hebrew)—skullcap worn by religious Jewish men
- Latkes (Yiddish)—potato pancakes. Traditional food eaten on Chanukah
- Mazel Tov (Hebrew/Yiddish)—congratulations and good wishes
- Mitzvah (Hebrew)—commandment or a good deed
- Nosh (Yiddish)—snack
- Off the derech (Hebrew)—strayed from the path; no longer observant
- Shabbos (Hebrew)—Sabbath
- Shalom Aleicheim (Hebrew)—song sung on Friday to welcome the Sabbath, or hello
- Shamash candle (Hebrew)—the candle used to light the other candles on the menorah
- Sheva brochos (Hebrew)—a week of celebration and blessings following a wedding
- Shul (Yiddish)—synagogue
- Simcha/simchos (Hebrew)—happiness or a joyous occasion such as an engagement, wedding or bar/bas

mitzvah

- Sufganiyot (Hebrew)—jelly donuts eaten on Chanukah
- Talmud (Hebrew)—the oral laws of the Torah that were later written down. It's comprised of the Mishna and Gemara
- Tefillin (Hebrew)—Phylacteries. They are worn by male observant Jews during weekday morning prayers
- Tzitzis (Hebrew)—a garment worn by observant men
- Yeshiva (Hebrew)—Jewish day school for boys

About the Author

Chaya T. Hirsch is an Orthodox Jewish woman who lives in New York. She is the author of *Meant To Be*, *That Special Someone*, *Shira's Secret*, *An Unlikely Match*, *Dina's Choice*, *Aviva's Pain*, *Malky's Heart*, and the *Losing Leah* series. She is currently working on her next novel.

Made in the USA
Middletown, DE
12 February 2023